RUBBLE

BRACKEN RIDGE REBELS MC BOOK 5

MACKENZY FOX

Copyright © 2022 Mackenzy Fox

All rights reserved. No part of this publication may be reproduced, distributed, or transmitted in any form or by any means, including photocopying, recording, or other electronic or mechanical methods, without the prior written permission of the publisher

Please purchase only authorized electronic editions and do not participate in, or encourage, the electronic piracy of copyrighted materials. Your support of the author's rights is appreciated.

This book is a work of fiction. Names, characters, places, brands, and incidents are the products of the author's imagination or used fictitiously. Any resemblance to actual events, locales, or persons, living or dead, is entirely coincidental.

Cover by: Mayhem cover creations
Formatting by: @peachykeenas (Savannah Richey)
Editing and proofreading by: Mackenzie - nicegirlnaughtyedits.com
2nd proofread by: Kiki Edits
ASIN E BOOK: B09KV8YKXK
ISBN PAPERBACK: 9798411433579

For everyone who has supported my writing, this one is for you. I hope you continue to enjoy my books for many years to come and I thank you for your support, it means so much to me. Much love.
MF x

AUTHOR'S NOTE

CONTENT WARNING: Rubble is a steamy romance for readers 18+ it contains mature themes that may make some readers uncomfortable. It includes violence, possible triggers including drugs use, alcohol abuse, miscarriage, rehabilitation, violence including knives and guns and as always…. LOTS of steamy love scenes!

** Please note, Rubble and Lucy's story begins 6 years prior. We don't get to the present day until Chapter 15. This was unavoidable being that Rubble's background story was just too deep and detailed to skim over it in a few chapters and a lot went down which relates to the present-day situation. This is where the story wanted to go and I'm merely a vessel!

It won't impact the telling of the story, but I thought it deserved an explanation.

BRACKEN RIDGE REBELS M.C. – Enter at own risk…….

ABOUT RUBBLE

ABOUT RUBBLE – Bracken Ridge Rebels MC Book 5

Bracken Ridge Arizona, where the Rebels M.C. rule and the only thing they ride or die for more than their club is their women, this is Rubble's story

Rubble:

When I first laid eyes on her I thought she was an angel.

One I shouldn't try and corrupt. One I should leave well alone.

But I'd never been very good at staying away from things that I shouldn't, it only made me want her more.

I pursued her. Taking her. Making her my ol' lady and we left my violent past behind.

Or so I thought.

Old threats from the grave I thought were long forgotten come back to haunt me and endanger everything I hold dear. My old club's debt for one, even if it's not my debt to pay.

All that matters is her, my woman, and our unborn baby, they're all I have. I'll do everything I can to keep them safe, even if it means starting a war.

Protecting the ones I love isn't a threat, it's a promise, and it's one I'm willing to die for.

Lucy:

I knew he was the one the first time our eyes met that night across the club.

He was everything that I shouldn't be attracted to.

Rugged. Dangerous. Mysterious. Those three things spelled trouble.

Worst of all; he belonged to a notorious motorcycle gang the Phoenix Fury. A club I shouldn't get involved in, but I did. And we fell in love. When the club fell apart, we left and moved on to Bracken Ridge, leaving the past behind us.

But like all fairy tales, there's always a villain, someone who wants to take the things most precious to you away.

It seems our fight isn't over yet; it's just beginning and now there's nowhere left to run.

I'll always stand by him. I'll always be his woman until the bitter end, until I take my last breath, if that's what it takes.

NOTE: This book is book 5 in a series but is written as a stand-alone with no cliff hanger and a HEA. Recommended for mature readers only has adult content. Bracken Ridge Rebels rule...enter at own risk!

PART I

THE PAST...

1

LUCY

SIX YEARS AGO

"I really just don't see what all the fuss is about," I declare, waving my new nails around in the air. I went for leopard print because it's flashy, gaudy, and the perfect amount of southern trash, just how I like it.

Two of my friends, Emerson and Jemma, the only ones who aren't trying to get it on with the guys at the bar like my other friends, look at me pointedly.

"You were with Gary for two years," Emerson says, looking at me with sad eyes, reaching her hand across the table to squeeze mine. "You've got to feel something?"

I know my friends think that because I just broke up with my boyfriend of two years, a man I was not in love with nor was he with me, that I should be acting or feeling a certain way.

Hence why we're at the *Apple Pie,* a strip club in downtown Phoenix where all the lowlifes hang out. We didn't come here on purpose; it just kind of happened on our girls' night out while trolling the bars.

This is exactly what I needed.

Not that I'm into female strippers, but it seems like a bit of fun, and there are plenty of cute guys around, willing and able to buy us drinks. I haven't had a whole lot of fun in the last two years. Gary was everything I thought I wanted.

Strait-laced.

Conservative.

Responsible.

It's like he invented the missionary position. Don't get me wrong, there's nothing wrong with a man who is any of those things. I admire loyalty and strength; I don't dislike dependability.

But I don't want to be in bed with a man who only knows one position. Frankly, I've had more excitement receiving a demand notice from the IRS. And it wasn't like Gary and I had a fight when we decided to break up. We were past our due date.

I also hate how everyone just expects me to be freaking heartbroken and at home drowning my sorrows, unable to get out of bed, unable to eat. That has never been my style. Never was, and never will be.

"Like what? Relief?"

Jemma shakes her head. "It might not hit you until his stuff's gone and you're really there alone," she reaffirms, because, while I love my friends, they all think I'm made of glass.

I'm not. I'm made of fucking steel, and I don't need them babysitting me and acting like I'm going to shatter the second I realize my relationship is over. It was over a long time ago. I just didn't leave when I should have, I tried to stick it out.

Yes, it's awkward, but I always look on the bright side, and it just means there's something better out there for me.

I'd rather know now than in another two years' time, or

heaven forbid, twenty years' time. They just can't seem to grasp it.

"Look," I say, trying not to sound snarky. "I'm not sad or alone. You're carrying on about this break up like I'm a freaking teenager. I'm fine. I'm actually relieved that it's over now and we can both move on. I love you guys, but you need to stop. My Prince Charming is out there somewhere, and that's all that matters. So shut up, quit bitchin', and let's drink some cocktails."

I down a shot just to emphasize my point while they both gape at me.

My friends shouldn't be surprised. I've always been upfront and in your face. It's who I am.

And I've always known what I want. Gary and I met when I was going through multiple setbacks, and he helped me out, being nice and shit. We never should have crossed the line.

The truth is, we don't even hate each other.

"As long as you're not going to go home and hang yourself from the shower rod," Emerson continues as I roll my eyes. "It's always the ones who protest that they're fine that really aren't."

I know she means well. She cares about me, and I dig that, I really do. But I'm here to have fun, not think about Gary or any of my other fucked up relationships.

"If I change my mind, Emmy, I'll be sure to call you first before I do it. Deal?"

She shakes her head. "That's not even funny."

I down another shot of tequila and look up at the naked woman twirling around the pole on the stage. I've got to take my hat off to strippers; they sure know how to work a crowd.

Most of the guys in here have their eyes glued to the

stage, though as I look around, a few cast a glance over at our table, and I turn away quickly.

I just want to drink and forget about my problems for a while, like all normal people. I'm not here to hook up.

"How about we order some more drinks and play truth or dare?" I suggest.

Jemma claps her hands and jumps up. "I'll get more drinks!" she declares. The other girls in our group are all still hanging at the bar. So much for sisterly solidarity.

Three more rounds of shots, and one game of truth or dare later, and I'm almost ready to hop up on stage. Well, I'm not going to, but I *could.*

I'm only four-nine, but what I don't have in stature, I make up for with big boobs and big hair. My two biggest assets. I've yet to meet a man who can keep his gaze at eye level.

Some say if talking was an Olympic sport, I would take home a gold medal, though most guys never get to find out.

I make my way to the bathroom while the rest of the girls join our table, then disappear through the crowded room. I avoid making any eye contact because I know the tight pink and white bodycon dress I've got on with a cut-out below my chest reveals a lot of skin and draws attention. My ex didn't like most of my clothes, especially ones that were tight-fitting, so this is a tribute to him.

I have wings, and now I want to fly.

I fix my makeup in the mirror before I leave and swing out into the hallway… immediately running into a brick wall… or in this case, the brick wall being a chest.

When I glance up, Mr. Dark and Dangerous stares down at me in surprise.

Well, hello there, sunshine.

He's cute.

He's got dark, disheveled hair, at least a three-day stubble and cheekbones you could ski off of.

Ding-dong.

I purposely don't apologize for running into him, and he catches me by the shoulder, preventing me from stumbling.

"Watch where you're going there, little lady," he drawls. "Could've squashed you."

Like clockwork, his gaze shifts down to my breasts.

I resist an eyeroll.

"That's all right, I've got inflatable air bags to help break my fall," I quip.

His eyes work their way back up to mine. I can't tell the color in this dim light, but then I notice he's wearing a motorcycle jacket with the words: *Phoenix Fury M.C.* on the top left breast pocket.

He's a biker?

I've never seen such a hot biker before. I thought they were all old guys with long beards and fat bellies.

His lips smirk. "What's your name, princess?"

I quirk an eyebrow. "Really?"

He shrugs. "Why not?"

I shake my head. "Not happening."

"That's a funny name. I'm Rubble, by the way." He holds out a hand, and I almost laugh.

A polite biker? Never met one of those before either, not that I've met many in my time, but the Phoenix Fury are known for many things in this city, and staying on the right side of the law isn't one of them.

Still. He is cute.

I shouldn't touch him, but what the heck. I shake his hand, and he smirks again. I hate being a forgone conclusion.

"What's your deal, Rubble?" I shout over the music.

His eyes stay on mine, and I realize I like them; they're

full of mischief. "Here with some friends. It's my birthday today."

I roll my lips. "Well, happy birthday, Rubble. If you don't mind me asking, why did your mama call you that, or is that just your cool biker name?" I laugh.

He quirks a brow. "My cool biker name?"

"Yeah, y'all have all kinds of weird names like splinter, zero, hammer…" I trail off as he smiles, amusement in those dark eyes. *Sexy eyes.*

I'm momentarily caught off-guard by how good that smile looks on his face. He's quite possibly the cutest man I've ever seen, and while he's not a giant, compared to me, he towers over my tiny frame. I can see the muscle behind his wide shoulders and the snake of tattoos running up his neck from below his shirt, the leather jacket making him look like a badass.

My nether region has a little flutter.

"I got mine 'cause my real name's Barney."

"Barney?" I stammer. He doesn't look like a Barney.

He grins. "Yup. Barney, so I got Rubble. Barney Rubble. Those fuckers just wanted to mess with my head."

"It's kind of original, I guess." I shrug.

His eyes flick to my lips. "You here with anybody?"

Wow. Straight to the point.

I shake my head. "Girlfriends. We're celebrating too."

A patron tries to get around us, since we're blocking the entryway to the restrooms, and he maneuvers me with a hand to my hip.

When he touches me, it's like a bolt of electricity jolts through my body. I normally don't let random men just paw me, but there's something about him that's kind and sincere, and a little lost… *Oh shit. Here I go again.*

I've always been a sucker for the underdog. It's kind of a thing. I'm a sucker for a cute face and gnarly bunch of tattoos too, so it seems. I really need to check myself with this guy, though. He smells divine but also like bad news.

"What are you celebrating?" he asks, his mouth to my ear.

I try not to shudder at his low, sexy, voice but it's a little hard not to. "Umm. My breakup, actually."

He looks down at me and grins like the cat who got the cream. "What a shame."

"You don't mean that."

He hasn't removed his hand from my hip, and I try to ignore the way my pussy clenches at his touch as I try not to focus on his face.

I don't need to be getting involved with an outlaw. I've had enough drama in my life to last a lifetime.

"No," he agrees. "I don't. Will you have a drink with me? Since we're both celebrating."

Stay strong, girl. Do not show any weakness.

"Can't." I shrug. "Gotta get back to my girls. They'll probably be looking for me by now, so I should go…"

He bites his bottom lip as I back away, and it sends fire to my belly because I know that look. "Give me your number," he says with a chin lift.

I give him a wave instead. "Have a nice night, Rubble. It was nice to meet you." *You're cute as fuck.*

"What's your name?" he calls after me. I turn and look over my shoulder to see his eyes scanning my body, and I know he likes what he sees.

"Whatever you want it to be, darlin'." I give him a wink and sashay off, leaving him, hopefully, in a wet puddle on the floor.

I know the effect I have on men, and it isn't me being conceited, it's just a fact. And maybe I like him looking.

At least he's cute, and if my friends weren't here, who knows. I may have been inclined to get to know him a little better. The club patches on his jacket were a little terrifying, though.

I've heard some not-so-great things about that motorcycle club, so there is no chance in hell I'm getting involved with a criminal. Cute or not, I'm not going down that road.

When I return back to the table, the rest of our posse have finally returned and more shots are being handed around.

I glance over Emerson's head, and I see Rubble sauntering back to a booth where a large crowd of men are all sitting in a circle. They all have on the same leather jacket he does. One of them has his back to me, so I study the image; a Phoenix rising from the ashes with a big billow of orange flame chasing its tail as the wings spread across the haze. It's really cool.

Some scantily clad strippers are scattered around here and on the main floor, and some are getting very friendly. I watch as one crawls onto Rubble's lap and straddles him.

I don't know why, but I can't tear my eyes away.

I watch as she basically dry humps him on the seat, right there, for everyone to see. I know we're in a strip club and all, but they have private rooms for that. I guess anything goes here.

I sip my cocktail as I continue to watch her move, her hips swaying in bootie shorts and her boobs pushed up in his face. His hands settle on her hips, and I have a sudden surge of jealousy come over me.

I down another shot in between sips as I keep watching.

She leans down and whispers something in his ear. He opens his eyes and grins at her, then, like a siren calling to him, his eyes flick to mine across the crowded room.

Shit.

I look away quickly, and when I have the gall to look back again, he's still staring at me.

Fuck. He really is beautiful to look at.

I watch as he kisses her, his eyes still on me, and he's making a real show of it, too. Bastard.

I feel my insides churn as I watch him clutch her head and tilt it so I can see him stick his tongue in her mouth. I've never seen anything so erotic in my life. He knows it too, as his eyes dance with even more mischief.

It's like he's doing all of this just to show me what I'm missing out on. And missing out, I am.

I swallow hard when he grabs her butt with both hands and squeezes. My mouth drops open when he pulls away from her mouth, and he gives me that sexy, cheeky grin, followed by a wink.

I look away, slightly embarrassed.

What the hell was that?

Out of my periphery, I see someone throw some money on the table. The girl claps her hands excitedly and dismounts from his lap, pulling him by the hand to stand. He gets up too and follows her, the guys around him wolf whistling and patting him on the back as they pass by. It looks like they're heading to the VIP area.

Apparently, this is a no sex club, but I seriously doubt anyone adheres to rules like that around here, judging by the clientele and the willingness of the girls.

I feel another, much stronger, surge of jealousy as I think about this complete stranger sticking it to some other girl. Still, she's pretty and has these annoying legs that go all the way up past my armpits.

I could've had him. My annoying inner voice tells me. *Urgh. Like I'd want to.*

However, I've had enough drinks to wonder what the hell is back there, and what it takes to get into the VIP area.

I disappear quietly as my friends are distracted and cross the floor toward the sealed off area.

The bouncer takes one look at me as I flutter my eyes up

at him and flash him my big smile before he unclips the rope, letting me through.

I mouth a thank you as he smiles back, with his eyes, of course, on my tits. Once I pass him, I roll my eyes at how easy that was.

It's much smaller and quieter back here. There are people hanging out at another bar, some are drinking out of martini glasses instead of beer bottles. It seems kind of upscale.

The classy part of the club – I almost snort with laughter.

I pass by multiple rooms with sheer curtains, and I try to peer in without looking like a stalker. There are strippers giving guys lap dances and girls on another stage practically making out while guys in the front seated area stare at them and throw money at their shoes. The guys in here must have serious money because they're all in suits and ties. Ah. So, this is where the married men pay more to hang out in secret, where they won't be seen.

I'm out of my depth here, but I don't want to turn back. I want to see what he's doing; I want to watch.

I pass another bouncer, and he doesn't give me a second glance as I do.

I get to the last room, and that's when I see them.

The scrawny blonde is giving him a lap dance, or she's trying to, anyway. I don't know if she's new or what, but I've seen a better hip roll on my eighty-year-old grandmother. Or maybe I'm just being catty.

I should walk away.

I really, really should.

Instead, I stand and look through the curtain as she takes her top off, and I'm surprised when I see that Rubble doesn't really even look that impressed.

His hands lay by his side, and I can see that he's clutching his phone in one of them.

Is he really just not into her? Was all of that out there just for show?

Surely not. Why would he care about getting to me? He doesn't even know me. She's still pretty, despite her lack of coordination. And he kissed the face off her when he was staring at me.

Then an idea hits me.

No. *NO!*

But before I can stop myself, I peel the curtain back and step inside.

Rubble immediately looks up as the girl continues dancing, and we stare at each other as a slow smile creeps across his face.

"There you are, sweetie," I drawl as the girl flinches and turns around, shrieking when I come closer. I look at her and shrug. "Sorry, babe. This one's mine."

2

RUBBLE

I stare at the buxom blonde and hope I didn't smoke so much weed that I'm hallucinating.

The hot chick from the hallway that wouldn't tell me her name is now telling my stripper to scram. I can't help the smile that spreads across my face. The sheer balls on her… it's admirable.

How did she even get in here?

I glance down at her fine rack, suddenly understanding how.

The chick on my lap isn't the world's greatest performer, and I'm nowhere near being hard, not like I was in the hallway when I touched Blondie and tried to get her to have an innocent drink with me.

I smile at the thought. Yeah, nothing innocent would be going on with us. She's hot, and I want in.

"You heard her, babe, get outta here."

Blondie smiles at me triumphantly.

"Hey!" the girl, still standing between my legs, says as she grabs her top to cover up her free-flowing tits. "You can't do that!"

I shove a fifty-dollar bill at her. "Yep, she can, now beat it."

"Asshole," she mutters, before barging past Blondie and storming down the hall.

I lean back farther on the couch.

"Well, well. Change your mind, sweetheart?"

"No." She rolls her eyes. "But she was doing such a shit job, I thought someone had to rescue you."

My eyes drop, gazing down at her body. She's fucking perfection personified.

Small, how I like 'em.

Tits, just how I like 'em.

And a bad fuckin' attitude to boot.

If she has a dirty mouth, I might even ask her to marry me.

"I was doin' just fine."

She narrows her eyes. "Looked like you were gonna fall asleep, sugar. That's a little harsh with it bein' your birthday and all."

"You follow me in here?" I know she did. Devious little woman.

She shrugs. "Maybe."

"You wet in the panties, babe? Watchin' me with her?"

She swallows hard, and I know the answer to that, even when she doesn't respond.

"Well, you cost me money, so I hope that means you're gonna get over here and finish the job. You owe me a lap dance."

To my astonishment, she moves closer toward me, and I feel my heart rate kick up seven hundred notches.

Shit. Is she gonna oblige me?

It's my lucky fuckin' night.

"Just because it's your birthday, I might consider it. But only if you ask nicely," she purrs.

Her sexy voice goes straight to my balls, and that's where I want to be, balls deep.

I bark out a laugh. She's got sass, it's fucking wonderful. Nobody talks to bikers like this, especially a patched member with the Phoenix Fury, but this chick has probably had way too many shots to care, and that's fine with me.

My dick kicks in my jeans as I imagine her naked.

While there's pussy and tits being flashed all over the joint tonight, and at church every night, I've seen enough of it to be picky about what I do and don't like.

And I like her.

I like her a lot.

"Gonna tell me your name, beautiful?"

"I'm not having sex with you," she states, ignoring me again.

Seems like she doesn't take to questions very well, which probably means she doesn't like taking orders too much either, most women don't, unless it's in the bedroom. Something tells me she'd like bein' in charge, and that'd be fine with me, more than fine.

Too bad she's hell bent on *not* wanting to fuck me. We could've had some fun.

"That's a pity. Look what you've done." I point down to the hard bulge in my pants, and her eyes follow. Her tongue darts out to her bottom lip, and I know she's thinking about it. Saucy little minx. I try not to picture her mouth around my cock...

"How do I know I did that and not her?"

I sit forward. "Because she ain't my type."

She quirks an eyebrow, assessing me.

"Get over here," I say.

My demand doesn't make her run, which is strange. She ought to. She ought to do a lot of things where I'm concerned.

But then, to my delight, she steps closer.

"I shouldn't be in here," she whispers, her eyes studying my body, and then roaming over my patches. "I really should go…"

"Yet here you are."

She moves into my space, setting her drink down on the table behind her as she stands in between my legs.

Her eyes are blue. Bright blue like the ocean. Her face is fucking gorgeous. She looks kind of angelic. All that's missing is a pair of wings behind her back.

It's then I notice she has on the highest pair of heels that I've ever seen, making it seem like she's much taller than she really is.

"Have you been a good boy, Rubble?" she asks coyly as I watch her slide her hands up the side of her body, skimming her huge tits as they glide up to her long, platinum blonde hair as her hips wiggle to the beat of the music. She's teasing the shit out of me, and it's fuckin' working.

My mouth goes dry.

"I'm never good, sweetheart. Haven't you heard? Bad is way better."

She smirks as she presses her hands to my chest and shoves me backward.

I lose all the breath inside my lungs as she turns and then scoots down, rubbing her ass right over my lap, without touching, and I instantly move my hands to her hips because I have to touch her. It feels like I've got a volcano going on, not just in my pants, but through my entire body. She lights up everything inside of me like a firecracker.

I'm so fucking turned on.

"You're beautiful," I tell her, pulling her back farther so she can feel my wood. I can't be sure, but I think she gasps. Yeah, I don't wanna let this girl go. I hope she wants more because I certainly want to take her to heaven and back.

She lifts up the bottom of her dress, and as I see a peek of her ass cheeks, I groan.

I need to fuck her. I need to hear my name on her lips when she comes.

She wiggles that butt around, lifting her hair as my hands move up and down the sides of her body. I want to reach around and feel those big ass titties, but I know I'll probably get a punch in the face, so I somehow restrain myself. Something else that can't be restrained for much longer is my aching cock.

She turns back around, straddling over me and leaning to my ear. "How am I doing so far?"

It feels like I swallowed sandpaper.

I move her hand to my dick, and this time, I do hear her gasp.

I laugh as she tips her head back, swaying her hips still, pushing her tits in my face as I stare down at them. The temptation to take them is right there, and I deserve a gold fuckin' medal for behaving myself.

If I could have anything in life right now, it would be to have those babies out because I need to see them. Play with them. Suck them. Do what I want to them.

But she ain't no hoe. I gotta try to hold on to my sanity, what little there is left of it. She could've slapped me when I shoved her hand on my cock, but she didn't. Instead, she tugs me by the hair and yanks my head so I'm forced to look at her.

She leans forward and bites my ear gently, then sucks the end of it, pulling it with her teeth. I feel it all the way from my cock to my toes.

"I wanna fuck you," I say, my voice strangled.

She shakes her head as she rubs her body up and down mine, and I hold my hands on her ass as her dress rides up even farther.

"Lap dance only. You want more, you gotta take me out to eat first."

"I'll fuckin' eat," I growl. "I'll eat your pussy till you don't even know your own name, and you'll be screaming my name till I'm done with you."

Her eyes go wide as she rests her hands on my shoulders. She opens her mouth, then closes it again. "I'm not having sex with you."

I puff air into my cheeks. "Then why are you bein' such a cock tease? You not attracted to me?"

She bites her lip as she smiles at me, and she's so fuckin' cute. I don't wait for an answer, as I reach up and press my lips to hers, kissing her with full force. She tries to pull back at first, but I grip her harder, squeezing her ass as she presses that sweet little pussy into my dick.

Oh, holy hell. I've never wanted something so bad as to lose myself in her. If she really doesn't want to come home with me, or at the very least, to the backseat of her car, then I don't know what I'm gonna do. I may weep like a baby.

Her lips are sweet, soft, tentative as I explore her mouth, letting my tongue slide in, and to my surprise, she lets me.

My hands beg to reach up and squeeze her tits, but since she made it clear we ain't having sex, touching them is only gonna make me suffer all the more.

When she pulls back, I let her this time.

"Happy birthday, Rubble. I gotta go, baby." I like the way she says that. I also like the promise in her eyes.

I move my hands to her hips. "Don't go, not just yet. I'm so fuckin' hard for you."

"I have to." She waves to the door. "My friends…"

"Give me your number, for fuck's sake." I sound like I'm begging now, and I don't really give a shit.

She contemplates, probably wondering if this is a bad idea, which it is.

I'm not a good guy.

She relents, and I watch as she pulls her phone out of nowhere and asks me for my number. I reel it off as she saves it in her phone. Then I hear my phone buzz in my pocket a second later.

Glad that she didn't blow me off with a fake number, I grin.

"There, you have my cell. Don't make me regret it."

My heart's racing that she's leaving. I don't want her to go.

"I don't usually let a woman walk out on me without getting what I want," I tell her, knowing I sound like an asshole. "What makes you think you can?"

She runs a long nail over my dirty patch. "You may be a biker, but I know you won't hurt me."

I shake my head. "You so sure about that?"

I don't like the fact she doesn't really get it that I *could* be just anyone; she has no reason to trust me. I'm not gonna hurt her or do anything without her consent, but she's lucky she got me; some of the other brothers in my club may not be so accommodating. There's a lot of guys out there just for themselves, especially ones who don't appreciate a cock tease.

She stares at me and I smirk at her bravery.

"I guess you could say I trust my instincts."

"Oh, yeah?" I cock a brow. "What's that instinct tellin' you, babe?" I guess if it were to run a mile, she wouldn't still be here.

She taps her chin. "Maybe that you're dark and mysterious, but you've got a soft side."

I balk. "Don't repeat that to my brothers, they'll kick my ass."

She bites her lip, driving me crazy. "And your bark is worse than your bite."

"You just got me all figured out don't ya, doll?"

"It's not that hard."

"Is that so?"

She seems unconvinced. "It's not really your fault. I'm always attracted to the wrong kind of men."

I shake my head, fascinated by this little creature. "You're mouthy."

She has a hot little mouth; one I want to command. I like that.

"I'm from the south," she says by way of explanation.

My shoulders shake with laughter because, what the fuck?

"Maybe you just haven't met your match yet, beautiful. Maybe you need a dirty biker to fuck you just how you want it, no strings attached."

She tips her head back and laughs. Fucking laughs at me.

I have a good mind to put her over my knee and spank her. I tell her as such and her eyes register shock as well as a little heat, if I'm not mistaken. I already know we'd be good together in bed, especially if she enjoys a little kink.

I got news for her, and it's all bad.

"Is that your best line?" She pecks me on the lips, not taking it any farther, much to my disappointment. "And for the record, who says I'm looking?"

"You're here, aren't you? And don't worry, I got plenty more lines. You'll be hearing them soon."

"You're optimistic."

This woman has principles, and I'm not used to that. Usually, chicks are crawling all over me, and I have to shove them off. There's only so much of me to go around. But not this chick.

She doesn't care. She seems immune to my charms, which is an odd experience. I don't think I've ever been rejected by a woman before.

As I gather those feelings, I wonder if someone did a number on her. She seems pretty strong and sassy. The women of the club might be made of tough stuff, but they know their place in the pecking order, not sayin' I agree with it but I don't make the rules. Tex, the club Prez does. They know not to talk back and are respectful, even when we don't deserve it, which is most of the time.

I can tell this girl's mouth would get her into a whole lot of trouble, and that's what excites me the most.

"Nah, babe, more like inevitable."

She backs away, even when I reach out, and gives me a lingering finger wave as she gets closer to the curtain. It takes all my strength not to get up, drag her back and fuck her hard, bent over on this couch. That's what I'd do if we were at church.

I wonder, not for the first time tonight, when I turned into such a goddamn saint?

More to the point, what the fuck's gotten into me?

She's yanking my chain and pressing all my buttons at once.

I know I drank a lot tonight, and I did a line before I got here, but still, my dick didn't wake up until she ran into me, and we're in a fuckin' strip club. That's got to mean something.

I need to get laid. If it's not gonna be with her, then I gotta find someone to offload on. Trouble is, she's got me too wound up, the thought of fucking some other chick just doesn't work for me. If I did, lord knows I'd just be picturing her face, her body, her smell.

I want the real thing.

She disappears from view, and I sigh out loud, tempted to pinch myself in case I just dreamt the whole thing up, but I know from the way my body's pent up and alert that I fuckin' didn't.

It's then I realize, I still don't have her name.

I reach for my phone and punch her number in as *Blondie*. That's kind of fitting, though I should call her *Dirty Mouth*. I smirk at the thought.

I adjust myself in my jeans, and I know there's no way in hell that that's going away anytime soon.

I didn't want to let her go, but I've got plans.

I'm going to get to her. I'm gonna get into her head like she's now in mine.

Call it a hunch, or maybe I'm just a glutton for punishment, but I always like a challenge.

I'm not afraid to admit I like a woman that's got a little bit of a spark in her, a woman who's a little hard to tame. How I'd enjoy having her straddle over my lap while I spanked her ass for sassing me. Fuck yeah.

The only problem is, I don't want my brothers getting wind of her. If she comes to the club, then she's fair game, and one, or several, of the patched members will want her and try to hit on her, regardless of if she's with me. I'd probably have to fight them.

She's fucking spectacular. Something tells me my girl won't be ready for that kinda shit.

She already told me she wasn't looking for anything serious, so I doubt she'd be interested in a gang bang. The thought of sharing her makes my hands curl into fists. Yeah, that's not happening in this lifetime. A woman like Blondie isn't to be shared. She's to be kept for yourself, selfishly, to cherish and worship on multiple surfaces.

With her, I fear it's a waiting game, and though I'm not usually known for my patience, I'll ride this out just so I get to see her again. Buy her fuckin' dinner.

I sound like a fucking schmuck, I know it. But I need to keep her a secret for the time being. No point in alerting my brothers to anything that's going on in my head or how much I want this mystery girl. It could all be for nothing. She may forget me in five minutes. She may never call.

To think I've just been dumped on my birthday of all days, it's unfair really. Bad karma or some crap. Maybe it's all the shit I've done finally catchin' up with me, who knows.

But what I do know is this is pure and utter punishment.

Some guys just can't get any kind of break.

3

RUBBLE

The following week is one I'd rather forget. We got a shipment coming in and a drop-off. The club dabbles in drugs and guns, and we do a couple of large transactions every few months. It's dangerous, but the club's Prez, Tex, has been doing this for a while.

The run is smooth, prepped, planned out and swift. We've never had to abort a mission, but there's always the chance of the van being pulled over, and with me being one of the newest to get patched in, I'm usually the driver or the handy sidekick.

Prez and the Vice Prez ride in a black SUV to ensure there are no complications should the van be pulled over. If we did, I'd be in jail for a long time with what we're hauling, hence why I'm always glad when the drop is over and done with.

Truth is, I didn't excel in high school. Never got a good education. Not that I'm stupid, but I never had any ambition to do anything that other kids my age were doing. I guess I fell into the wrong side of the law from an early age and never managed to climb my way out.

My dad was an abusive drunk, my mom a battered wife. He drank himself to death when I was fourteen, and my mom ended up being unable to care for me, as well as herself. My older brother, Rusty, did his best, but I wasn't exactly a model child, and he was only seventeen himself.

I lived on the streets for a while. I learned how to survive by doing a lot of illegal shit to get by. Then I fell in with the club, prospected for over a year and earned my stripes.

This club is ruthless, but nothing compares to being homeless and having nowhere to call home. I'd prefer to go out in a wooden box rather than ever do that again. There's no honor in dying cold and alone.

The club has been good to me, though often I feel like my moral compass is compromised. The boys are into some pretty heavy shit, stuff that'd make your eyeballs fall out, and women aren't exactly considered hot property nor are they very respected at the best of times. Smokey, the V.P., seems to be the one who throws the most punches when some of the sweet butts get handled roughly, but Tex doesn't really give a shit. I'm not the nicest guy in the universe, but I'm also not the meanest and would never hit a woman or do something she didn't want to do. Being around my dad doing that to my mom was enough to make me realize I never wanted to be that kind of asshole.

Being a larger club, there's plenty of hot pussy to go around. New chicks come and go all the time. Some end up being permanent hang-arounds; those are the girls that come to the club and party with us, drink and hook up, otherwise known as sweet butts. Some are more daring than others. Some girls that come once, you may never see again.

Some just aren't cut out for club life.

I wonder how Blondie would take all of this. A part of me knows deep down this kind of life wouldn't be for her. She stumbled into the Apple Pie by chance, and she definitely isn't from the wrong side of the tracks.

I haven't been able to stop thinking about her since the weekend, and I texted her with no reply. I can't say I blame her. If she were smart, she'd stay away.

The lap dance she gave me has been all I can think about all week, and the fact I never got laid. She was all sweet as pie until she started wiggling her butt over my lap and cock teasing me. It remains to be seen how much of a bad girl she really is. She didn't let me fuck her for one, so maybe I'm losing my touch?

There's a big difference between easy and hard to get, and she's somewhere in between.

Unlike most of my brothers, I know how to be patient. A woman like her is worth a few sleepless nights, not that I'll admit that to anyone.

Every now and again a woman comes along that blows your mind, and considering our encounter didn't end in all night sex just goes to prove that I've got it bad. And I know it's because I couldn't have her. Now I'll make it my mission in life to add that notch to my belt.

I know I can.

"You daydreaming again while on the job?" My counterpart, and tonight's sidekick, Hoax, chuckles. We're buddies. He's not a bad dude, and we've got each other's backs, but he likes to talk a lot. He's tonight's designated driver.

We sit and wait for the others before the drop off. It's the usual routine.

I contemplate telling him about Blondie, only 'cause he won't make a big deal out of it.

"Met a chick on Saturday night, and she's got me all wound up," I admit.

"Not that skinny bitch that Pirate fucked in the men's stall?"

I give him the side-eye. "Nah, dude. Someone else."

"What's the problem, then? She frigid?"

I shrug. "Playin' hard to get. Nothin' I can't handle, but she's fuckin' with my head."

"She been around the club?"

"Nah, man. She's not from around here." Best to play it down, just in case. I don't want anyone else interested in her.

"Once you fuck her, it'll be old news," he says.

He's probably right. "Yeah, I know. I guess I like the chase more than I thought."

He shifts in his seat. "Got my sights set on that new sweet butt, Bambi."

I don't know why the girls choose such cheesy names for themselves. Bambi is usually a name used by strippers, but all I think about when I hear it is that fuckin' Disney movie.

She's new to the club, curvy, a brunette, likes it in the ass, or so I've heard. She's the flavor of the month with the guys. Most of the club members don't give a shit that they've all boned the same chick, but sometimes it's an indulgent thought about having a woman of your own. Very indulgent.

In this club, if you bring a woman to church, she's fair game unless she's an ol' lady. Other brothers will hit on her and try their luck, and unless she's your woman, or you want to fight it out, he's got every right to take her.

Of course, the girls are usually willing, but I sometimes wonder what would happen if they weren't. I couldn't stand by and see that shit goin' down. Tex has been known to be a brute to women and though not all the guys are like that, nobody stops him.

"She's cute."

"You tapped her?"

There's no jealousy here, not when the chicks are passed around and don't care whose bed they end up in. Only ol' ladies are semi-respected, and even then, that's a push. No patched member has a claim over any chick unless they claim her, or if they're Prez of course. He can do what he likes, but it's not like he sets the best example for the rest or the prospects.

"Nope."

He looks back to the front window, facing the garage door. "Plan on it?"

"Would it be an issue?" Don't want him gettin' the idea I'm hung up on Blondie. If she agrees to go out with me, it's inevitable at some point she'd have to come to the club. They're my family. They may be the scum of society, but so am I. Tex has been good to me, considering my year and a half of prospecting was no picnic. I don't wish to ever relive that period.

He shrugs. "Not if I get first dibs."

I grin at him. "Greedy fucker."

"You gonna bring your girl to church?"

I shift in my chair. "She isn't my girl." *Not yet, anyway.*

Not only does that thought hit me straight between the eyes, but I realize I know nothing about her. Not even her name.

Maybe I'm not the Romeo I thought I was, but then again, a strip club isn't exactly the kind of place where you get to know a woman on a personal level. She may have the face of an angel, but her body is that of the devil. Ready to punish my every waking moment because I didn't get what I wanted when I wanted it. I plan to remedy that soon and wonder if I should shoot her another text, as desperate as that might look.

I've never chased a woman before in my life, and I figure that is the basis of the appeal; that she isn't falling over herself to get with me. I still want her, though. I want those huge tits out so I can play with them. I wanna squeeze that sexy ass and hear my name on her lips. Just the thought of it makes me hard.

"Should just tell her to get her ass over to church," Hoax says after a beat.

I snort a laugh. "Trust me when I say this chick isn't the type you can tell to do anything."

I see his eyebrow shoot up in my peripheral. Yeah, she's a handful, that much I got.

"Might not be M.C. material, my friend. Does take a certain type of woman."

Which is exactly why I don't plan on bringing her to church.

"That it does. Probably why she's ghosted me." Yeah, it's obvious I shouldn't admit that, but I don't care. Hoax ain't a bad sort; he knows how women work.

He turns to look at me quizzically. "Did she do a number on you, bro?"

I snort. "Fuckin' hardly," I lie. "Anyway, I was pretty out of it Saturday. Would rather remember a night with her for the spank bank later, than for it all to be a blur."

He points at me. "You're not wrong there. Nothin' worse than passin' out and not remembering anything. Though sometimes, with the chicks I wake up next to, I may not wanna know what I did or how many times I did it."

I snort a laugh.

Most of the boys are notorious for being with plenty of women and crave variety, and I've had my fair share, too. However, I ain't sharing Blondie, even if she wanted to. I know for a fact that a jealous streak runs through my body wherever she's concerned, a new emotion I'm dealin' with. There seems to be a lot of firsts with her. Things I'm not used to, such as waiting around like a goddamn schmuck for this woman that I don't even fuckin' know and she can't even return a damn text. Maybe we didn't have as much of a connection as I thought.

I run a hand over my face. "See my dilemma, then. Damned if you do, damned if you don't."

He chuckles. "Yeah, sure, but you're never gonna get a taste of her pussy if you just keep sitting like a little bitch whining to me."

I know he's right.

"Plus," he goes on, like the son of all wisdom. "Chasing a chick can be kind of a fun experience. It's different than having bitches jump you the minute you get inside church. Shit like that can get boring. A man likes a bit of a flirt, you know what I mean, a bit of a tease. Ain't nothin' that can keep a man's attention like a woman he can't have."

"Fuckin' philosopher." I laugh. "Wastin' your time in the M.C. when you come out with shit like that."

He pounds his chest with a fist. "Had a mama tell me there ain't nothin' a man can't fix without a little attention. She also told me to be wary of the quiet ones; they're the ones you gotta watch out for. Some chicks are just harder to come around, brother."

"You can say that again. The quiet ones are also the craziest." I smile when I think about Blondie and that dirty mouth of hers. My smile turns into a grin when I think about her plump lips around my cock. Nah, she definitely wasn't quiet, so hopefully, she's not a psycho. I've had my fair share of those, too.

We don't get to say anything else as Tex, the V.P., Smokey, and Griller, the Sergeant at Arms, enter the garage.

Tex comes over to the window. "We all set?"

"Nitro packed the goods. We're good to roll." Nitro is the club's Treasurer. He likes to make sure shit's all in order. The man creeps me out a bit, but he's been around for years. Keeps to himself, doesn't say much.

"Good. You know the drill. Here's the location."

Each drop is different, and nobody has the coordinates until we're headed out. Safer that way.

I've done this so many times that I don't even register anymore what we're carting or how risky it is. A shitload of jail time is the short answer. But this is business; it's part of the duty of the club. It's not like any of us want this to ever go bad. Paydirt is a good day for everyone and keeps the club coffers full and the Prez happy. If he's happy, then we have a short amount of peace until the next drop.

Being a criminal isn't all it's cracked up to be, but I've never been a nine to five kinda guy.

I don't like the idea of being locked up. I also don't like the idea of where all this shit ends up out on the street, but I try not to think about that part. My momma always said I had a soft heart, even though I've been trying for years to prove to myself that I don't.

It ain't my job to be anybody's else's mother, though, even if I do feel like shit when I see some kid go on a shootout and gun people down for no reason.

A part of me wonders if the gun was one of ours. I argue with myself that kids can get guns from anywhere now. It's easier than trying to buy alcohol when you're underage, but I try not to dwell on it too much. Shit just gets too real, and I don't need that on my shoulders.

The drop goes off without a hitch as we wait in the van for the exchange. Everyone's packing, which is normal, though I've never liked the feel of cold metal against my skin.

Prez doesn't always come on the runs, but occasionally, he likes to stay on top of the deliveries, making sure everything's running as it should. He's in his late forties, but he's known the club since being a kid. It's in his blood.

He's a badass and a little reckless. He'll blow your head off if you look at him the wrong way. Sometimes I go out of my way to avoid him if I can, which sounds cowardly, but if he doesn't like the look of your face, you may just get shit thrown at you for no apparent reason, other than he felt like it.

We get back to church, and since the drop went well, it's a good enough excuse to have a party. Realistically, it's just another Saturday night.

The money from the drop will be divided amongst the members after the club holds a meeting.

Since Hoax and I have the riskiest job, we get a little bit of a bonus, but not much.

The pitfall of being newly patched in is you still have to keep proving your worth. If you slack off in this club, you won't last long. The brotherhood is as strong as it is ruthless, and nobody in this club will appreciate anyone who doesn't pull their weight.

I grin into my beer when I see Bambi straddled across Hoax's knee. He gives me a thumbs up while they're lip locked, and I turn away from the spectacle. It isn't beyond some brothers to fuck right there on the couch, which is another reason why the chicks you bring here have gotta know the life. Most chicks would be shocked out of their mind to walk in a club and see shit like that, but it's normal around here. Most turn a blind eye or stand around and watch.

A primal feeling courses through me when I think about Blondie. About anyone watching her on my lap. I don't know what the fuck these feelings are going on inside me. I crack my neck, trying to shake it off when my phone buzzes.

It's Weasel, one of the prospects.

I frown.

"Yo, Rubble," he says. "Got some chick out the front here askin' for you.

I frown some more.

"Which chick?"

"Dunno, but I let her in. She's not from around here, though, dude." He snickers, and I don't like it one bit.

"How'd you know that?"

He snorts. "I'd remember that fuckin' huge rack anywhere."

My blood runs cold.

I hang up and make for the back door, the one that leads around the side of the clubhouse.

I know it's Blondie, but what the fuck is she doing here? At church?

Is she fuckin' insane?

My heart races in my chest as I go out to intercept her, if she even makes it up the driveway without being accosted.

When I get outside and jog to the front, I see her halfway up the drive.

I breathe a sigh of relief, but it doesn't last. I gotta get her out of here.

She waves at me. Fuckin' waves.

As I get closer, my eyes drop to her rack. Weasel wasn't fuckin' kidding. I'm not sure if she should be wearing skintight clothes like that because it only accentuates those assets, and that's all fine and well, but around here, it makes you seem easy.

As I approach, I smile at the sky-high stilettos she has on, giving the illusion of long legs, which she hasn't got. I don't know how she walks in those things.

A grin splits my face as she totters toward me.

"You lost, sweetheart?" I call as I reach her.

She bites her bottom lip, fucking perfect. My dick kicks in my jeans, not willing to be a bystander this time round.

"I dropped my phone down the fucking toilet," she says as I laugh. "I lost your number."

I rest my hands on my hips as I assess her. She reaches out to me, and fuck me, we hug.

She smells so fucking good, like candy apples. I want to take a bite…

"You mean to say, you came out to the HQ just to find me?" I marvel. "Thought you were ghosting me. I texted you a couple of times."

She nods, a coy smile on her lips that does wonders for my ego. Here I was worried I was losing my touch. I'm thrilled to know it's still alive and well.

"That's incredibly brave," I go on. "Not like this is the yellow brick road over here, darlin'."

"I knew that when I met you," she tells me, her eyes flicking down my body ever so slightly.

I'm wearing a cut with nothing on under it, being that it's fuckin' hot in Phoenix at the moment. Her eyes graze my torso, and I'm suddenly glad I don't skip out at the gym when her gaze heats.

"You did?"

"Yes, Barney, I did."

I laugh again, then lean toward her. "Don't be sayin' that too loud, I got a reputation to hold up."

She casts those bright blue eyes at me, and I'm a goner. Seriously, I'm fucked.

She pouts, and I want to lean down and take her mouth, but I can't. And I need to get her out of here before….

"Hey, Rubble, who you got there?" I hear Smokey call from somewhere behind me.

Oh, fuck no.

The V.P.

Smokey's cool, but I don't want him knowing about her.

I turn around and give him a chin lift, then turn back to Blondie.

"Do you trust me?" I say, staring down at her.

She frowns. "I uh… I barely know you."

"Know this. I'd never put you in harm's way, but you came here, baby, and now I've gotta smooth this over."

She peers over my shoulder, and her eyes go wide.

"Okay," she whispers.

"Whatever I say, go along with it, yeah? And for fuck's sake, keep that smart mouth shut."

She nods. "Uh, all right…" She sounds about as unsure as I feel, but we don't get any more time.

Smokey is slapping me on the back while he eye fucks my girl, and I now have to think of something fuckin' quick before he manhandles her.

"You brought us a present, brother?" He grins as I watch the smile fade from Blondie's face. She holds her own, head held high, and I know she wants to spit fire at him. That won't be tolerated here, though.

"Nah, brother, this one's mine."

He snickers. "You sure, she looks a little startled."

I hold my hand out to her. "C'mere, baby, meet Smokey, our club's V.P."

She smiles tentatively while taking my hand in hers.

"Nice to meet you, I'm Lucy."

Lucy.

Sweet as sugar.

I grab her chin, tilt it up and kiss her rough, hard.

It's gotta be done; he needs to know she's fuckin' mine or this will end badly.

I grope her ass while she lets out a strangled noise in the back of her throat. I don't even get to enjoy it though, because my heart's racing like a fuckin' freight train.

I feel like a fuckin' prick for just taking her like that, but I've no choice. She came here, on my turf, and now I've gotta try and work a way out of this situation.

When I pull back, she stares at me a little wide-eyed.

Smokey snickers, patting me on the back again but

nodding at her. "Well, when you're done, feel free to send her my way. If you're willin' that is, sweetheart."

I grimace as I pull her to my body. Her big tits squash against my chest, and I glance down at them. Fuck, she's beautiful.

She's still staring at me wordlessly. Yeah, I've no doubt I'm gonna hear about it soon enough.

"Well, don't be a stranger," he goes on, "come on inside. She should meet everyone."

Fuck.

This is exactly what I don't want. Yet, I know that if she comes in, and I show her around, nobody will care, and then we'll get to leave. If I make a big deal about gettin' outta here, he'll smell a rat.

In this club, if you show weakness, you're as good as dead.

I don't think Lucy is ready for what he's got in mind, but it doesn't stop me. And I won't let anything happen.

I nod once, then tug her along as Smokey walks away, toward the party. We follow, dread filling me each and every step.

4

LUCY

It's not the kiss that assaults my senses, or how he just took it without asking, but the fact I actually enjoyed it.

After suffering at the hands of men who don't know what they're doing, I find my body aching for him, the strong attraction blindsiding me even though he just kissed and groped me in front of a complete stranger.

I press my fingertips to my lips as we follow behind a big, scary looking man who looks like he wouldn't be very kind if you got him alone in a dark alley way. I guess bikers aren't meant to be boy scouts.

"I don't know if I want to do this," I whisper as Rubble slings his arm around me.

"You and me both," he mutters.

I could just demand for him to get me out of here, or I could just run back the same way I came. But something about the danger of it all, and the fact Rubble just went all alpha on me has piqued my interest tenfold. His brutal kiss has me tingling all the way down to my toes.

"Is this safe?" I whisper again, relishing in the smell of

him; leather, cigarettes, and his faded cologne. If you could bottle sex, this is what it would smell like.

"Safe enough. If you're askin' if I'll protect you, then the answer is yes, baby. Like I said, keep your pretty mouth shut, stick with me, and feel free to grope me if you want to." He looks down at me with heat in his eyes.

My chest flutters when I know it shouldn't.

Keep your pretty mouth shut?

I shouldn't be here. I had no business coming here, but I had to see him again, and I wasn't about to go back to that damn strip club, just to see if he'd show up one night.

The fact is, I came here for him. I sought him out. I knew what I was getting myself into when I arrived at the heavy gates declaring it to be 'Phoenix Fury HQ.'

I could have turned tail and ran then, yet here I am. Wrapped up in Rubble's arms after he just assaulted my lips and groped my ass while I'm being led to God knows where. The viper's den for all I know.

Rubble was so sincere when he asked if I trusted him though, and it's probably stupid since I don't know him from Adam, but there's something in his eyes that tells me all I need to know. That he'd never hurt me. Or maybe I'm a fool. I'm starting to think the latter as we get closer to the double doors at the front of the building because I couldn't imagine Hell being any less intimidating.

The party's in turbo mode, the music pumps so loud, it could make your bones clatter. Rubble's arm tightens around me.

As soon as we enter, it looks like pure chaos.

There are bodies everywhere and a bar is in full swing. To my left, there's a bunch of pool tables surrounded by bikers. To my right is a makeshift dance floor where girls are strewn here, there and everywhere, and there are half-naked bodies in every direction you look.

This makes the Apple Pie look tame by comparison.

Rubble leads us to the bar, his hand caressing slowly down my back, and I'd hazard a guess he wants to grab my ass again.

He leans to my ear. "What's your poison, beautiful?"

His eyes meet mine, and I see fire there that makes my insides squirm.

You came here looking for this, girl. Now you've got it, so don't act all fucking coy.

"Don't suppose they make apple martinis?"

He snorts a laugh.

"Fine, I'll take a bourbon and Coke, please," I say, trying to keep my attention solely on him, and not on the surrounding areas.

He nods to the scantily clad bartender, who may as well not even be wearing clothes, and orders our drinks. He turns back to me and is about to say something when another dude sidles up besides us and stares down at me, confusion marring his face, but it's quickly replaced with a big grin.

"This her?" the guy asks. He's broad and looks like the kind of man you'd see on the door of a nightclub.

Rubble gives him a cold glare, then rolls his eyes. Ah, so he's been talking about me.

There go those little butterflies again…

"Yeah," he mutters, then says, "Lucy, this is Hoax, he's a buddy of mine."

I give him a nod back, glad I'm pressed into Rubble's body. His hand's now resting on the small of my back.

"She's pretty," he says, still staring at me.

"I am standing right here," I fire back.

Instead of Rubble telling me to watch my mouth, he rumbles with laughter, and so does Hoax.

"You're not wrong about that smart mouth," he comments,

slapping Rubble on the back. They seem to do a lot of that around here. Then he leans to Rubble's ear and says something else I can't decipher. He nods and Hoax takes off.

"What did he say?" I ask once he's gone.

Rubble nods to the bartender as our drinks arrive.

"Nothin'. Let's go find a seat," he says, handing me my drink.

He keeps his arm slung around me. In fact, it hasn't left my body, and we weave through the throng of bodies to a less crowded part of the club.

He slides into a booth and pulls me onto his lap. The close contact has me feeling not just the flutter inside, but now my pussy is on fire for him. I know I'm flirting in dangerous territory but I can't stop the adrenaline running through my veins.

"What?" He shrugs.

I shake my head. "You're just too cute for your own good, aren't you?" I say close to his ear.

He grins as I glance down at him. He's at the perfect height now for my tits in his face, which I guess was the whole idea, though his eyes stay on mine.

I sip my drink as he takes a big swig, then places his glass on the table.

He motions with two fingers to come closer, and when I bend to his ear, he whispers, "I'm sorry about before, but I had to. It sends a message. He had to know you belong to me, even if it is make believe."

I run a hand over his bare chest as I move my mouth to his ear. "Don't be sorry, the bad girl in me kinda liked it."

When our gazes lock, his look tells me everything, and this time, he doesn't need to apply brute force. Our lips meet, and a groan escapes me as we kiss, his stubble scraping my mouth deliciously. It's a good pain and not as rough as the first kiss. *That* kiss was all alpha, but this one is him showing me he has some kind of restraint.

I think I like it when he takes charge.

I grip onto his pec as one of his hands grips the back of my neck, deepening the kiss, the other squeezing my ass cheek.

I feel his tongue seek entry, and I let him. I cup his face as the kiss goes on and feel my insides turn to jelly and my pussy throb. Dirty kissing like this always does it for me. When I pull back, my panties are wet and my nipples stand to attention.

He smirks, his eyes gliding down my body, then he comes back in for more. This time, he takes charge, holding my face with one hand. It's then I notice he has a pair of knuckle dusters encrusted over four fingers; I don't want to think about why he's wearing that too closely. The other snakes its way up my torso and grips one of my tits. He gives it a squeeze as my pulse races at his sensual touch. It's like he knows exactly what I need. And fuck me if I don't swat his hand away for groping me in public.

There is no doubt about it; I'm going to have sex with this man. It's what I came here for when it's all said and done. I haven't been able to stop thinking about him since that night.

We keep making out right there in the booth, with chaos all around us. Though I should be scared and not doing this in plain sight of others, the excitement only fuels my thirst, and I grind into him.

He moans, gripping my breast even harder. I so badly want to be naked with him, have him suck my tits and make me come with his mouth.

"You're killin' me babe," he says, nipping my ear as I squeeze his biceps, noticing how muscled and sculpted they are, like the rest of him. He's got a body built for sin.

I place my drink down and straddle his lap as I push him

back against the booth, grinding my pussy into him. Fire lights his eyes when I look down at him and smirk.

"You like being on display, baby?" he asks, gripping the back of my head and pulling me down to kiss me harder. With our bodies pressed together, I can feel his dick, hard as steel, digging into me, and we both look down at the same time.

"Looks like you've got something there for me, sugar," I say, arching my back, placing my tits in his line of sight. He takes the bait, moving his hands up my body and gripping them both as I glance around quickly. Nobody seems to be noticing what we're doing.

I'm not going to have sex with him here, but I need friction between my legs, and I need it now.

I grind into him harder as my dress rides up, and I know by now half my ass is hanging out.

"Fuck, I need these puppies out, baby." He presses his face into my chest as I imagine riding him, having his hard cock inside me as we go at it fast and furious.

I lose all sense of reality when I say, "Take me upstairs."

His lips meet my neck as he sucks on my pulse, and I wrap my arms around his shoulders.

"No fuckin' way, it's a shithole," he says, disgusted.

"I don't care," I whimper.

"Got you that hot, beautiful?"

I tip my head back. "Mhmm..."

He moves a hand from my breast down in between us, snaking his hand up my thigh, and it disappears up my dress.

I feel his fingers play with my soaked panties. Any slight movement is going to get me off super quick, but what I can't get over is how he stares at me with those *undress me* eyes.

"Want to see how wet you are," he says, then pulls my panties aside and swipes two fingers through my soaking wet heat as I hiss at the contact.

He closes his eyes and does it again, mouthing *fuck* as I stare down and wonder what the fuck I'm doing. Acting like a two-bit whore, yet here I am, past the point of caring and the point of no return. I've lost my damn mind.

He brings his fingers out, then puts them in his mouth and sucks. I whimper as I watch him, biting down on my bottom lip when he groans. He moves his hand to my mouth and shoves his fingers in, his eyes turning molten as my lips wrap firmly around them.

He works his fingers in and out of my mouth as I suck, swirling my tongue around and around as he licks his lips.

All it takes is a moan from me, and he yanks his hand out, running the other through his hair. "Upstairs. Now."

Smiling triumphantly, he shakes his head at my grin and kisses me chastely.

"I thought they say it's the fuckin' quiet ones that are trouble."

I climb off his lap and pull my dress down. "No sugar, it's the ones that know what they want and go out and get it."

He downs the rest of his drink, adjusts his dick in his jeans, and grabs my hand.

We hurtle through the sea of bodies, passing people in all kinds of undress as the music throngs through the entire building.

In a few moments, we're heading toward another door on the far side of the room. Rubble produces a key and unlocks it.

When we're through the door, he turns to me.

"This is where a few of us live, so we keep it locked for parties and shit."

I nod, knowing I'm fucking crazy for even being here or taking it this far.

But I need, no, I *want* to feel him inside of me.

He bends down to kiss me quickly, and then we're

mounting a flight of stairs. You can still hear the music, but it's quieter, so at least I can hear myself think now.

We get to a landing, and he takes the first door on the left, unlocking it as he tugs me inside.

"Sorry about the mess," he says. Picking up some clothes in the doorway and tossing them in the corner. "I wasn't exactly planning on company."

I arch an eyebrow. "Oh? Don't you usually bring girls up here, Romeo?"

He licks his bottom lip as he stares at me, then bites it as he reaches for me. His thumb swipes over my lips as I stare back at him.

"Nah, baby doll, I've been creaming in my own hand this last week, wishing you'd call me."

My mouth goes dry at the thought of him jerking off to me. Whether it's true or not is irrelevant. We're here now. I'm not going anywhere.

"I would have, if my phone didn't go swimming."

He shrugs his sleeveless jacket off as I stare at the tattoos covering his body. They are comprised of various swirling patterns of rose covered vines that wind up his neck and disappear onto his back. His arms are covered with the same.

He is, without a doubt, the sexiest man I've ever laid my eyes on.

"You're brave, little one," he says, stepping into me so we're flush up against one another. "Comin' here like this could have been very bad news."

"Maybe I like bad news." I shrug, sounding much braver than I feel.

He shakes his head. "Does your mouth get you into trouble a lot?"

"Yes, but something tells me you like trouble, sugar, and I'm not usually the kind of girl that just sleeps around, just so you know. The truth is, I've been wanting to jump you since that night at the strip club."

He runs a hand through my hair, then caresses my face. "That's like music to my ears, Lucy."

It's the first time he's used my name and I like how it sounds when he's aroused and looking at me like I'm his next meal.

I run my hands up his ripped stomach and squeeze his pecs. "Yeah?"

He watches my movement as he grunts; it's so fucking sexy. "Yeah, baby."

"Did you imagine me doing this?" I run a hand south and grip his dick through his jeans, and he hisses at the sudden contact, his eyes meeting mine.

"I like your hands bein' on me," he confesses. "Feels fuckin' amazin'."

I smile, squeezing him as I rub my palm over his length. Every single movement has me wanting to climb his body like a tree.

"I think I like it too," I breathe softly.

I go for his buckle as he watches me undo it, sliding the zipper down, and skating my hand over his boxer briefs as he groans.

"Pull it out, baby."

I give his jeans a tug and pull them to his knees, his pubic hair coming into view as his boxers slide only halfway down. I pull them too and his cock springs out, and like the rest of him, it's fucking hot.

Big. Fat. Juicy.

Oh shit this is gonna be good. My mouth waters at the sight.

I fist his entire length in my palm as he groans; I think I like that sound.

"Jesus," I whisper.

"Like what you see?" he mumbles as I jerk him off while he watches.

"I think I'd like it better in my mouth," I whisper, a smile creeping on my face.

I'm about to drop to my knees when he yanks me up by the shoulders.

"Get that fuckin' dress off first. I need to see those tits," he tells me.

My core clenches at his dirty words as I grab the bottom of my dress and roll it up.

I wore a pink G-string and a matching, sheer pink bra. I fling the dress behind me as he stares down at my body like he wants to eat me whole.

I waggle my finger in his face. "I'll get these out." I cup myself and squeeze my tits together while his eyes burn. "After I've had a taste of you."

I guess you could say I've always been pretty confident with my body, but I've never acted like this in front of a man. Gary was very strait-laced and not really into kink. It's like I have this need in me to fulfill all my desires with Rubble. He brings out the wild side in me.

The danger. The deliciousness of what we're doing. I can't get enough.

His eyes darken when I drop to my knees, and I'm face-to-face with his cock.

It's a beautiful thing, the tip plump and succulent as I rub my tongue over it.

He growls again, and I think I'm beginning to crave only that sound.

I grip him with one hand and tease his tip with my tongue, flicking his slit and licking my way down his shaft. I know, like any man, he wants to ram it down my throat, but I like the idea of making him wait.

He doesn't thrust, though. Instead, he cups my head and gently holds it while I caress his balls with my other hand.

"Jesus, Lucy…"

I like it when he says my name, and I want to be a bad girl for him. I want to show him I'm not as angelic as he thinks I am.

I slowly work my lips over the tip and suck him into my mouth, glancing up as I do it. He watches me with those fiery eyes. A thrill runs through me at the thought of him between my legs, pleasuring me, and it only drives my hunger. I suck him deeper, then pull back, letting him go with a pop as I continue to grip him at the base.

"You're so fucking beautiful," he tells me. I smile, sheathing him as I let go momentarily and reach around to undo my bra straps. I pull it off and fling that too, letting my breasts fall out.

"Want to see my party trick?"

"Only if it's for me and only me," he growls.

I like the way he's so fucking domineering when we're alone, it's like he knows what I need, what my body needs.

He groans as he watches me, and I cup them together. I reach toward him and suck him back in my mouth, and this time, I go deeper. He hits the back of my throat, and I do it again, loving how salty he tastes, how utterly addictive he is. I pull him out and move up even closer to his legs, sliding his cock between my tits as I jerk him off in between them. Seeing his cock move between them sets my pussy on fire. I want him so bad.

He makes a noise that's so primal and fucking delicious, I spare a glance up, not that I needed to, his grip on my hair tells me all I need to know.

"Fuck, Lucy… Fuck…" I know he's going to come, so I keep rubbing him, his dick poking out the top every time I bob down, and when I suck him into my mouth again, he pumps his hips, harder, faster, then pulls out and shoots his load all over my chin and my tits. The grunt he makes has me so horny, I don't just want him, I *need* him.

I need him like I need water. Like I need air. Like I'll die without him inside me.

I dared to play this game, and now I have to finish it.

5

RUBBLE

THE WOMAN IS A MINX. I HAVE NO OTHER WORDS FOR HER sweet torture.

She gets me all worked up in front of my entire club, practically dry humps me for everyone to see, then sucks me off, and I come between her beautiful, big tits.

If I die tonight, I will die happy.

That move was fuckin' gold. I've never seen anyone do anything like that before, and I know I want her to do it all over again. The only thing that stops me is the fact that I need to clean her tits up so I can please her right back.

Grabbing a shirt from the floor, I toss it to her so she can wipe herself clean.

I lean down, untying my boots, then remove them and my socks, and all the while she's eyeing me like a tiger. Next, I pull my jeans and boxers the rest of the way off. My dick is at half-mast, but it's still hard, and I yank her up off her knees.

"That was very naughty," I growl in her ear. "But fuckin' beautiful. I want to taste you too, baby. You deserve it after that."

A soft moan leaves her lips as I reach for her and kiss her

hard, my tongue in her mouth, and she kisses me right back with just as much fire. Fuckin' spitfire.

I palm her tits, pulling on her nipples as she moans.

"I know you want me to touch you here," I say, cupping her sex. "But I'm not going to. You're gonna beg me, baby. I wanna play with these first." I pinch her nipples hard as she gasps.

She groans as I lift her, and she wraps her legs around me as we move to the bed. I sit back against the bed frame as she straddles me, and I run my hands down her tiny little body. Her slim waist and wide hips have my dick at full tilt and ready to rumble all over again. That didn't take long.

I never go twice in one night, but with her, I don't think I have any limits.

"Did you like my dick in your mouth?" I ask her as we kiss, and she grinds down on me.

She nods. "Best dick ever."

I snort as I cup her tits, feeling their weight, loving how big and natural they are. I bring her with me as I rest back, and I move my mouth to her nipple as I tweak the other with my fingers. I suck as I squeeze, licking her dark pink bud, trying to get as much of her as I can in my mouth. I move to the other, paying it the same attention as her hands slide into my hair as she tugs.

"You like that, baby? You like me playing with your body?"

"Yes!" she cries out, grinding into my cock as I rub my chin over the sensitive peak, loving how she bucks in my lap when I do it.

I suck like a fuckin' baby, going from one to the other, squeezing and lifting. *Jesus*, she's too fucking divine.

"Can taste myself on your mouth," I grunt. "Bet you like that too."

She leans down to my ear. "Spank my ass."

I glance up, gripping her ass cheek with one hand. "You wanna be spanked, baby?"

I circle one cheek as she anticipates it.

"Yes," she sighs. "Spank me while you suck."

Fuck. I'm in some kind of heaven and I'm never coming down.

I do just that. I give her a good hard smack on one cheek and suck hard on her nipple. She grabs both tits and holds them in my face while I move from one to the other. I spank her plump little ass as I move from one nipple to the other, and she presses her hot, wet little pussy into my dick. I know she's going to get off.

"Ride my face, baby," I tell her as I reach down and rip her G-string off.

I slide down the bed as she stares at me, unsure.

"Ride. My. Face."

She climbs over my head and grips the headboard as I lick her folds, sliding my fingers through her wet heat, her legs either side of me. She's so fucking wet, she's dripping. I suck her into my mouth, and she cries out. Then I swipe my tongue over her clit, and she cries harder. I insert a finger and swirl my tongue at the same time, and she detonates in three seconds.

The sound she makes is like nothing I've ever heard before.

I don't let up. I eat her out as she grinds against me, trying to get another orgasm in before I flip her over and fuck her senseless. I part her with my thumbs, spreading her wet juices with my tongue. Her tits look fucking fabulous from this angle as she rocks forward, and I suck on her clit this time and don't let go.

She comes again, locking eyes with me as I insert another finger and fuck her hard, fast, and brutal. Her orgasm goes on and on, and when she's done, she collapses onto my chest.

RUBBLE

I waste no time flipping her over as I fumble around in the nightstand for a rubber.

She helps me rip the packet open when I don't do it fast enough, then rolls it on me.

I line up and push into her, still on my knees, her legs around my waist, the force making her gasp. It's deep in this position, and she bites her bottom lip as I still, letting her adjust to my cock as her tight little hole swallows me.

I glance down to where we're joined and pull out, slamming back in again.

"Oh God," she cries as our eyes meet, and I lift her legs over my shoulders, gripping the mattress as I stare down at her body while she plays with herself, and I ram into her hard and fast.

I need to come. This is too much. Her body is insane, it should be illegal.

No way will I have her wearing a bodycon dress like that ever again in this clubhouse, not that I want her back here again. I want her for myself. If Tex sees her, I don't know what he would be capable of, and I don't want that. I'll fuckin' slit his throat if he even looks at her.

It's bad enough that I brought her up here to this shithole.

I pound in and out, moving my hips back and forth as her breath hitches, and I'm not quiet either. I let her know what she's doing to me, telling her how fuckin' sexy she is and how much I fuckin' want her. The headboard creaks and protests as we go at it.

"Not gonna last, you're too fuckin' beautiful," I say, reaching my hand between us as I pinch her clit. It's all she needs, and she comes hard, calling my name. If it weren't for the music, the whole clubhouse would know my name, too.

I jerk and spasm my release so hard, so violently, that I momentarily forget where I am.

Fuckin' Heaven, that's where I am.

A cold breeze wakes me as I slowly open my eyes.

Long, blonde hair is strewn across my chest as Lucy cuddles into my side.

We spent all night fucking.

One can hardly blame me when she acted like a little deviant. Here I was thinking I had to wine and dine her first, when in reality, she just wanted some good dick.

I smile up at the ceiling, thinking I still got it, when I know it was mostly her.

That sinful body sent shockwaves through me as I rode out her orgasms, one by one.

I've never wanted to please a woman so much in my life. Yet, I spent all night doing it.

She rode me the second time as I held her hips and bounced her up and down. Her tits are so fuckin' beautiful. I can't get enough of them.

She cried out like a woman possessed while she watched me suck on her rosy peaks. Safe to say that she likes what I do to her.

I stroke her shoulder as she sleeps soundly.

This is a first for me, too, having a woman in my bed.

The girls I bone usually take off, one: because I don't actually like sleeping with them, and two: we're not like this; swept up in each other's arms.

Lucy has this hold on me that's instant and, quite frankly, alarming.

I don't know if it's her sense of adventure that's got me all riled up, since she did, after all, seek me out. I know it's definitely that hot body of hers and that pert little mouth, but more importantly, the feeling I get when she's around. I can't explain it.

The tightening in my chest tells me all I need to know, even when I don't exactly know what it means.

She stirs in my arms as I return from the bathroom, taking a leak as quietly as I can, but when I crawl back into bed, her eyelashes flutter.

She's lovely in her sleep, angelic looking.

"Hey, sleepy head," I whisper as her eyes meet mine.

A smile curls up on her pert lips that has my dick awake again.

"Hi yourself," she says, stifling a yawn. "What time is it?"

"Who the fuck cares?" I reply, then I add, "You good?

She nods into my chest. "Yup. Though I think you broke my vagina."

I burst out laughing. "I fuckin' hope not. I happen to like it."

I get the feeling she likes the thrill of being here, being in my bed. I hope it is me and not just the dirty biker notion she's got goin' in that head of hers. But she came here to seek out sex with me, that's gotta count for something, right?

"I've not had that many big O's since…" She yawns for real this time. "Since forever."

I think I like hearing about how long it's been. Imagining her with some other dude doesn't exactly appeal to me, and in fact, it makes me want to rip someone's throat out.

"Good to hear," I mutter into her hair. Even that smells like candy.

"Not for me it isn't," she says. "Though I guess that's what bullets are for."

"Bullets?" I question.

"Vibrators, honey. A girl's got needs too when there's no man around."

Shit me till Sunday.

55

Imagining her using that on herself has me getting all kinds of ideas.

"Is that right?"

"Uh huh. Gotta take matters into your own hands sometimes, sweetie."

"Here I was thinkin' you were some kind of angel in disguise. I'm shocked to the core."

She smiles into my chest. "Looks can be deceiving."

"I'm thrilled to find out you're not," I add, a little startled at how normal this feels.

It's like I've known this chick forever. I don't want to kick her out of my bed and send her packing, not that I've literally kicked girls out of my bed, but I have kinda hinted it was time to go. I'm not a total asshole.

I stare at her, unable to focus. I'm not sure what it means. Everything feels different now. She looks up at me with those big blue eyes, and I feel my heart patter faster.

"What are you thinking?" she asks.

We lie still for a while as I try and put together what the fuck I am actually thinking.

"That I shouldn't have brought you up to this shithole," I admit, unsure how she even agreed, and I feel slightly smug that she hadn't even had two sips of her drink. It was all lust and not alcohol fueled.

I run a hand through my hair, unsure what to say next, and I'm totally avoiding the question. This isn't like me.

I don't get involved with women that aren't from the M.C.; it makes things less complicated that way, even if I'm wondering when I'm going to see her again and if she wants to see me.

I've been told I'm good in bed. I'm not a selfish prick like some of the brothers in the club, but I can safely say I don't usually eat chicks out. It's not usually my jam to be doing that in a club where women sleep with everyone.

But with Lucy, I wanted all of her. Images of her riding my face make me want to do it all over again. She's got a perfectly pretty, bare, tight little pussy, and I can't get enough of it.

I smile when I think about her tottering up the driveway in those heels.

"It's not so bad," she sighs, though, it's still dark in here. She can't see the mess.

I vow to never bring her up here again.

I'm not ashamed of where I live, or my club, but I'm sure she'll never return once she realizes where she is. It was worrying at first with all the brothers eyeing her up last night, which is why I whisked her away to a booth so we wouldn't draw so much attention.

I never intended we'd make out and end up fucking on the first date. Not that it was a date.

Even if I feel like I'm the luckiest man alive.

"You gotta work?" I ask.

"Yeah," she sighs. "I start work at eight. Oh crap, what's the time?"

I glance at my watch.

"You've got hours yet, baby," I tell her, but really, I just want to keep enjoying holding her, which is so fucking lame.

I know I need to shut this down. But a part of me just doesn't want to.

I may not deserve it, but I'm gonna relish in it anyway.

Next time I see her, and I will be seeing her again, we can meet on her turf.

Yeah, that's a much better plan. The last thing I need is any of my brothers sniffing around. Getting rid of Smokey was bad enough. And then Hoax didn't help matters; fucker ratted me out.

I don't even know this fuckin' chick, and I'm already

getting jealous about any other guy hittin' on her. Not happening. She's *mine.*

An hour later, she uses my bathroom and passes on a shower. I can't say I blame her, as it's not that nice in there. She dresses in last night's clothes, which I find very amusing. She looks like she just got fucked big time.

"Don't look so pleased with yourself," she says when I rest my hands behind my head and watch her dress.

"Why not?" I reply, loving how she bends over, giving me a bird's eye view of her ass. "You had a good time, right? Pretty sure we almost broke the bed."

I watch as she tucks her luscious tits back into her dress, and I just about cry when she covers them up. I like her naked and sated.

"I think you know the answer to that," she retorts as I reluctantly swing my legs off the bed and pull my jeans on.

I'm thankful, as we leave and take the stairs, that nobody is around in the clubhouse this early.

There's a lot of mess, and as we make our way through the quiet, dark room, I see bodies strewn about on the couch and a chick asleep on the pool table.

I lead Lucy out to the front gates where she left her car last night. As she locates her keys in her purse, and I give her a chin lift.

"So, when am I going to see you again?" she asks out of nowhere.

I can't help the race of my chest as the words wash over me.

Feeling like a smug son of a bitch, I run a hand through my hair. "You want a real date, princess?" I grin.

She gives me narrow eyes, but her lips are twitching. "What did you have in mind?"

Fucking you again.

"What do you like doing?"

I know nothing about her, and I find myself itching to know what she does for fun.

"How about you take me out for a Guinness next Friday night, and we'll see where we end up."

I stare at her. "Guinness?"

She smiles, and I reach out and flick her hair off one shoulder. I need to touch her.

"Yeah, I like Guinness."

I frown. "Isn't that like, stout, or some shit?"

She laughs "Yes. Girls drink stout, you know."

I rub my chin.

Not for the first time, I wonder what I've gotten myself into.

Here I was thinking she was a martini or margarita girl. A good girl from the right side of the tracks. But I was so so wrong. She's got the mind of a devil and a body that could send me to Hell. And I'll do anything I can to see her again.

Waiting until Friday to see her is going to be absolute torture, though.

I like how she's flirty; it's sexy. She's got a confidence to her that I'm attracted to. I like a woman who knows what she wants, and it's not something I'm used to. I'm used to hard and fast. Women that are good in the sack but have absolutely no substance. It's a shock to the system as the realization dawns.

So is the fact that I want to keep her to myself, and that feeling is even more prominent this morning. I don't want anybody getting close to her, talkin' to her, lookin' at her. It was risky last night, and I don't want that to happen again. Not until I see where this goes.

I peck her on the lips. "I guess I'm forgiven, then?"

"What for?" she asks, surprised.

"For kissing you without permission and manhandling you like that, even if it was for the greater good."

She laughs and playfully swats me on the chest. "Only because it was for the greater good, otherwise I'd be super mad."

I know she's too pure for me. It's glaringly obvious.

"You got a new number?" I ask, remembering she killed her phone.

She rummages around in her purse until she locates it. "Yup."

She reels it off as I punch it in my phone, then call her.

"Till Friday," I say, wishing she didn't have to go and wondering why I didn't fuck her again this morning.

"Friday," she agrees, climbing into her car. She gives me a little wave through the window. I tap the top of the roof as she starts the car and drives away.

I watch her until she's almost out of sight and her taillights disappear.

I've no idea what that thudding is going off in my chest. It's got no business there.

I should try and control myself, but what the hell… It's a darned sight better than how I usually feel after a party at church. I always drink too much and wake up regretting most of what I did and who I did it with.

This feels good, though, and let's face it, I haven't had a lot to feel good about in a long, long time. So, I'm gonna allow myself this one indulgence. It might be short-lived, but what the heck, I'm goin' to Hell anyway.

6

LUCY

I STARE OUT AT THE STREET THROUGH THE RECEPTION AREA window. It's almost summer, yet the rain pours down. It's typical Arizona weather; you never know what it's going to be from one day to the next.

I curse myself. What I'm really trying to do is distract myself from Rubble.

I can still feel him all over me.

I can honestly say I've never been worshiped like that by a man before. He played my body like a finely tuned instrument; the thought makes me tingle from the tips of my toes. Remembering what he did to me... feeling his body... his tongue... I've got to stop, I'm at work.

Looking back, it probably wasn't the smartest idea turning up at the clubs HQ and asking the kid at the gate if he could call Rubble for me. I mean, I've done some dumb shit before, but that took the cake.

I wasn't even drinking, which is worse, but I just knew I had to see him again. I guess when I want something, I go out and get it, no matter the consequences.

It sounds crazy, but we have a connection. Sure, it might

just be physical, but when I met him in the strip club, we had a moment. And he was just so sweet, despite the fact he's in a criminal club and wears dirty patches on his jacket. In fact, I'm sure his rap sheet is as big as my shoe collection.

This is exactly why my relationships never work, not that I want a relationship with him, but I go for the completely wrong kind of guy. Every. Single. Time.

But it's like my thoughts aren't my own when it comes to men. I'm a sucker for a pretty face and a dirty pickup line.

I cringe when I think about how I straddled his lap in front of total strangers. Okay, sure, they were busy doing other things, and it was dark, mind you. It wasn't like anyone cared; they were doing far worse, but I know that's just a justification for my bad behavior.

I'm starting to think I like being bad.

I knew I wanted to be a little reckless. I knew I wanted fun, but I didn't know I wanted *that*. And now that I've had a taste of it, I want more.

Is it the danger?

Is it the unknown?

Is it the fact that I'm doing something totally out of character? I'm not sure. But I'm always telling everybody else to be a little bit sassier, live a little, don't worry so much, and here I am playing Mary Poppins every day.

I won't lie, it felt good to be wanted. And it felt even better when he held me in his arms.

I know that he's been with a lot of women, and he'll likely forget me tomorrow. He probably won't even make that date on Friday, but I can't find anything inside of me to regret any of it.

The minute his hands were on my body, I was a goner, and I regret nothing.

The way he looks at me; I can safely say no man has ever looked at me like that before.

Sure, I get guys gawking at me all day long, lusting after me, treating me like a bimbo because of how I look. They wouldn't know their ass from their elbow, or what to do with a woman like me, but with him, there's something else in his eyes. Some desire that I can't decipher. I know I shouldn't, but a part of me wants to get to the heart of this rough and rugged man that I can still feel between my legs. I almost want to get inside his skin and know all about him, and that is a very bad idea.

Just as I'm fantasizing about exactly what he can do with his tongue, my boss flings another file on my desk, and it lands with a thud, causing my coffee cup to spill. "Thanks, Bob," I call after him sarcastically.

"You're welcome," he sing-songs like the asshole he is.

"Always a pleasure," I mutter under my breath when he's out of earshot.

I don't take it personally. Bob is hot and cold, and most of the time, I just want to staple things to his head. He's going through a divorce, so that means all women are gold-digging, money-grabbing bitches, even the ones he pays to run his office.

I only stay because I basically get to do my own thing, and most of the time, he lets me get on with it. Oh, and I get to yell at the boys in the workshop. They're used to me by now; I've been here for four wonderful years.

I work at a car detailing business. It's busy. There's lots of people, mainly obnoxious businessmen and corporate women, but the worst clients are parents with kids. The guys hate it when a mom or a dad comes in and needs their car overhauled. It takes them a whole day to clean the car. I don't know why they whine; they're getting paid by the hour.

"Hey, Luce," says Jemma, my friend and coworker. She's twenty minutes late, but I covered for her when Bob asked earlier where she was. As soon as you mention women's cycles, they shut up pretty fast. In reality, she forgot to put gas in her car and had to make an unexpected stop on the side of the highway.

"Hey, babe, how's it hanging?"

She dumps her stuff on the other side of the desk and shoves her purse underneath.

"God, I'm so fucking late!"

"Don't worry about it," I say, taking a sip of my coffee. "I got your back. If Bob asks, you're bleeding heavily, okay?"

She snickers. "Thanks, doll, where would I be without you?"

"I have no idea," I say, humming a little tune to myself as I process the next invoice.

A few moments later, I feel her staring at me. "What?" I ask when I turn to look at her.

"You did it, didn't you?"

She is the one person who can smell my bullshit radar like nobody else can. Jemma was there the night I met Rubble, and it's all I've been spouting on about.

It's like a gift. She should go on America's Got Talent or something.

"I don't know what you mean," I try, innocently.

"You fucking did it!" she cries as I roll my eyes. "What happened, tell me everything! I want details!"

I shake my head. "Why am I so transparent?"

"Easy, you never hum, and you're chirping like a goddamn canary."

I make a mental note to never hum again.

"So, was it good?" she presses when I don't respond. Jemma is boy crazy, and like me, she picks all the wrong kinds of guys.

"Oh, girl, you've no idea," I say, because why lie? It's the truth. "He's a fuckin' magician."

She scoots over on her chair on wheels and claps her hands together.

I drop my pen down on the keyboard. I can't hold it in any longer. "Oh God, Jem, I did a very bad thing."

Her eyes go wide. "You slept with him?"

I bite my lip. "Yes, but that's not the very bad thing… I… I went to the clubhouse on Saturday night."

Her eyes go wide. "Luce, what the actual fuck?" she screeches as I tell her to shush at the same time. "Are you out of your mind?"

"Apparently so." I shrug.

"Let me get this straight. You turned up at the Phoenix Fury's HQ and just waltzed through the front doors?" She stares at me incredulously.

"No, the kid at the gate called him, and he met me halfway up the driveway. In my defense, my phone died, and I had no way of calling him."

Her eyes go wide. "And?"

"And what?"

"How was the fucking sex?" she whisper-shouts.

"God. He was so good, crazy good, we were like fucking bunny rabbits." And that's saying something.

"Where the hell did you do it? Don't say the clubhouse!"

I bite my lip. "Upstairs, in his bedroom."

She slaps her forehead. "Lucy, that place is so dangerous! You don't even know this guy, and that clubhouse is notorious for wild parties and drugs. What if you'd run into trouble?"

"I didn't though, and Rubble was there. He would've protected me, he's not like that."

"Rubble?" she shakes her head. "Seriously, Luce, I love you and all, but I am starting to think you're going through a midlife crisis a little bit early. You're not getting any hot flushes or weird cravings or anything, are you?"

"You're just jealous because I had rough, hot sex all night Saturday, and you probably didn't even call what's-his-face because you're too chicken to make the first move."

"That isn't nearly the same thing," she argues. "Not even close."

"Why not? I got laid, didn't I?"

"You could've been killed."

"That's a little dramatic, Jem."

"Fine, you could have been raped and buried out in the desert. Those guys don't have the best reputation around here. I've heard any woman that goes into that club is fair game. They like to share women and stuff... it's so gross."

My face pales at such a thought. I definitely don't want to be shared around a biker clubhouse, and I can only imagine the ones that do must agree to it. Right?

I open my mouth, then close it again. She does have a point.

"I admit, it was reckless," I concede. "But on the other hand, I had an amazing night, and I'm going to see him again on Friday."

She gapes at me. "Tell me you're not."

I nod. "We have a date at the White Pony."

"Oh, Lucy, I'm starting to get worried about you."

"Why? I'm fine, and he probably won't even show. I look at it this way; it was fun while it lasted, and it isn't going anywhere. It's just sex."

She leans on my counter and sighs. "I wish I could have uncomplicated random sex and not regret it," she says. "You know, just once, to see what it's like."

She is right about one thing; there is reckless and then there's stupid.

I have heard the rumors about the Phoenix Fury's clubhouse too, yet I went in there unarmed and determined to find Rubble. I'd have the very same concerns if it were her in my shoes right now.

"Well, it's very good if you can get a guy who actually knows what a tongue is for," I say, just as Jimmy sticks his head out of the workshop.

"What are they for?" he asks as my eyes go wide, still facing my computer screen.

"Licking the icing off a cream cake, sugar," I drawl.

His eyes glance over to Jemma, like they usually do, and I feel the urge to nudge her to get her to say something. These two have been dancing around each other for six months since Jemma first started working here.

"Does that mean you're buying cakes?" he asks with a hopeful look in his eyes.

"Not on your life, but Bob's not in a great mood today, so I'd avoid asking him anything unless you really have to," I go on. Not that they don't already know his mood swings by now.

"If you can ring Mrs. Parish, let her know her car's ready to collect," he asks Jemma, his tone suddenly all polite, like butter wouldn't melt in his mouth. Something tells me he's thinking about what her tongue is made for.

"Sure," she says, giving him a smile.

He smiles back, then heads back into the workshop.

I turn to Jemma. "You two seriously just need to bang it out and get it over with."

She turns to me, startled. "What? *Jimmy?* Are you kidding?"

"He's crazy about you, you just can't see it."

"He's my coworker," she says, like I'm nuts. "And keep your voice down!"

"So what?"

"You know that's not a good idea if things don't work out.

It would be kind of awkward seeing him every day. What if he's a dud, then it could get really weird."

"You do actually have a point, but he's still really cute."

She glances back to the workshop, and sure enough, Jimmy glances away the second she does.

He's got it bad.

I giggle. "Aww, that's so sweet!"

"It's not sweet," she whisper-shouts. "I don't want to lead him on."

"Well, now all he's thinking about is tongues and licking." I smile.

"You're not helping."

"You'll thank me when you're the one humming," I say, giving her an encouraging smirk.

The phone rings and Jemma makes her escape while I finish the rest of the invoices.

My new year's resolution this year was to not get involved in another relationship that I knew would never last. My problem is, I'm too loyal. I try to stick things out, make them work, and in the end, I'm the one who ends up suffering for it.

Really, sleeping with Rubble could be the best thing I've done in a long time. I took control.

Even if I never see him again, it was a turning point that night, and I feel kind of empowered.

I block out the idea that we met in a strip club called the Apple Pie. I also do not care to alarm myself *once again*, that the Phoenix Fury are criminals, and Rubble is probably into all kinds of bad things that girls like me should know nothing about.

I should stay well away.

I *should*, yet I find myself getting ready for my date on Friday with a spring in my step.

I texted him earlier to make sure we're still on. The White

Pony is a quaint, quiet little place downtown, but it's kind of hidden away. Definitely not his kind of hangout.

I'm even more surprised when he sent a reply earlier in the day saying, *Can't wait. See you then, angel.*

Is it so wrong that my insides turn all gooey when I read the words? They turn into molten lava when I think about our sex-capade, too.

It was so fucking hot.

I'm not denying myself. If we're fuck buddies, then so be it, I'll take it. It can be my dirty little secret.

I decide to dress casually, in just jeans and boots, a bodysuit, and a short denim jacket.

I keep my hair natural, in a long flowy ponytail.

I've been looking forward to seeing him all week, and I know that's really stupid.

The dangerous situation only makes it all the more appealing.

It's sex. I keep telling myself. *I'm not going to have a meaningful relationship with him.*

He's not boyfriend material. Hell, I'm not that crazy.

I'm barely out of the car when I hear the loud engine of a Harley Davidson approaching from up the street.

I watch him pull up as I lock my car, and he parks right outside the bar. He's wearing his cut, a helmet, and some goggles.

I try not to stare.

Him sitting on his bike is the sexiest thing I've ever seen in my life.

He kicks the stand down, cuts the engine, tears his goggles off, and removes his helmet. He has a bandana on, holding his hair back off his face, and he adjusts it, pulling himself together.

I tug the lapels of my jacket over my chest and take a couple of deep breaths.

Where there's fuel, there's fire, and where there's fire, someone's bound to get burned.

I cross the street just as he swings his leg over and puts his helmet on the handlebars.

"Hey, stranger," I say, as I get closer to him.

He turns and gives me a smile that melts my panties and has my heart rate accelerating all at the same time. He's drop dead gorgeous, towering over me, even though I'm wearing high heeled boots.

"Aren't you a sight for sore eyes," he replies, giving me a once over. His eyes darken when he gets to my boots. "Fuck, baby, I don't know where you've been hidin' this whole time, but I should keep you locked up at home, so nobody else gets to look at you."

I shake my head, giving him a playful smile. "That sounds awfully caveman of you. Hopefully you won't club me over the head and drag me off to your lair." *I'd come willingly, though.*

He smirks. "Nah, I like my women fully conscious, heightens the experience when you can't anticipate what I'm gonna do next."

My mouth goes dry at the thought. "You're awfully sure of yourself, anyone would think you're a badass biker."

He snorts. "I don't know about badass, but speaking of which." He shrugs out of his leather jacket. "Best to tone it down if we don't want any trouble."

He turns and puts his jacket under the seat and pulls out another, with just a Harley Davidson emblem on it.

"Will they not let you inside?" I ask.

"Best not to tempt fate, plus," he says as he shrugs it on, then adds," if another club sees me in my colors without my club brothers, things could get a little nasty."

My eyes widen as he chuckles. "Don't worry, Sparkles. I'll protect you."

I glance down to his belt and wonder if he's packing heat as well.

Adrenaline courses through my body.

I don't know whether to run away or jump into his arms.

He glances up when I don't say anything, then holds my chin with his thumb and forefinger.

"You gonna give me some sugar?"

I bite my lip.

"Isn't a kiss meant to be after the date? Depending on if it goes well?"

He leans forward to my ear, his dark, musky scent washing over me. "After where I've had my mouth, baby girl, I think it's safe to say that it's gonna go well."

I have that feeling again, right down in my core. "I don't know," I tease. "Maybe I should make you earn it?"

He pulls back and brushes his lips over mine so gently that I'm not even sure if they touch.

"You teasin' me isn't helpin', sweetheart." He grins against my lips. "But have it your way. I'm not a patient man, though, best warn you now. When I see somethin' I like, I tend to take a bite."

He lifts his head to mine and kisses my forehead. The gesture is so contradictory to what he just said that I don't know if I just imagined it.

He holds out his hand, and as I take it, I wonder if I'm not making a deal with the devil. Though the thing that worries me the most is the fact that I don't even care.

7

RUBBLE

An angel sent down from Heaven to torture me, that's what she is.

I watch her drink a large glass of Guinness and wonder where in the world she's been hiding.

She's smart.

She's funny.

She has a fuckin' cute accent I can't get enough of.

And she's as sweet as pie.

She talks with her hands, and literally tells me her life story all by the time she's finished her first pint.

She also makes me laugh, something I'm not used to doing on a regular basis.

I know she's got a sister who she barely sees, and a stepbrother who she hasn't seen in years. He ran away as a teenager and nobody's seen him since; I can tell she misses him and that her heart is broken because she never found out where he was, even after all these years of trying. It's like he just vanished. Her parents are separated and they still live in the south, and it doesn't seem like she had a good relationship with either of them. She's lived in Phoenix for almost five years.

I don't divulge too much about myself, I tell her I have a brother and we grew up in Wisconsin. I got into the club after school, when I was a runaway.

I can't tell her anything about the club, just that they're like a family and we stick together. Luckily, she doesn't ask me too much about the club; maybe she doesn't want to know.

I know my brothers won't be happy if they find out I went to a bar with her, even though I took my cut off. Nothing like club colors in a downtown bar, *any* bar, that attracts unwanted attention that could start a war.

I'm not that stupid. I also want to keep her for myself for a bit longer, just us without prying eyes.

"I've been meaning to ask you somethin'," I say; it's been on my mind since we first met.

She glances up from her fries. I'm glad the woman likes to eat, 'cause there's nothing worse than a stick figure who's watchin' her weight.

"What were you really doin' at the Apple Pie?"

A grin splits across her face. "I already told you, I was having a breakup party."

"Can't tell you how happy I was to hear that." I raise an eyebrow. "It's just an interesting place for girls to hang out."

She shrugs. "If there was a male strip club in town, trust me, we'd have been there."

I can't help but grin at her. "That shit get you goin?"

She shakes her head. "Nope. And I know it didn't get you goin' at Apple Pie either because you had limp dick till I straddled you."

I shake my head at her lip. "Limp dick?"

She smiles, triumphant. "I don't hold it against you. In fact, it's a compliment that you got it up for me and not her."

My mouth goes dry, and I imagine her wrapped around me while I bury my dick inside her sweet little pussy. She's not wrong that she gets me goin', every fuckin' time.

"What happened, with your ex?" I prod.

She looks down at the table. Quiet for a moment. "We just lost our way," she says eventually. "We're still friends, we just weren't happy together. We were not headed in the same direction.

I feel a pang of jealousy hearing that they're still friends. The urge to rip his throat out is coming in as a close second because I don't like the thought of anyone else touching her.

I can't imagine any red-blooded male this side of the planet that would be happy about losing her. She's a fuckin' ray of sunshine.

"He's a douchebag," I say. "Anyone that could let you go obviously has something wrong with them."

She glances up at me. "Do you say that to all the girls?" Her tone is playful but I feel like her eyes give her away. She wants to know if this is real.

I need to tread carefully. I don't want to hurt her, but where women are concerned, I tend to hurt them by just being myself. I don't mean to; I'm just not made for anything serious. With her, though... with her, I'm out on a ledge.

"Don't look so worried." She snorts with laughter when I don't answer.

I bring my attention back to her. "I was just picturing all the ways to torture him for being such a dick."

"How do you know he's a dick?" she asks, raising an eyebrow.

I lean forward on the bar, closer to her. "It's not a hard one to figure out."

She swallows hard, and I almost kick myself for not playing it cool. All that talk in my head about treading carefully and not wanting to hurt her, but I know what I want. And I want her.

She circles the rim of her glass with her ring finger, and I watch her as I take mine up to my mouth.

"Penny for your thoughts," I say when she goes quiet again. She seems to do that when she's nervous about something, or when she's lost in thought.

She glances up at me. "I was just thinking about how nice this feels."

The comment floors me, and my heart hammers in my chest. Fuck.

This is how normal people get to know one another. I've never been on a real date before, so this is a first for me, and I kinda feel a little bit guilty about dragging the sweet butts up to my room and bangin' them without even knowing their name. Since meetin' her, there's been nobody else.

My eyes dart to her lips. "I was thinkin' the exact same thing."

Her brow furrows. "You were?"

I lean toward her again. "Hate to admit this, but this is the first real date I've been on in a long time." No need to sound like a total sap.

"No shit," she whispers.

I grin again. I seem to do that a lot around her. "So, is now not a good time to ask what we're doin' later?" I waggle my eyebrows as she laughs.

"Is that a roundabout way of saying you've got bad ideas going on in that head of yours?"

I chuckle. "Not like I can help it; you get me wound up so fuckin' tight." I drag my eyes down her body and whistle low. "Can't argue that it's never limp around you, Sparkles."

Her cheeks flush a little, and I don't know if it's because we're talkin' about my dick or if she's actually embarrassed.

"I like you, Rubble," she admits. "But the biker club thing

scares me a little bit. You're different around them, harder. And I get it, but I think I like you like this."

I smirk. "That's why they say women make men weak," I muse. "Guess we don't need to put that theory to the test."

"I'm serious."

My eyes flick to hers. "I get it. The club isn't for everyone, but we're havin' fun, aren't we? And if you come to church, then it's best if it looks like you're mine. It'll keep the other guys away from you, and I won't have to break any faces."

She levels my gaze. "I'm not a woman who wants to be passed around, Barney. I know what goes on there. Let's make that really clear. All this talk about keeping the guys away from me and making it look like I'm yours, it sounds a little freaky. You can't tell me you don't do bad shit."

I like how she uses my name when she's serious. It's adorable. But when it comes to the club, she doesn't know the life and we definitely do bad shit.

"No, I can't say that I don't, you're right about that." I run a hand through my hair. "But I don't do anything bad to innocent people, if that helps, and I'm careful. We all are."

She looks slightly bewildered as she leans on the bar closer to me. "Do you kill people?"

I frown. "I've never killed anyone in my life," I say truthfully.

"This feels like more than just fucking," she says, her voice still low.

Her words make my dick stand to attention.

She knows just how to get me. Every single fucking time.

"Maybe it is." I shrug like it's nothing. "I like you, Lucy. I want to see you again, and that might mean comin' to church now and again. I mean it when I say the club may be scary, but I won't let anything happen to you."

At least if I lay it out on the line, she can't say I didn't tell her.

She nods like she believes me, and I feel a little better.

"Let me ask you somethin' else." I give her a chin lift.

"Okay," she breathes.

"Did you come around the club lookin' for me, or just for sex?"

The color rises in her cheeks ever so slightly, and it makes my heartbeat thud louder in my chest.

Her perfect lips part. "I came looking for you."

Fuck.

I'm glad she didn't ask why it matters.

"Couldn't stay away," I muse.

She rolls her eyes. "Very funny. And it was a first for me. I've never done anything that reckless before, but I wanted to see you again." She looks down at the table then back up at me again. "I thought you were cute."

I raise an eyebrow. "Cute? Puppies are cute, and kittens, and little kids with ringlets and shit. Could've gone with insanely handsome or incredibly sexy."

"Fine. I thought you were insanely handsome and incredibly sexy," she repeats, laughing at me again.

"It's not the same when I have to prompt you."

She smirks. "You're really good in bed."

Now we're on the money, and I don't want to spoil it by saying I've had a lot of practice.

She'd make a good ol' lady. *Wait, what the fuck?*

I lean in, my hands gripping her knees, and her breath hitches. "You showed up lookin' like every man's wet dream, then practically rode me at the table, Sparkles. I wanted to spank that little ass red while you rode me, those tits in my face while you moaned my name… and lucky me, I got my wish." Her eyes go wide and I revel in her reaction at my dirty words. I want her now. So fuckin' bad. "I wanted you to ride my face so bad because all I could think about since I met you was how good your pussy would taste on my tongue."

Her mouth hangs open as I brush my nose against her neck and then bite it gently.

I need to get my dick wet and soon.

"You're so dirty," she whispers as I kiss where I bit her.

I tighten my grip on her knee. "And you seem to like it. Bet your pussy's wet right now, isn't it, babe?"

She bites her lip, and I like how easily I can turn her on.

"Women like me can't be tamed," she says. "Haven't you heard?"

Her words go straight to my dick. "I need to get the fuckin' check," I mutter, downing the rest of my bourbon. "We're leavin'."

"Why are we going so soon?" she counters, a smirk on her lips.

"Need to fuck you," I say, wondering if that'll shock her. Nope. It doesn't. She wants it too.

She shakes her head. "Fucking on the first date?" she mocks. "What kind of girl do you think I am?"

"A prick tease is what," I reply, standing and holding my hand out to hers.

I'm not gonna be able to hold back forever in keeping her away from church, but for now, at least she knows the deal. She will have to go there. Even if the way Smokey looked at her makes me want to choke him, and I can't, because he's my V.P. Not to mention the other interested eyes roaming all over her, checkin' her out. As I say, I've never been a jealous man. Until now.

Just as my feet hit the pavement, my phone rings. I internally groan when I see it's Tex.

Fuck. Looks like our date is gonna be short lived.

"Yeah, Prez."

"Got a shipment goin' down tomorrow, need you back at the warehouse tonight to keep watch."

"What about the fuckin' prospects?" I got a girl to bang.

"They're out doin' other shit. It's an unexpected paydirt, and risky, need all hands-on deck."

"Gotcha."

"Be there in a half hour, Griller will be doin' the night shift too."

"Alright." I hang up and run a hand through my hair.

"Everything okay?" Lucy asks.

I turn to face her. "Bad news, baby. I gotta go."

She pouts. "And you haven't even gotten to first base yet."

I'm frustrated as all fuck, especially when she stares up at me, her eyes almost begging me to reconsider.

"Yeah, don't remind me."

Her eyes sparkle. "I guess that means I have to decide if we're goin' on another date, then?"

I pull her to my body and take her mouth, walking her backwards to the building and pressing her against the wall.

My kiss is brutal, my tongue seeking entry, and she lets me. I don't care if anyone sees, let them watch.

When I pull away, she's breathless and panting, her chest heaving. I glance down at her glorious tits, and I want to fuckin' curse Tex all the way back to the Midwest.

"Text me your address," I say. "I'll see if I can try and come by later."

She nods, her lips swollen. I think I like her like this, sated and waiting for me.

I hold her head as I go in for another kiss. It's less brutal this time, but I gotta stop, 'cause if I don't, I'll be heaving her across the road to fuck her in the back of her car.

"Don't keep me waiting too long, sugar," she whispers as I push off the wall and bring her with me, walking her across to her car.

I fuckin' curse the ground with every step.

"I'll text you when I can," I say. Though, I don't really know when I'll get to see her again.

This sucks ass, but pussy comes second where my position in the club stands.

I kiss her again, and her plush lips are like Heaven. I can't remember a time when I wanted a woman this badly.

"Okay." She climbs into her car and gives me a small wave before pulling out onto the road and driving away.

Running a hand through my hair, I take off back to my sled and gun it all the way to the warehouse.

It's two days later and way past what anyone would consider a decent hour, but I still circle down Lucy's street. I text her and tell her I'm outside. I know it's not much notice, but I've been busy, and I didn't think I'd come to her like this; bloodied and bruised.

She'll ask questions, but I need to see her.

All the bad shit I do and can't atone for, I'll make up for by pleasing her.

She doesn't reply, and all the lights are out, but I see her car parked in the lot.

I climb the stairs, and when she still hasn't replied to me, I bang on her door like a caveman.

A few moments later, the light goes on inside, and I hear movement.

She opens the door, with a chain still attached. Good girl, at least she checked first.

"You gonna let me in, baby?" I ask.

"Rubble?" She stifles a yawn. "What the hell, it's almost two a.m.!"

Yeah, I'm a selfish prick. When I want something, I go get

it. Fuck the consequences, though I hope she doesn't tell me fuck off.

She closes the door, unlatches the chain, and pulls the door open.

My mouth waters as I glance down at her silk pajamas and the tank top that barely contains her tits.

I kick the door shut with my boot and stalk toward her as she backs away.

"I missed you, princess, what else can I say?"

She frowns, noticing my battle scars. "Rubble, what the hell happened? Your face is all cut and bruised."

Yeah, some shit went down with the drop off. We got out alive, but Prez has started a turf war, one that is only just beginning and the club's abuzz with more fury than ever. Everyone knew he was biting off more than he could chew and now we're divided. A shit storms coming, I can feel it in my bones.

"You should see the other guy," I mutter.

When she's backed up against the kitchen wall, I tug my cut off and then peel off my shirt.

She stares at me wide-eyed. "Are you shittin' me right now?"

I stop in my tracks. "Does it look like it?"

Something crosses her face; it's in between looking really pissed and even more pissed, then her eyes drop to my chest.

I know she wants to look away, and probably tell me to get the hell out of here and never come back.

"Is this some booty call?"

"Nah." I grin. "A booty call is only when you technically meet up for sex. I came barging in wantin' to see you and that beautiful face that I've missed, so it doesn't count."

"Cocky ass," she mutters.

I reach for her jaw and crash my lips to hers. My other hand snakes up to cup one of her tits, and I give it a squeeze.

I feel her hands run up my stomach and slide all the way up to my pecs, feeling my muscles as she makes that little groaning sound that I can't get enough of.

"Like your sleepin' pajamas," I tell her when we break free. "But I like you better without them."

I lift her and sit her ass on the countertop, peeling her pajama pants off as I go.

She's wearing lacy panties that make me want to be an animal and rip them off her.

"Tell me why the hell your face is all cut up and bruised like that?"

I nudge her nose with mine. Even though my face fuckin' hurts, I won't stop. I move my hand into her panties, and she spreads her legs like a good girl, giving me full access.

"That doesn't matter. All that matters is that I'm in you as soon as possible. You're all I've been thinkin' about; all that's on my mind twenty-four seven, like you've put some kind of fuckin' spell on me."

"You mean to tell me you haven't fucked anyone since we last did it?" she asks, as my fingers slide through her wet folds. Jesus, she's always so ready for me.

"Nope. Never been a one-woman kinda guy till I met you. I'm fuckin' lovesick." It's the truth. I don't roll that like. I can't fuck another woman if I'm craving someone else, and I've never craved anyone like I do her.

I've also been drinking; she can no doubt smell it on me, but I'm not completely wrecked. I got here without crashing.

She shakes her head. "I should clean up those cuts."

I find her clit and circle it as she presses her nails into my shoulders. "Wanna suck on this baby. Wanna make you come so hard that you won't ever question me again why I came here so late."

She moans in response, reaching for the hem of her tank

top and pulling it over her head, her huge tits spilling free in my face.

"Oh, I'm so fuckin' home, sweet cheeks," I say, as I cup one breast and suck her nipple into my mouth.

She doesn't know yet, but I'm here to stay.

8

LUCY

Rubble plays with my body like he's tuning a freaking guitar. I've never met a man so good with his hands. I come twice on the kitchen counter, and seeing his hand between my legs while he sucks on my tits is like a fantasy come true.

It's raw.

It's sexy.

I can't get enough.

He carries me to bed, his bruises and bloodied hands long forgotten as he sits on the end of the bed while he shucks his boots and then rips off his jeans.

I peel my panties away and climb aboard.

He rolls a rubber on straight away and pushes up into me the minute I sit on him.

We both moan in unison like long lost fucking lovers.

I'm losing my marbles; this definitely isn't normal.

I should yell at him to get the hell out of here, and who does he think he is barging into my apartment in the dead of night? Rolling up here on his Harley, waking up the neighborhood.

But I don't say anything of the sort. I want him.

I let him ravage my body like it was made for him. Like I'm a freaking fun house.

I need this, though; my body craves his touch.

I need the danger. I need the rawness of it. I need him to please my body any way he wants. Everything else can just go to hell.

"Fuckin' missed this tight little cunt," he says as I grip his shoulders and begin to ride him.

His filthy words rip right through me as I give in to the sensations. His cock is buried so deep and feels so thick inside me that I can barely hold on to my sanity.

"Oh, God," I wail as he holds my hips, and I push my breasts into his face as he grins up into me.

I should be pissed about my beauty sleep being interrupted, but being woken up to this kind of sweet torture is hardly something I can be cross with him about. In fact, he could wake me up like this more often.

He plucks my nipples as I squeeze him tight inside me, moving up and down as he tells me how good it feels, how beautiful I am. His words wrap around me like a tight, warm blanket. And I know I shouldn't get so caught up in him, I don't want to be on the rebound and get weird feelings, but I can't deny that this feels really fucking good.

So what if he is a rebound guy?

It's not like I'm going to marry him.

It's just sex. Yeah, I keep telling myself that, and even in my own head, I sound like a broken record.

He grips me harder, moving me up and down faster. "Not gonna last, babe," he says as I hold onto my breasts and he buries his face in them as I come, screaming his name as he stills and grunts his release, slowing me down as I relish in the fact I just made him come undone, again.

A satisfied smile creeps across my face.

"Wow, house calls might be something I could get into," I

say, pushing the hair from his eyes, his forehead all sweaty. We kiss again, and I can't help the tight feeling I get in my chest.

"You're a fuckin' sight for sore eyes. Every damn time," he tells me. He peppers my breasts with little kisses as I try to still my beating heart.

I slowly, and reluctantly, slide off him and reach for my robe. Wrapping it around me, I go fetch the first aid kit. When I come back, he's discarded the rubber and has made himself at home on my bed. Lying on my comforter completely naked.

I never in a million years would imagine a man like him in my apartment, let alone in my bed. That thrill runs through me and I don't care to fight it.

My eyes rake his body. He has tattoos up his legs too, and all down his torsk. No, he's got it all wrong. *He's* the one who's a sight for sore eyes.

"Did those all hurt?" I ask, sitting down on the edge of the bed, knowing I need to go get a wet washcloth so I can clean his cuts and his hands properly.

"The bruises or the ink?"

"The ink." I don't want to think about how he got hurt.

"Some more than others." He gives me a wink, and I roll my eyes.

I don't have any tattoos, but I've considered the idea. None of my friends have been game enough to get one with me.

I stand and go to the bathroom and run the sink, tipping in some disinfectant as I wet a washcloth. I come back to him with a towel and begin cleaning him up.

"I could get used to this," he says, as I lean forward and dab his face first, then his knuckles. I remove a couple of his rings that have blood embedded into them. I don't want to think about that too closely.

"Well don't, I'm not your nurse," I tell him. "I'm sure you won't even tell me what happened to get you in this kind of a mess, not that I'd even want to know."

"Shit gets rough sometimes." He shrugs. "But I had to see you. I'm sorry…"

He's so sincere that my heart constricts.

Idiot!

I clear my throat. I have to be level-headed about this.

"So, did you just come here to fuck me?"

His eyes go wide, and then he throws his head back and laughs.

I shake my head. "What's so funny?"

He winces as he holds his ribs, and I realize he's hurt there too. "I like a woman who's upfront, baby doll. It's kind of refreshing, to be honest. Speakin' your mind, especially when you curse."

I get up to rinse the washcloth and settle back down next to him again.

"Don't the women you usually sleep with talk like that?"

He grunts. "No, baby, they know their place in the club, as bad as that sounds, and it's not usually for back talkin'."

They sound like a bunch of misogynistic assholes.

"That sounds extremely sexist."

"Might be sexist, but it's true. Prez is old school. He likes his club run the old ways, and women don't always have a high ranking in the club, but"—he squeezes me around the middle—"that doesn't mean we all think like that. I don't treat women like shit, I never have. I happen to fuckin' love a little bit of lip, especially when it comes from you."

I can't help but smile, even though I want to sock him one. His precious Prez sounds like an asshat.

"You would say that because I'm cleaning you up and riding your dick. Not like you're gonna say otherwise."

He gives me a devilish grin that melts my insides, then he

pulls on the tie of my robe. It falls open, and his eyes dip down to my breasts.

"Fuck, I love your body," he tells me, his eyes meeting mine. "And I'm not just sayin' it. I couldn't wait to get over here and be inside you. Just to hear your voice, have you wakin' up just to let me in. Ran three red lights."

"I should tape up your hands," I reply, ignoring him.

"I want to eat you out, in front of that mirror," he says, reaching out, fondling one of my breasts as my body begins to hum all over again. It's like my body is now craving him, and I've no say in the matter.

I glance over to my dresser and my pussy clenches.

He's so fucking dirty! And it's so damn hot, I could scream.

"Rubble..."

"Yeah, baby?"

He pushes my robe off my shoulders and dips his head, sucking a nipple into his mouth, his hands lifting my breasts up so he can fondle and squeeze them.

"God," I whisper as I drop the washcloth unceremoniously on the floor. My hands go to his hair, and I tug.

I watch as he licks one nipple, savoring it, his eyes coming to mine as he sucks, lifting and squeezing at the same time. It's so fucking hot; I can feel the wetness slick between my legs.

I reach my hand down and begin to touch myself, my other hand reaching for his dick, and I fondle him at the same time. His eyes darken as our hands feel each other, exploring, pulling, pinching.

His dick is perfect. Thick, long, and hard. I want to do very bad things to it. I want him to stick it anywhere he chooses when he plays with me like this.

He moves his hand to my pussy and groans when he finds me wet and ready for him.

"Finger yourself," he mumbles, and I do, sliding two fingers inside myself as he groans, watching me. He's so dirty and animalistic, and I love every second of it.

He releases my nipple with a pop, kisses me chastely, and grabs me by the hips, rolling me over.

"On your knees," he growls. "Face the mirror, Sparkles."

I do as I'm told and see myself on all fours, with him behind me.

He kisses my ass cheeks, rubbing a hand all the way up my back as I whisper his name.

"Need me to soothe that ache, baby doll?"

"Yes," I moan. "God, Rubble, please…"

He grins at me in the mirror, and I feel him part my ass cheeks, palming me there as I shudder. His tongue replaces his hand as I call out, the sensation something I've never felt there before.

He licks all the way down to my wet center and my clit, sucking my lips as I make noises I've never made before.

Watching his head between my legs as I try to not hyperventilate is like a full-on live porn show.

"Ever had someone in your ass?" he asks me out of nowhere. He gives my cheek a slap, then the other one as I groan. "Answer me."

I shake my head. "No."

"Soon, baby, I'll go there. We'll work up to that."

I swallow hard knowing I want him to.

I feel his kisses all over my ass cheeks where he just slapped me. He inserts a finger into my pussy, and then I feel the smack again. He repeats it on the other side, then licks this time.

"Fuck," I say. "Oh, fuck…"

"Bet I can make you come like this."

I feel his tongue again at my ass, as his fingers rub my clit, and I rub against them, needing friction, needing to come before I combust.

"I need it… baby, I need it…"

He slaps me again and inserts a finger, then he reaches around and pulls on my nipple, squeezing my breast hard.

I need him inside me. I groan as his fingers slide in and out of me at a maddening pace and his thumb now works my clit.

"I want you to come first. Watch yourself in the mirror, watch what I do to you, Lucy…"

When he says my name, I begin to fall.

He slaps my ass one more time, then kisses the skin and inserts another finger, making it three as he moves his hand deeper, finger fucking me into oblivion as I feel his tongue again on my back entrance.

"Fuck, Rubble…" I cry. "Fuck, oh God, oh, oh, oh…." I come so loud and for so long that I don't know where my body ends and his begins, but I close my eyes because seeing him behind me and me splayed out with my breasts swaying and my pussy being rammed into is too much.

He chuckles as he licks me clean, then lifts off the bed and rolls on another rubber. He comes over the back of me and lines himself up behind me.

"You take my dick so well, baby," he says. "Your pretty little pussy likes it rough, and soon, I'll take that little ass, too." He spanks it again, and I groan. God, I love the sensation of pain and pleasure. I never knew this kind of thing existed. I'll let him tie me up and do whatever he wants if this is how hard I can get off every time.

He sinks into me hard, fast, and without warning, and I grip the duvet as he rocks his hips into me. His eyes meet mine in the mirror, and his face is the most beautiful thing I've ever seen.

He looks at me like I'm his queen.

His fucking queen.

He only dips his eyes to watch his dick disappear into me, but brings his gaze back to mine again right after.

He moves a hand up to grab my breast and pulls my nipple hard, then his other hand reaches round and grabs the other one as he pounds into me from behind.

His moans are indecipherable as we fuck like maniacs.

I call out his name, close to the edge, begging him to let me have it.

"You're mine," he grunts.

I cry out, so fucking close to detonation.

He spanks my cheek again. "Did you hear me?"

"Yes!" I cry. "Fuck me, Rubble, fuck me harder…" I come, keeping my eyes on his as he smirks, watching me moan his name over and over.

This only fuels his need as he pushes my head to the mattress and grips my hips, pulling my ass higher in the air. He plunges into me harder, fucking me with everything he's got, the bed protesting as it bangs against the wall in fury.

Watching him do this to me is so freaking hot that I come again, my clit rubbing on the mattress only heightening my pleasure, or maybe the orgasm never ended, I can't tell.

I hear him grunt, then he pounds harder, his face a picture of pure ecstasy, then he stills, unloading his cum into me as he groans *baby doll* over and over like I've just made him my king.

And maybe I have, without even knowing or caring what that means.

I don't know when things changed.

We've been seeing each other randomly for the past two

weeks, but it was tonight, wrapped around him on his Harley, that brought me to my knees.

I always liked the look of a large, loud motorcycle, but I've never been on one before. When he took me for a ride out of town, along the highway until there was no traffic, just us on the open road, I felt exhilarated. Wild. Free.

Rubble brings out things in me that I never knew existed.

He lets me be who I want to be, without questioning it or wanting to change me. He likes me just the way I am, and that makes me feel things I shouldn't.

I can't fall for him, not in that way.

Though I haven't been back to the clubhouse since that night, it's only a matter of time.

Even if he did want to see me for real, I don't know how I feel about getting involved with a motorcycle club, especially outlaws. It scares me.

Everyone in the city knows that these guys are bad news. So bad, in fact, that they have a guard at their freaking gates and a huge high security fence that's built like Fort Knox.

I don't know the details, but they must run drugs and guns. I hope that's all it is, not that any of those things are good, and I can't believe I'm justifying it. I can't imagine Rubble being part of that, but the realization is this: he is.

He's part of the M.C. and refers to them as his "brothers."

It worries me about getting too involved, I don't want to look the other way.

I want to ask Rubble about what they do, but every time I even get close to asking anything about the club, he changes the subject and avoids talking about it. I get it's to protect me, which is what he says all the time, but I know nothing about the club because of that.

I can't make a judgment on something that I know hardly anything about, only rumors and innuendo. If I'm trying to give him the benefit of the doubt, he's making it really freaking hard.

I do know, the more time I spend with him, the more I like him.

He makes me feel good, and I know I shouldn't rely on him to be my crutch, but fuck it, he's my dirty little secret.

I haven't really told anyone except Jemma and Emerson, but they think I'm just screwing him on the side. Once Jemma got over her initial shock she's been okay with it, as long as I don't go back to the clubhouse again by myself, which I know I'll have to if I want to keep seeing him.

As I cling to his body and wrap myself around him, I know my heart is going to want what it wants, and that's exactly what I'm afraid of - and I know I'm falling fast, with nothing soft or cushy to land on.

9

RUBBLE

The last drop didn't go as planned. Shit went down. Punches were thrown, and Nitro got hit over the head with a crowbar. I copped the brunt of it but held my own. I never back down from a fight.

I'm six-one and not as brawny as some of my brothers, but I'm tough. Tougher than I might look. I grew up on the streets, I know how to fight, and I know how to fight dirty.

The fucker never stood a chance.

Rival clubs and other criminals can often try to get the drop on you during a delivery, and unlucky for them, we were a step ahead. We always have a backup van following, and other members scattered around should something go wrong.

Tex is pissed and, needless to say, the culprits were dealt with. He's more jacked off that he didn't get to torture them for information, but we all know between the Dragons M.C., who want to control distribution, and the Cubans trying to get a finger in the drug trafficking trade by being the supply chain, that isn't up for negotiation. Tex wants to rule all. This is the problem and has been for a while. He's playin' them from all sides.

It was messier than it had to be, but we got away unscathed. *This time.*

The only part of that night I care to remember is Lucy patching me up.

Her answering the door like a goddamn angel. Her hair tousled from sleep, her robe hanging open, her body begging me to take it. And take it, I did. All night.

I realize putting my dirty, bloody hands all over her was wrong. I shouldn't have taken my shit to her place. She'd only ask questions, quite rightly as I was still bleeding, but like a selfish asshole, I can't say I regret the decision.

There was nothing wrong about sticking it to her, that felt very right, but the way my chest tightens when I see her, or worse when I *don't* see her, has me questioning everything. And the fact I'm keepin' shit from her, which shouldn't affect me because I barely know her, yet it does.

I haven't stuck my dick in anyone since her, and I don't plan to; there ain't no sweet butt on the planet that can cure what I got. The funny thing is, I don't want anyone else. I haven't since we met. She's got me where she wants me, even if she has absolutely no clue that she's doing it.

It's not normal.

Before her, I was capable of all kinds of mayhem. I had different women in my bed every other night. I did a lot of shit without conscience sometimes. But now, it's like she's managed to anchor me to her, and I'm goin' willingly. And it's got me beat.

In any case, the sweet butts have never, and I mean *never*, turned me on like she does. She's special. She's completely innocent to club life, and I can't fuckin' get enough of her. *Sparkles.*

The clock is ticking on avoiding church and getting her

to meet some of the members, not that the sweet butts will be impressed with new competition shoved right under their noses, which is how they'll see it. I try not to let what Lucy might think bother me.

I'm going soft. I shouldn't give two hoots what she thinks. If she wants to be with me, then this is the life. The question is, does she want to be with me? I go into overdrive wondering if she feels the same way, and what I'll do if she doesn't.

That would mean no fuckin' around at the club, and I could do it. Hell, I *want* to do it if it meant she'd be mine. There's no man on the planet that I'll let have her unless it's me.

Most of the guys have regular women on the side, girlfriends, wives, and they also have sweet butts. I know for a fact Lucy wouldn't be into me having any other pussy but hers, which is understandable, but unless I claim her as my ol' lady, the guys won't let it slide.

I wouldn't leave her alone in the clubhouse unless she was my ol' lady, that goes without saying. Touching another brother's ol' lady is a no-go area, one of the only rules the brothers tend to stick to or it can get messy. If you do, you're fucked. If she does, she's fucked too.

As her arms tighten around me, I feel the swell of her breasts pushing into my back and the course of blood rushes to my dick.

Honestly, I'm like a dog in heat when she's around.

When I come around in the middle of the night, she lets me in, and sometimes we don't even exchange words. We just worship one another all night. It's the best part of my day.

I seriously doubt I'd ever get sick of her hot little body, and when we're not busy at it, we talk for hours. I've never had this type of relationship with a woman before because

I've never really been interested enough about a woman to listen to her or what she's got to say.

I just never cared.

With Lucy, I want to know all about her, what makes her tick, what she likes and doesn't like, and I know I'm a fuckin' pussy for even admitting it.

So I've decided after a month of sneaking around, tonight, we're going to church. I can't hold off any longer, and I know I'm going to have to put my game face on because nobody, aside from Smokey and Hoax, have really seen her or know anything about her. Just that I've been skipping out for weeks.

I do a line with Hoax in the men's room before Lucy arrives later that night. Another thing I've not done in front of her, and tonight, she'll be a little bit shocked if she looks too closely at what the guys get up to. I don't shoot up, I never have, but snorting a little bit of coke takes the edge off. It makes me a little more cavalier, sure, but I know my limits. I can handle it.

When she texts me that she's out front, I meet her at the gates and show her where to park.

When she exits the car, I stare at her body. She's wearing a short skirt with ankle boots and a tank top, her long hair free-flowing, hanging over her rack.

"Jesus," I mutter, pulling her into my arms. I kiss her hard, and her soft lips let out a moan as we embrace and I push my hips into hers. "Might not make it to the party, beautiful. You look too fuckin' good, good enough to eat."

"Play your cards right, and you may get your wish." She gives me a wink as I laugh and wrap an arm around her shoulders. She's tiny, even in heels, and I love how I tower over her.

The clubhouse is pumping with the usual busy Friday night music and bustling bar. As we enter, I see two of the prospects having an arm wrestle at one of the tables, someone is hauling a sweet butt off the pool table, and a row of my brothers are takin' shots at the bar.

They all turn our way when we enter.

May as well get this over with.

Every single one of the fuckers stares at her rack as we approach, and I feel my anger boil. Though I don't show any of it on my face.

"Rubble." The road captain, Ratchet, gives me a nod. "You brought us a snack, brother?"

My arm tightens around Lucy's shoulders.

We had the talk earlier. She knows that the men of this club aren't exactly the kind of men you meet in a normal bar, in a normal club, and while I love her sassy remarks and smart mouth, they're not going to show the same enthusiasm I do.

"Nah, Ratchet, this one's mine. Everyone, this is Lucy."

A few of the brothers give her a chin lift, the ones that can lift their eyes from her chest.

I don't like the way other men look at her, but she's beautiful, and I can't go around smacking everyone in the face just because they're lookin'. Long as she's by my side that's all I care about.

And she's used to it; she holds her own.

She gives them a small wave.

Nitro is the only one looking at her like a human being, and that's saying something. I stare back at him because he looks like he's seen a ghost, but that is obviously just my imagination. Lucy doesn't know any of the guys here; she wouldn't lie about it. But there's something in his expression that rattles me.

I especially don't like the way Ratchet snickers to himself and shakes his head.

Smokey gives her a grin. "We meet again, little one."

I swallow hard.

If any of them want to fight me, tonight's the fuckin' night.

"You sure she's not up for a gang bang?" Popeye calls out, downing his shot. Smokey slaps him upside the head as he splashes his drink all over his lap.

I feel Lucy stiffen underneath my hold.

Fuck.

This isn't good. They're not gonna do that, obviously, but some of the prospects don't think before talkin'. Imagining Lucy with anyone but me just about starts a nuclear explosion in my head. I crack my neck side to side because if Popeye says one more thing, I'll end him and it'll be a warning to everyone else.

"If you want your nuts cut off, you're goin' the right way about it," I reply, taking a shot and downing it, enjoying the burn it leaves, then I add, "Cut it out, for fucks sake, I'm in the mood to crack your head, fuckface."

"Sorry man, didn't mean no harm," Popeye says, as Smokey shoves him off in the other direction.

The others snort and turn back to the bar.

"Where did you say you were from?" Nitro gives her a nod as he steps closer.

"I didn't," she replies as all the brothers snicker. *Burn.*

The corner of his mouth turns up into a smirk of his own, which only has me tightening my grip.

"Lucy though, right?" he prods.

I frown, wondering if I am gonna have to crack a skull after all.

"Yeah, in case you didn't notice, I'm from the South, grew up in Texas," she goes on. "But I haven't lived there in years."

He nods and looks like he's about to say something else until there's a commotion behind us.

"Nice fuckin' rack," Foghorn pipes up out of nowhere. More snickers ensue.

"Thank you, honey," Lucy replies. "Got them given to me."

He eye fucks her and says, "Oh yeah, beautiful? From Doctor Pump Me Up?"

They all laugh and Foghorn gets a pat on the back for his trouble.

She shakes her head. "Nope, darlin', from Doctor Blessed Me Naturally."

A few low mutters ring out, and I grin into her hair. Okay, you can take the girl outta the South…

"Touché,' Foghorn concedes.

Yeah, I'm one lucky fucker. Anyone can go buy big, huge, fun bags, but the fact they're natural makes me puff my chest out. This may not be a pissing competition, but it's still satisfying to make them weep. It won't teach them any manners but I've drawn a line in the sand.

"Fucker," I hear Smokey mutter.

"So, Lucy, where'd you meet a pussy boy like Barney?" Rachet asks, giving me a smirk.

She pauses then says, "We met at Apple Pie on his birthday. I gave him a lap dance because the stripper in question wasn't doing a very good job. Needless to say, he liked what he saw, and he got my number. The rest is history."

Smokey spurts out his drink at the lap dance part, and my girl leans over and gives him a sharp pat on the back. He grins up at her. "Multi-talented, huh?"

I know exactly what he's thinking, what they're all thinking, and it's time for us to move on.

"You've no idea," she replies cheerfully.

I give her a smack on the ass as she turns and pouts at me. As she does, all the guys lean back to check out her ass. I shake my head, giving her a quick kiss.

She plays the part of a smart-mouth a little bit too fuckin' good, though the brothers seem to be bedazzled by her too. It's obvious she's too pure for this place, for any of us, but especially me.

I'm shooting so far above my average that I'm sure something's gonna give soon. She'll see right through me.

"You makin' her your ol' lady?" Tex asks me, sidling up and hitting me on the back, hard.

I bristle when his eyes land on her. He likes blondes. And he likes fresh meat.

He gives Lucy a nod.

He's a big man. Large and wide, his dark, heavy-set brows make him look menacing, and he is, if you cross him.

Tex has been trying to expand the club's dealings of drugs and guns through multiple avenues for the better part of a year. The trouble with expanding too fast, too soon, means risks can happen, and added to that, rival clubs don't take too kindly to the Fury moving in on their potential turf. Sometimes I wonder if Tex might have a thirst for anarchy and violence, but all he knows is the old ways and that isn't always the way to do things. The tension around here has been mounting for some time and after the shit that went down with the last drop, everyone is on tenterhooks.

"Workin' on it," I tell him as Lucy squeezes my ass with her hand.

He's about to say more, but Candi, one of the sweet butts, comes up behind him, and he turns his attention to her. Saved by the bell, thank fuck. Last thing I need is Tex eyeing up my girl any more than is necessary. It rolls my stomach because he's shitty to the women, even when some don't even mind bein' roughed up. After I saw my dad beat my mom as a child, I swore I'd never be like him. *Never.* I'll die before I ever do anything like that. Hence, I should respect my Prez, but a lot of the time I simply don't.

I order a whiskey for myself and a vodka for Lucy. Glad

that Tex is distracted, I pull her hand to mine as we make our way through the club. Everyone we pass by gives me a chin lift and then looks at her quizzically. She definitely sticks out like a sore thumb.

What's worse; sweet butts and girls who look like strippers are strewn everywhere. While I'm used to chicks parading around half naked around here, even having sex on the couches or in one of the booths, Lucy definitely is not.

But this is my club. It's how it is. It shouldn't matter what she sees or what goes on here, but my gut twists at the notion she'll be disgusted and want to leave.

It's then that I realize what I'm even saying to myself.

That I want her around.

That I want her to be mine.

And it's only been four weeks.

I run a hand through my hair and take a hold of my senses, what's left of them.

I introduce her to a couple of the club girls who'll be cool with her, avoiding the sweet butts and hang-arounds, since they won't be allies... or God forbid, friends.

It's every woman for herself in this club.

The thing I can't get over, is how well she fits in. Sure, she doesn't look like a club hang around, she's classier than that, but she's totally herself. Relaxed, even though there's chaos going on around us.

I know she's a bit of a wild child, as she likes the adrenaline rush from the crazy things we get up to together, and now she digs my bike and the runs we go on, but a part of me knows deep down that she may not be cut out for club life. That's if I did want her to be my permanent, my ol' lady.

Every time I think about letting her go, I just have to imagine another man with his hands on her and that makes me calm the fuck down.

We're havin' fun. She seems to be okay with the club; she

didn't run away screaming. She's overlooking the fact Hoax is gettin' a blow job over on one of the couches from some chick, and there's a ghastly smell of weed in the air.

She seems to know how to have a good time without getting into any of that shit. I think that's what I like about her. I like how she's clean. She's not into any bad shit, she barely drinks, doesn't smoke, and has probably never done any drugs in her whole life.

When she throws her arms around me, and I kiss her, not caring who sees, I think she gets the fact that I dig her. I dig her a whole lot.

"What?" she asks when I pull back.

"Just lookin'."

She bites her lip. "Yeah, I know that look."

"Oh, you do, do you? You just got me all figured out, don't you, babe."

She nods, triumphantly. "I like to think I'm a pretty good judge of character."

"Is that right?"

She leans up and kisses me lightly, her lips grazing mine, and I don't know why she's holding back. I want to take her upstairs and nail her into the mattress, but the truth is, I prefer her bed. I've had too much to drink, and with the other shit I took, it's probably not a good idea to jump on the bike and go to her place, so I kick myself for not thinkin' about that part sooner.

"Your club is crazy," she mouths, as I stare down at her. She glances around, but I've only got eyes for her.

When they meet mine again, I ask, "Does it make you wanna run away, baby doll?"

She looks like she's thinking about it, and I hate the way my heart constricts while she deliberates. I wasn't even fuckin' aware I had a heart until just recently.

Another thing she brings out in me.

"No," she says, finally. "It's dangerous, Rubble, I get that, but you're different. I feel different when I'm with you."

"I hope that's a good thing," I question.

She nods.

I move my mouth to her ear. "I warned you to stay away from me."

Her breath hitches.

"Do you just like the danger, baby?" I continue. "Or is any of it me?"

I kiss her neck, not wanting to see the look in her eyes for fear that it could just be the danger of being with a biker that she's after, that the lure isn't me at all. That it could just be with any one of my brothers here.

I don't know why I need her fuckin' reassurance, and it alarms me the way my thoughts are heading.

Sure, I didn't have a very loving childhood, and I've never really been nurtured by anyone, so is that what this is? Do I like the fact she is easy to love. *Love?*

What the fuck is wrong with me?

Should've fuckin' run when I had the chance.

She cups my face with one hand. "It's all you, Barney," she whispers. "I wouldn't be here just for the danger or the excitement. If I wanted *just* that, we would have been a one-night stand and nothing more."

I push my hips into hers, and she groans.

"So, what are we?"

"I don't know," she says, "but I think we just went way past complicated."

I know one thing; if she rips my fuckin' heart out, I'll really know the meaning of pain because imagining not seeing her feels like someone shoving a knife into my chest.

I've been beat up pretty bad in my time, but nothing would compare to that.

"I want you," I whisper, biting her pulse point. "I want you now, on your knees."

She pulls my jacket, and our lips meet. "I want to be your everything," she says against my lips, her words rushed. "I shouldn't, and I don't know why I want this so bad…"

"Fuck," I moan. Her words are so pure and honest, and I know I'm gonna drown her in my dirty, despicable world, and taint her forever. And I'm selfish enough to do it.

She squeals as I lift her up, and she wraps her legs around me as I make for the stairs.

I need to get up to my room so I can worship her like she deserves. I don't give a shit about this fuckin' party, I just need her wrapped around me in bed.

I know without a doubt, and I'm fuckin' stupid for admitting it, that I'm irrevocably falling in love with her. And I know because I've never felt like this before.

I've never felt like I would put my life on the line for anybody else but my brother Rusty, not even some of my club brothers, but I would, for her. For her, I'd take a bullet, and I'd die a happy man because she blessed my life, even for this short amount of time.

I'm fucked.

That's all I know.

10

RUBBLE

It's always the same, when one part of your life starts to go right, another part falls spectacularly apart, and by some miracle, you live to tell the tale.

The following week, we're watching the warehouse again while Tex and Smokey check the goods. They don't usually store much shit here, it's too isolated, and that would mean the prospects would spend all of their time guarding things. It's mainly guns and ammo, since all the drugs are kept in a few different locations, one being the bunker under the clubhouse, but not out here. Not until recently, that is.

We're making a big drop later tonight, and Tex dropped a bombshell on us, telling us we we're doing business with the Vipers, a rival club that operates on the other side of Phoenix.

We've never had a beef with them as such, but we're not exactly best buddies.

It explains why Smokey has been acting weird all week, Griller too. They may have voted it in at the table, but that doesn't mean that they like it.

Still, it's gotta make you wonder, with the turf war

already goin' on with the Dragons and the Cubans, now adding the Vipers to the mix? I get a feeling in my gut that isn't good about any of this.

Tex is shady. I know because I've been around shady people my entire life.

He doesn't always think about the club as a whole, but more about what he can gain. I should trust my President. I should trust him with my life, since he'd expect me to put my life on the line for his, but the fact is, I wouldn't.

I also had a fight with Lucy last night and that's got me on edge.

She caught me using. I tried to explain that I don't do coke on the regular, just socially or when I need it, but she freaked out. Totally.

I don't like to see her mad, or disappointed. In fact, I don't know what's worse.

I'm not an addict or anything, but sometimes getting high takes the edge off all my problems. Since I've met her, I've been doin' less and less.

During the fight, she asked me if I'd ever used before coming to see her, and of course I haven't. Maybe I've come down a bit once or twice like the night she came to the club to meet everyone, but I don't have to be high to see her. It seems she didn't appreciate my honesty. She kicked my ass out and wouldn't let me back in.

I'm fuckin' pissed, and now I've been stuck on warehouse duty.

I didn't get any kind of sick pleasure out of seeing her pissed at me, far from it. The woman is scary. Her kicking me out is not gonna fuckin' happen again, though. I texted her to let her know she's gotta be at the clubhouse tonight or it's over.

No way am I gonna let her decide what our future holds.

Her ending things isn't a decision that I'm going to entertain just because I fucked up.

I knew that when she found out I dabble in drugs, it could be a problem, and for the first time since I was a kid, I wondered what it'd be like to stop. To be clean.

I shake my head and take another large gulp from my hip flask.

She's gonna get her ass spanked red raw for what she did, and this time, I'm gonna make her count. That'll show her that she can't be tellin' me what to do or just dismiss me. I don't tell her what to do, even when she wears those cut out tops that should be for my eyes only.

I know how stubborn she can be, though, and once she's got her mind set on something, that's pretty much it. However, I tend to fully explore her stubborn little mind, and her body, when she's laying across my lap. This isn't over.

The warehouse is out of the city amongst a bunch of other industrial sheds used for shipping containers and commercial supplies. This is where the truck with the shipment arrives first, then it gets split up and we take it to several smaller locations.

It's not always a good idea to have the one big haul in the one area.

There's a bunker under the clubhouse that's completely hidden and purposely built to store guns, ammunition, and to cut some of the drugs. Tex also has a huge stash of hydroponic dope growing down there. Some of that shit's lethal and it'll get you off your head faster than you can blink.

"You get that feelin' that shit's gonna go down for real one of these days?" Hoax asks, running a hand through his hair. He always gets a little nervous guarding the warehouse, more so than doin' our drops in the van.

"It comes with the territory, doesn't it?" I reply, stubbing out a cigarette. "One of these days, it'll catch up with all of us."

"Talks going around about Prez."

I glance around, but nobody is near us. We shouldn't be talking like this at all, but shit needs to be said.

"Yeah, I know."

"Three shipments in a week?" He shakes his head. "I don't fuckin' know, dude. Why all of a sudden are we gettin' repeat business? Who is he rippin' off? The Dragons aren't gonna take it, and if the Cubans get less than their share, it'll be all our heads on the chopping block. A line's being drawn."

I don't want to think about it. If he is playin' one against the other, a shitstorm will rain down on the club.

"I hope it's not the Cubans; they'll bury you out in the desert up to your neck and let birds peck you to death."

"You're not even fuckin' wrong about that," he replies in a whisper. "And here I was thinkin' Tex was the most ruthless son of a bitch I've ever laid eyes on."

The rumors about him were long and heinous, but like all good M.C. Presidents, you have to be feared in order to be respected.

I just hope I never do anything to end up on the wrong side of him. He's been askin' a lot of questions about Lucy lately, and when I'm bringing her around next. I don't know what the fuck for. She's fuckin' mine, even if she is still currently mad at me and not answering my calls.

It isn't beyond him to just take whenever he wants to but that's where I draw the line. I'll fuckin' kill him before he lays a finger on her. Unease fills my gut and I wish we had someone like Smokey runnin' the club. He's a good guy, has everyone's back and the members trusts him. I don't know why they don't hold a vote and get Tex out.

"It takes a tough motherfucker to run an army," I say. "I wouldn't want that job, not for anything. There's too much hate out there, too much jealousy. There's always some fucker tryin' to dismantle the club and take over turf."

The Fury is less than twenty years old, not that old in the grand scheme of things. Tex had a lot of connections from his time in the joint too, which I guessed was where some of the intel came from when new buyers wanted in.

There is always a deal to be made, and though the drugs were good, another rumor that isn't so secret is that Tex has been cutting and mixing the coke with some other shit. Unless you really know what you're doin with that kinda thing, you're playing with fire. Last thing you want is new shit out on the streets that could be deadly.

I don't want to think about it. I don't want to think about Lucy makin' me feel like less of a man because she booted me. The worst part is it stung like hell. More so than any club shit that's gone down. More than some of the beatings I've taken.

I'm gonna rectify it soon…

"If there's safety in numbers, then maybe that's why we're all here," he says, then adds, "But to be honest, I can't shake the feelin' in my gut."

So, he feels it too. I try not to let that get to me because gut instincts are rarely ever wrong.

The rumbling of motorbikes in the distance has both of us stopping in our tracks.

I look out of the top window where we're situated and use the walkie to alert Rachet, Nitro, and Griller, not that they can't hear the fuckin' things. It ain't any of our crew.

"How many?" Griller growls back when I tell him we got company.

"Least a dozen."

"Fuck."

The drop was so significant tonight that Tex came along, though he doesn't do any of the heavy lifting like we do, and guns are hard to come by. I guess that's the only other valid reason we're all here. If shit goes south, then it'll be a fair contest.

"Told ya," Hoax says next to me. "This is some fucked up shit. Fuckin' Vipers."

"Let's not get ahead of ourselves," I reply, pulling out my 9mm pistol from the holster around my shoulder. I always carry whenever we're hauling or watching the warehouse, though luckily, I've never had to fire it at anybody.

"Whatever you say." He does the same but cocks his gun. "But this ain't gonna be good."

What I don't understand is why we need to have the Vipers involved in anything. Something isn't right here.

It's then that Griller comes back over the walkie and tells us to stand down on orders of the Prez.

Hoax and I share a look.

"Fuckin' gut instinct." He points at me. "Shady as fuck."

"Don't be sayin' that too loudly," I retort. Nobody in the club should be talking shit about Prez. Lucky for Hoax, I'm not gonna rat him out and cause trouble where there doesn't need to be any, hell, I feel the same way, but it feels off. All of it does. And now it feels like we're sitting ducks.

We watch from the overhead hanger as sure enough, the Vipers pull up.

Tex greets them with Smokey, Griller, and Ratchet, with Nitro hanging somewhere in the back. I don't know what they're saying, but a few moments later, Tex and their Prez walk into the hanger underneath us.

The floors are a steel mesh below us, so we can only partially see through.

I don't know what the fuck's going on.

There's never been any beef with the Vipers, but that doesn't mean that there isn't going to be any after this if he's double crossing the Dragons.

"We doin' business with the Vipers exclusive now?" Hoax asks, confused. It's true, it's not like the Dragon's got a meet n' greet.

I shrug. "Beats me, but you were right about somethin' not bein' quite right. It stinks like a whole lotta bullshit."

He points at me like he told me so.

What gets me too is that Griller seems more than a little pissed when he asked how many of them there were. He must have known about it; all the board members would have known. It's odd that Tex didn't fill the rest of us in or that the Vipers were the buyer.

I rub my chin. "A heads up would've been nice," I mumble. "Dragons hear we're sellin' guns to the Vipers, it's gonna be an even bigger shitstorm, they already think the Cubans are tryin' to muscle them out."

"Maybe that's how Tex wanted it," Hoax whispers.

I fear he is exactly right.

We've all had this feeling, not to mention the extra deals he's cutting without having inventory. I don't know if this just cements the fact that he's shady and really can't be trusted and should stand down, or if he'd purposely put the club at risk by switching tact.

I still hold my pistol because I don't trust anything that's going down right now.

When you don't even trust your own Prez, that ain't good.

At least ten minutes go by, and I can see them walking to the goods. Prez takes out a gun, and they both examine it.

"So if they're buyin' who are they sellin' to?" Hoax goes on, like I didn't hear him the first few hundred times he's said it. "Gotta make you wonder where the extra shipments are comin' from to service all of the players."

I shake my head, I've no idea what Tex is playin' at but he's playin' a dangerous game.

We don't have to wait too long to find out because after the two Prez's shake hands, the Vipers take off.

Shouting inevitably follows, and when Hoax and I dismount the stairs, Griller is being held back by Smokey and Nitro as he points in Tex's face.

"...didn't fuckin' agree to this!" He's yelling when they come into view. "The agreement was we bring in new clients and work with the other M.C.s to distribute. Not fuckin' come in and sell the entire inventory to the Vipers. Knowing them, they'll turn around and use the weapons on us!"

The tension explodes as Griller roars at him, his voice ringing off the walls.

"We need the Vipers to expand farther south into Mexico, and they've got the connections we don't," Tex growls back. "We voted. You don't get the final say on when or what club I get to appoint to distribute."

"Really?" Griller struggles against the two fairly big men holding him back. "'Cause I didn't fuckin' sign up for this shit. Pretty sure when we voted, it didn't include Viper territory bein' included into the equation, they were helpin' distribute, not buyin' in. You know they're shady as fuck, you know that fuckface will double cross you the minute he thinks he can get the drop, everybody knows it."

Tex does not look rattled, not one bit, yet unease settles over all of us. He has to feel it; the tension mounting in the club feels like it's reached boiling point.

"He's right," Smokey says, as quiet ensues, so much so you could hear a pin drop. The V.P. going against the President isn't something you see every day, but he has to speak up, he's the next in charge. "You weren't exactly forthcoming in tellin' any of us the Vipers were the new buyers. That's gonna reflect badly with the Dragons. They'll see it as a threat, we've already got the Cubans threatening to blow us up, once they hear about the Vipers takin' inventory, shit's gonna go south real quick."

Tex glares at him. "Let them. I've known Grave for a long time, we go way back. This will be good for the club as it means we won't be gettin' our hands as dirty. They'll expand and distribute through Mexico without us having to do shit. The deal was, I find the contacts, set them up, and get the deals. There's enough to go round. My side of the agreement is done. You'll all be singin' a different tune when your pockets are lined stupid with cash, we're makin' more than we ever have before and if we don't keep up the demand, they'll go elsewhere. We gotta take the deals while the going's good."

Griller looks at him like he wants to beat his face in.

Tex turns to us. "What the fuck are you two still standing there for?"

Hoax palms the back of his neck. "We'll take the rest of the gear back to the clubhouse," he says.

Tex gives him a nod, then turns back to the others.

He wants us gone, trying to save face without everyone knowing what the fuck went down. But everyone's gonna know by the time we get back.

Not for the first time, I get that feeling that this club is falling apart at the seams. It's like Tex has his own agenda and that's superseding everything else. He's not givin' the full story before makin' secret deals, that shit's not gonna fly.

We head out, dump the boxes off at the bunker, and then I'm at a loose end.

I glance at my phone to see no text from Lucy.

Once I get to the bar, I down a bottle of Jack and decide to ride over to her place. Probably not a good idea since I'm tanked, but I need to see her.

When I get there, all the lights are off, but that doesn't stop me from banging down the door.

After about five minutes of pounding, I realize she's not here.

I slump against the door and sink down to my ass. I dig out my phone and dial her number.

To my surprise, she answers.

"Rubble, it's three o'clock in the morning!" she yells down the phone.

I pull my phone away from my ear. "Needed to see you, baby. I'm at your place, and you're not here."

"I don't want to see you right now," she says. "I need time to think."

"Think about what?" I stammer. "You're overthinkin' this. I told you, I don't do that shit all the time. I don't need it…"

"And I told you it's a hard limit for me," she replies. "My step-brother got involved in drugs when he was fourteen and ran away. I haven't seen him since, he's probably dead." I usually like the sass in her tone, just not when it's directed at me. And I know talkin' about her stepbrother upsets her because the two of them were close.

"I don't wanna discuss this over the phone. Where are you?"

"At a friend's."

"Whereabouts?"

"Rubble, don't do this. It's not like you've asked me to be your girlfriend or anything. So you don't get to ask me these questions."

"The fuck I don't," I growl, running a hand through my hair. "You've done something to me, Sparkles. Before you, I could make all kinds of decisions, but now, we have one fight over something trivial and you run away. I said I'm sorry."

"It wasn't trivial," she points out. "Like I said, it's a hard limit. I just can't."

I get it but it isn't like I'm an addict, a thought suddenly occurs to me. "I'll quit, then," I find myself saying.

The line goes quiet. "Why would you do that?"

"'Cause I want you to be my ol' lady, and I want you, right fuckin' now. Tell me where you are!"

"How do I even know you're tellin' me the truth right now. You're probably high and let's face it, we hardly know each other. You've no reason to do anything like that for me."

"But I will, if it means you'll be mine." The line goes quiet again. "Babe?"

"Rubble, you can't do this to me, I just don't know…"

"You do know," I cut her off. "I know because you're pissed at me. It tells me you care. Nobody's ever cared about me before, not like this, not enough to get me all fucked up and wake your neighbors up."

"I… I…can't…" she says again.

"Just think about it," I go on. "But I want an answer tomorrow. I want you to be my ol' lady, and I'll give up the coke." I won't be giving up bourbon though, but she doesn't need to know that. A man's gotta have some outlet.

"I'll call you tomorrow," she says eventually. "Don't do anything stupid."

I bang my head against the door. Though I want to see her, I know that I'm in no fit state to plead my case, and I already sound like a fuckin' pussy as it is.

"If you don't, I'll come to your workplace, pull your panties down, and spank your ass in front of all your coworkers," I warn. "And it won't be in a good way."

"Rubble…"

"You got me?"

"Tomorrow," she tells me again.

Once I sleep it off, it'll be the morning.

I close my eyes, not realizing that tomorrow will never come.

We make the drop just outside of Tucson. Though nobody's happy with Tex right now, this drop was already planned before the meeting with the Vipers last night. We can't back out now.

Tex sends another van behind us, along with Smokey, Griller, and Nitro.

Shit's been tense the last twenty-four hours, and you can feel it.

I know the guys are uneasy about Tex bein' so off the grid, but the exchange goes without a hitch, and soon enough, we're headin' back out.

Lucy texted me telling me she gets off work at six, and I take it that's a good sign if she's not ghosting me. It might be sudden, but I've never been so sure about something in my life. Not having her in it for just that full twenty-four hours was enough to send me crazy.

Imagining her with any other man could drive me to insanity, I don't want that.

I thought finding a woman to settle down with would make me weak, but it doesn't. It's the opposite. I don't know how it happened; it just did. And I don't regret it. In fact, I should drop a few more drunken truth bombs when I see her next. She doesn't just get to end things on her terms, though I can't help but feel a little proud she's got the balls to sass me.

That's my girl

I smile when I think about her plump, pink tushy and my hand marks on her cheeks. She'll be gettin' more of that for ignoring me all this time. I get that she didn't like what she saw, but we can talk it out. I'm not a total jerk.

Then I'll fuck that smart mouth of hers and make her gag. What's more, she'll love every single inch of it; I'll make sure of that. I'll show her what she's been missin' out on. The thought makes me want to run to her right now. But I don't get the chance.

The hit comes out of nowhere.

I'm in the passenger seat and Hoax is crappin' on about Bambi for the hundredth time, when there's a loud pop, then the tire blows.

"Fuck," Hoax yells as the van swerves.

"What the fuck?" I yell as another van out of nowhere sideswipes us, and Hoax struggles to hang onto the wheel.

The van swipes us again, knocking us off the road as the tires squeal when Hoax tries to slow down. Our van slides and skids, hitting the guardrail as it flips and slides down the embankment, rolling as the front-end crumbles, and we jolt forward.

I feel something in my body crack.

Then, everything goes black.

11

LUCY

Rubble never showed.

Twenty-four hours go by, and he's not answering his phone.

I guess he's more pissed at me than I first thought.

By the next morning, I'm pissed, too. So much for all his promises.

He doesn't get to blow me off like this. If anyone is going to be the one ending things between us, it's going to be me. Asshat.

I concede that kicking him out may have been a little harsh, and I shouldn't have been so naïve. Of course, he's into heavy, bad shit; he's in an outlaw biker club. Why would I think anything different? More to the point, I only care so much because I know I'm falling for him.

A part of me also knows that I'm being stupid to keep seeing him. It's not like this can really go anywhere, not as it stands. And I feel sick at having to end it. I don't want to.

When I lost my brother, everything changed. He got in with the wrong crowd and that was the last time I saw him. Home life wasn't great back then. We weren't beaten or mistreated or anything, but when mom and my stepdad separated, he lost his way more than any of us kids. He started doing drugs young and his dad couldn't handle it so he came to stay with us, that was short lived. Mom had inherited Adam so he was never really taken in with open arms, and my sister Tina was no better. Mom also didn't handle her divorce well, she started drinking and gambling more and more. When I was old enough to leave, that's exactly what I did. And I looked for Adam, Hell, I looked for him everywhere. My beautiful, sweet-faced brother who wouldn't hurt a fly. Dread fills me when I think of him lying in a ditch, or in prison, or worse…

I just can't deal with all of this. It's too much.

Rubble trying to say he only uses recreational drugs doesn't change things.

God knows what he does when I'm not around, probably plenty.

Yet, my heart flutters at the thought of never seeing him again. He'll never leave the club and I can't ask him to. They may be a bunch of assholes but they're his family, he's said it more than once. And I won't ask him to choose. We've known each other for less than two months. I know where his loyalties lie if it comes to the crunch, and it has.

None of them work regular jobs, and Rubble's always coming and going at all times of the night. *They're criminals.*

It may not be a big deal to some about my hang up on drugs, but that's because Rubble doesn't know anything about my past, about what I've had to deal with. About what I saw growing up in my neighborhood. And drugs are a hard limit for me. I can't change it.

After work, I decide to stop by the clubhouse and see him for myself.

If he thinks he can hide from me forever, then he's messing with the wrong bitch.

A guy at the guardhouse at the front of the gate assesses me with suspicion.

He's got the word *Prospect* written across a patch on the front of his jacket.

"Are you lost?" he asks, by way of greeting.

I try my hardest not to roll my eyes.

"No, I'm looking for Rubble."

He frowns some more. "Who are you?"

I put my hands on my hips. "A friend."

He snorts. "Rubble doesn't have friends that look like you."

"Fine. We're fuck buddies. Now can you let me in?"

He gives me another once over, almost like he's trying to gauge if I'm trustworthy.

"He's not here," he says finally.

My heart plummets, and my patience is wearing a little thin, though I keep my cool. He's probably armed and dangerous, like the rest of them.

"Where is he?"

He looks down at his feet, then back up at me as a slight shiver of fear runs up my spine at the look on his face.

"He's in the hospital."

My eyes go wide. "What? When?"

"The night before last. Some shit went down. The van he and Hoax were driving got shot at and ran off the road."

Fear grips me, and I hold onto the metal bars so I don't topple over.

He frowns again. "Are you all right?"

"Is he… is he…" I can't even get the words out.

"Nah, but he got banged up pretty good. The van rolled, and Hoax took a bullet. Luckily, they only got him in the shoulder, but they lost control of the wheel, and that's when they crashed."

The blood pounds in my ears. He's been in the hospital for almost two days.

"Is he going to be okay?"

He shrugs. "They said he fucked his spinal cord, might not walk again."

I slap a hand over my mouth. I don't want to cry in front of him.

"Which hospital?" I manage to choke out.

"St. Joseph's."

I don't even wait for more details, I high-tail it to my car and take off like a bat out of hell, racing as fast as I can across town.

He might not walk again?

Fear grips me at every turn.

I've known this man for a short space of time, and already he's wormed his way into my heart, under my skin, and into my life. And I came here to break up with him. *Way to go.*

The overwhelming and sinking feeling hits me all at once, but I hold it in. I'm made of strong stuff. I've had to be with the upbringing I've had. If I can get through all of that and make it this far, then I can get through this.

I think about Rubble lying in a hospital bed and press my foot down even harder.

I don't know how I make it to the hospital without incident, but I somehow swing my way into the parking lot and find my way to the reception desk and then to his floor.

I know it's the right floor because when I step out of the elevator, I'm met with a line of larger-than-life bikers and their prospective women, some clad in leather jackets declaring they're property of such-and-such.

I swallow hard and hold my head up high, making my way through the crowd.

I only get so far when I hear a nurse in the hallway.

"And I said if you don't step back and give us some room to work, we'll be forced to have you removed," a very brave nurse is telling Smokey. I'd recognize his scraggly, long hair anywhere.

"We just want to talk to the doc," he's saying. "It's been hours already; we need to know if he's gonna make it."

My heart plummets, and I gasp. Smokey turns around and immediately looks down at my frame.

His lips twitch. "Lucy," he begins.

Tears well in my eyes, and I lurch into his chest. I don't think he knows what to do with me because his hand pats my back awkwardly as I try not to cry.

I can't help it when a sob escapes me. "Please don't tell me... please..."

He takes a long breath. He smells like bourbon, cigarettes, and peppermint.

"He's all right. It's Hoax, he got shot. Rubble's been askin' for you, but we had no way of contacting you. His phone's fucked from the crash."

I pull back and wipe my eyes. This is too much... Hoax getting shot...

"Can I see him? Please, I just need to see him," I trail off.

He regards me with a frown as I clutch onto the lapels of his jacket, but he gives me a chin lift and says, "Come this way." He leads me down the hallway, away from the throng of people, then adds, "Though don't annoy nurse Nancy. She's got a stick up her ass."

The one named Nitro assesses me as I pass by him with that same displeased look about him that I don't like. He's always looked at me weird, and I don't know why. It's like I don't belong here. Little does he realize; I know that better than any of them.

I'm not one of them. I never will be. My heart feels heavy as the truth grips me.

The nurse shakes her head as we pass, and I give her an apologetic smile.

"The prospect kid said the van rolled, and Hoax got shot and Rubble may not walk again!" I cry, my words jumbling.

"Fuckin' prospects," he mutters. "If the pigs ask you anything, you know nothin', baby doll. You got me?"

I look up at him at the same time he looks down. In all of his giant six-six form, he means business. And who am I to argue? I don't give a shit, I just need to know Rubble's okay.

"I wouldn't say anything," I tell him. "I don't even know anything anyway. Rubble keeps all the club business to himself."

He seems to believe me and places a hand on the small of my back when we stop at a room.

He pushes the door open and I stare at Rubble.

He's got a million tubes coming out of him and a monitor beeping, along with a bag that seems to be draining fluid.

I'm shocked at his appearance. He's scraped, bruised, battered, and it takes me a second to realize he's blinking, so he must be alive.

"Baby," he whispers.

I try not to cry, but his banged-up face and split lip makes it really difficult.

I hear Smokey close the door behind me with a quiet click.

"Rubble," I whisper back, my hands over my mouth as I walk toward him.

"Come sit with me."

I shake my head. "How did this happen?"

"Shit happens," he replies, trying to smile. "You should see the other guys."

His long running joke isn't funny this time around.

I stand and loom over him, assessing him from head to toe, and I've no idea where to start or what to think.

"I stopped by the clubhouse because I hadn't heard from you. The prospect told me that you'd been shot and the van rolled," I go on, hardly daring to repeat the words. It pains me to see him like this. "And that I'd find you here…"

"Fuckin' prospect," he says, just like Smokey.

He tries to smile as I reach out and place my head on his arm lightly. I don't know where I can touch him without interfering with the tubes and things going into his body.

"What can I do for you?" I ask, frantic. "Can I get some water, a nurse…"

"I'm okay, babe…"

"You look far from okay!"

"I'm having my lungs drained, can't drink water just yet."

My eyes go wide. "What the fuck?"

He winces. "Yeah, perforated a lung. Smashed up my legs, and they think there's some damage to my spine, but it's gonna be okay, babe. I've been through rough shit before."

I can't believe how cavalier he's being.

"You call this rough shit?" I shake my head.

His dark eyes flick to me. "Give me some sugar."

I shake my head. "No, Rubble, I'm not giving you anything. I'll pull on a tube or a wire or something, and then the alarms will go off."

He chuckles but begins coughing and spluttering as he tries to sit up.

I help him and prop his pillows up a bit, so it's a little easier for him to breathe.

There are purplish bruises forming around his eyes, and I really do wonder what happened to the other guys if this isn't so bad.

"Don't try to talk," I say. "You should be resting."

"I've been lying here waiting for you, least you can do is give me somethin'."

I sigh and tilt my head, giving him a swift but soft kiss on the lips.

"Babe, that's not a fuckin' kiss."

"Stop it or I'll call that mean nurse in here. Don't think I won't."

He smirks, then sobers. "Any word on Hoax?"

I shake my head. "I heard her talking to Smokey. She didn't say anything, just told him to back off or she'd call security."

He rumbles a laugh again, at the same time grasping my hand. "Sit, babe, stay for a while. I need to hear your voice."

I perch on the plastic chair next to the bed and try not to notice how cold his hand feels.

"I've never been so worried," I say, brushing the hair back off his face gently. "I don't know what to say to any of this. Obviously, none of you are going to say what really happened, but I'm sure I can put two and two together. This shit could've got you killed."

His eyes look pained as he assesses me. "It didn't, though. I'm still breathing."

"Hardly. You've got five thousand monitors beeping away, a possible spinal injury and a bag draining fluid from your lungs. I don't think that counts as being A-okay."

His lips twitch. "You're so cute when you're mad."

"I'm not kidding," I say, my words less harsh. "I just don't know where any of this leaves us, because if I'm not imagining it, we're not just fucking, are we?"

He brushes a thumb over my knuckle. Even like this, banged up and left for dead, I still want him. It isn't just my body that calls to him, it's my freaking soul, too. It speaks to me on another level that even I don't understand.

"It's not very manly of me to admit it, Lucy." He smirks. "But you've done somethin' to me that I didn't think was possible. To think about someone else's needs other than my own, that's never happened before. It's not somethin' I know. I've only known the hard road, babe. With you, everything's easy. I like havin' you on the back of my sled. In my bed. I like you bein' with me."

I stare at him, unmoving, and I know that I never intended to break up with him, despite all the things I know. Maybe I am a sucker after all, but I feel the same way.

When I'm around him, I feel a light on inside me, and he's the one who flicked the switch.

"I like being there too, Rubble. But I can't handle you doing drugs. I'm sorry. One day, I'll tell you my story, but I can't right now. And like I said before, it's a hard limit… I can't go through what I went through before…"

He squeezes my hand. "Babe, I get it, I hear ya. I'm not gonna take that shit anymore if it means there's a chance you'll leave."

I look at him for any signs of him joking, but his face is completely serious.

"And I know now you think I'm just sayin' that so you won't go, but I meant what I said. The choice is yours, babe, you just gotta do what makes you happy."

I smile softly. "This is crazy, we barely know each other."

He shrugs, then coughs at the movement. Every time he moves, it looks painful.

"Doesn't matter about time; it's more about how we feel. And I've never felt like this before. You just gotta work out if you can be with me and the club, babe, because this is the life I live. It's all I know."

I can't help that feeling again sinking in my gut. *He's a criminal. He just got shot at. He could have died.*

"It's a lot, Rubble. Look at you, in a hospital bed, being shot at and left for dead!" I shake my head, anger boiling up inside me, tears pooling in my eyes. "It just isn't normal where I'm from. This shit is like something out of the movies, not in real life."

"I'm tough, baby, and I'd never let anything happen to you. You know that, right?"

I want to believe it, and I know he wouldn't. But even with no fault of his own, he can't guarantee that. None of them can. Look at what just happened.

I dread to think what it was about. *A deal gone bad?*

"Rubble, what about all the bad shit that goes down with the Fury. Don't you worry about going to jail, or worse? Hoax just got shot, and you're lying here, unable to walk. This is just the start of it."

He winces. "Two other clubs didn't see eye-to-eye, and we were in the middle," he grunts. "They just picked the wrong night."

"Rival clubs?" I snort. "Goddamn it!" Fear shoots through me at the thought of him lying there dead on the street. This is just too much.

"Babe, the less you know, the better. Trust me on this."

I stare at him, unimpressed. "You talk about me being your ol' lady," I snap. "But if I'm gonna be your ol' lady, Rubble, then you better not think you can keep everything from me. The other *brothers* in your club might think it's all right to keep shit from their women, but I don't roll that way. Not knowing if you were dead or alive just about did me in."

He brings my hand to his lips. "Talkin' like that, babe, might earn you a good spankin'."

I roll my eyes. "I don't think you're going to be doing any spanking until you're better, and don't dodge out of listening to what I said, I mean it. I know you all like to go around, beating your chests like cavemen, but shit like this is going to get you killed eventually. I just can't be involved with an outlaw club. I can't look the other way while you sell drugs that go on the streets that kill people, and that's just the start of it…"

His eyes still have that spark, even when the rest of him is beat up. "Do you trust me?"

I frown.

For some odd reason, I do trust him.

"You're not superman," I retort. "You can't fly your way out of this one."

"Maybe not, but I've got a plan up my sleeve, baby. If I can get out of this fuckin' bed and back on my feet, I'll show you what it is."

My heart fills with love for him, and I know that is very stupid. It's fucked up but imagining never seeing him again is worse.

"How do you know I'm a woman to be trusted?" I ask, as he caresses my knuckles with his bandaged hand.

He gives me a come-hither nod, and I plant a light kiss on his lips. "I knew it the first time I laid eyes on you. We didn't run into each other by accident."

I shake my head. "Did you purposely follow me to the bathroom at Apple Pie?"

He kisses me again, and I know he's incorrigible, so I pull back slightly. "I wouldn't say I purposely followed you, but I may have had my eyes glued to your ass from across the room."

I know he's making jokes to make light of the situation, and it doesn't make it any easier.

"Rubble…"

"Don't go feelin' all sorry for me. I won't know for sure if you're stayin' because you actually like me, or because I'm all banged up in hospital, lookin' like a homeless guy who just got robbed."

He's hard on himself, and I get it. But I'd never be with someone because I felt sorry for them. This wasn't exactly how I planned on meeting somebody. And I meant it - I don't like this club and the people in it, even if Smokey and Hoax seem like the only semi-decent ones.

"I feel shitty because you're banged up, but you probably know by now that I say what I'm thinking, and sometimes that lands me in trouble."

"Or into the arms of a bad boy biker, right?" He laughs, trying to tug me to him.

"Rubble, stop it, the nurse will come in and kick me out."

"I doubt anybody is goin' to be game enough to do that, sugar, with all the boys out there."

I give him a sobering smile. "I hope Hoax is going to be okay."

"Me too, baby, me too."

He closes his eyes as tiredness takes over him. I hold his hand and watch him sleep.

My heart constricts when I think about how I could have lost him. I'm deep in my feelings for him, and I know that I'm past the point of no return.

That doesn't scare me, but being without him felt like the scariest thing in the world.

A world I don't want to be in without him.

12

RUBBLE

I'M IN HOSPITAL FOR THE BETTER PART OF TWO WEEKS.

Thank fuck I get the use of my legs back. Although, I'm going to need rehabilitation, and I'm not looking forward to any of that. One of my legs remains completely shattered, so walking without assistance is nearly impossible, but on the flip side, I'm lucky to be alive, and that's all that matters at the moment. When the van flipped, all I could think about was Lucy and never seeing her again. When they say your life flashes right before your eyes, it's absolutely true.

Hoax pulled through, though of course, the cops got involved. Shit like getting shot is never easy to try and explain. I'm so fucking relieved; he's a good brother, loyal to the club, and he didn't deserve to die by the hands of cowards.

Things have been tense at the club ever since. Some of the brothers are questioning Tex's decision-making, and if he's putting too many lives at risk with switching distributions and being secretive about it. The Dragons have declared war because he undercut them with the Vipers, and as if things couldn't get any worse, some of the bricks were light on the shipment that we were guarding at the warehouse. Everyone there that night is under suspicion and has been interrogated. Now that we're doing deals with every cocksucking low-life under the sun, narrowing it down is proving to be hard. The shipment passed through two different check points before reaching its destination.

Someone has light fingers, and someone is going to be losing those fingers.

Lucy didn't want me to go back to that shithole of a room at church, and I couldn't get up the stairs anyway, so I'm at hers twenty-four seven. The stupid thing is, we can't do anything because I can hardly fucking move. The good news is, my spinal cord wasn't permanently damaged, but it is making walking impossible because everything has shifted.

Subsequently, I've started drinking a lot, most of it is to numb the pain, but also because of boredom.

Lucy's at work every day until the weekend, and I can't do club shit because I've got my leg in a fucking cast, with the other one elevated, so I take pain meds to ease the ache.

Lucy does everything for me. Helps me get to the bathroom, washes me, brings me food. She's a fucking saint. I don't deserve her, but I already knew that, and as the time passes by, it becomes more and more apparent.

My first physical therapy session didn't go well. Once the cast came off, it was time to put weight on my leg again. Thank fuck I still have one semi-functioning leg, not that it's going to get me up and moving, but I'll be damned if I'm staying in a wheelchair forever. It makes me feel like less of a man when we haven't had sex for so long that I think my dick has gone into hibernation. It's a little hard to get business done when I've had my leg in a cast, can't sit up and have three cracked ribs.

RUBBLE

I wonder if Lucy wonders what the fuck she got herself into.

I told her pretty much what happened. I know I shouldn't have, but I left out the major details. In the club, women aren't supposed to know club shit, but it's well known that the ol' ladies and sweet butts tend to hear more information between the sheets when the brothers are letting off some steam, so it isn't unheard of that they know bits and pieces about club business. I don't care anyway.

With Lucy, it's like I can't lie to her. And I know that makes her a liability and me a fuckin' idiot if we break up and she decides to talk, but I always want to be transparent. With Luce, it's like I can tell her anything, and she'll keep my secrets. Not that I'd let my club brothers know that; they'd string me up and hang me out to dry.

It's the second day of physical therapy, and things aren't going too well. I'm frustrated as hell. Adrian, my therapist, stands in front of me as I stand between two parallel bars.

"Just hold on to the bars, and push down," Adrian reiterates, like it's so fucking easy.

Lucy nods encouragingly, and I want to die.

I try to do what he says, and I have the upper body strength to hold myself easily out of the chair, but again, I can't balance any weight without toppling over, time and time again, as the gait belt I wear prevents me from hitting the mats on my ass. It's humiliating in front of my woman, to say the least.

"It's fine, baby," Lucy says as Adrian helps lift me back to the chair. "You're doing great."

"Doesn't feel very fine," I mutter, managing to keep a lid on it, but my anger's brewing.

I try again, reaching the bar this time, but my leg just gives out, and I hang onto the bar, hopping on my semi-good foot. It fuckin' hurts too. Everything hurts. My back, my neck, my legs, every damn thing.

Adrian moves behind me to help support me by lifting from under my arms, but it feels pointless. We make it to the bar again, and I hold on to each side as I try to move my fucked leg; even dragging it feels like a dead weight.

"I don't know why they didn't just cut the fuckin' thing off," I say.

"Just keep a grip on either side. It won't come straight away, just an inch by inch, a little at a time; there's no hurry," Adrian tells me, like that's supposed to feel like encouragement.

"An inch would be a fuckin' miracle at this point."

Lucy stands beside me on the other side of the bars for encouragement.

I turn to her. "You shouldn't be here," I say, because I'm a fuckin' prick.

Her face falls just slightly. "Why not? I want to be here."

I let out a long, deep breath. "Because I don't want you here, seeing me like this."

She rubs my arm, and I pull it away, and by doing so, I lose my balance and fall back, Adrian catching me before I hit the ground.

"Rubble!" she calls as I land awkwardly in his arms. Like a fuckin' pussy.

My patience with myself snaps, and inevitably, I take it out on her.

"I said get the fuck out of here!" I yell at her. "Just go!"

"No, I won't do that," she says, her voice firm. "We're in this together, like what we said."

I stare up at her. "I don't fuckin' want you here, all right?"

Her eyes go wide as my words cut her. It's best I let her off the hook. I'm nothing but a burden anyway, and while I don't want a pity party, this is just like chopping a man's balls off.

"You don't mean that," she whispers, then to Adrian, "Can you give us a moment?"

He plops me back into the chair and turns to leave.

"He doesn't have to go; we don't need a moment."

She narrows her eyes. "Why are you doing this?"

"I didn't sign up for this, neither did you."

"But I'm your ol' lady," she whispers.

I shake my head. "We haven't made that official yet, so you're off the hook."

She screws up her adorable little nose. "Off the hook? Is that what you think this is? That I want off the hook?" She has the decency to look horrified.

"Fuck's sake, Luce, don't you get it? They said I may never walk properly again. You really wanna be with a guy who can't even walk on his own two fuckin' feet?"

Her eyes glaze over, but she doesn't say anything.

"Just as I thought," I mutter.

She leans toward me. "You don't know anything about me or what I want if you think that, so fuck you! I get you're trying, but being an asshole just because you can isn't winning you any points. All you're doing is trying to push me away, and for what reason, I don't really know. I'm the only one around here that seems to be in your corner."

"It's because of this!" I yell, motioning down to my legs. "I'm fuckin' useless, to you, to my club…"

She shakes her head. "So this is what it's all really about? Your precious club, right? I don't see any of them here. I don't see your *brothers* here helping you get around, making sure you don't starve. Not to mention the work getting you to any place that a guy needs to go… so yeah, maybe it is fuck me. Maybe I am the stupid one after all."

I stare past her, furious at her tone, but I can't do anything about it.

"Thanks for rubbin' that in my face. I'll be fine on my own. I've managed to get this far in life without you."

She places her hands on her hips, looking down at me with scorn. "You're a fucking asshole."

I don't get to hurt her any further, as she storms out, her heels click-clacking across the tiled floor, and then the door slams, rattling the rafters as she exits with just about enough steam to power a rocket.

I rub a hand down my face.

Way to go, asshat.

She's right, everything she said is true.

After the upbringing I've had, what the fuck could I have to offer a woman like her?

I'm a criminal.

I've got very little money.

I've got no career, aside from being able to fix cars and bikes, but that's more of a hobby.

I'm a fucking loser, just like my alcoholic father said I was, and he was right, I did amount to nothing. My mom committed suicide because she couldn't handle me and my brother, that's the truth of it. I drive people away, it's what I do best.

Why I thought I was worthy of a woman like her, I don't know. Maybe I just need to get high. Write it off. Blow off some steam.

I have to push her away, she's only stickin' around because she feels sorry for me. If I can't ever walk again, she'll resent me in the end.

It's for the best.

Two long, miserable days go by, and I'm bunking downstairs at church, sleeping on one of the couches because I can't make it upstairs.

I've never been so fucked up in my life, and I'm still hungover. I don't know the difference between night and day, and I know I'm just like my father, a fuckin' drunk.

We partied last night, and a sweet butt crawled into my lap. I almost fucked her. Not that I wanted to, or even could, but to have a woman's arms around me felt fuckin' good.

It just wasn't the arms I wanted. I shoved her off though, I didn't want her hands or her mouth or anything on me.

I only want Lucy. And I can't have her.

She hasn't tried calling me, and I don't blame her. She deserves better; she'll thank me in the end. Instead of calling her, like I want to, I end up drunk again, and I pass out on the couch.

When I wake the next morning, I feel someone shake me.

I rub my eyes, and then I smell the coffee. Jamie, one of the girls who works the bar, waves a cup in front of my face.

"Morning, sleepyhead."

I groan.

"How is it morning already?"

"You look like shit," she says, taking the bottle that I'm still clutching from me. "Can't help but notice that you've been moping around here quite a bit lately."

I push myself up to a sitting position and take the cup from her. "No shit. Can't walk, remember?"

She rolls her eyes, earning her a glare.

"That's not what I meant, and you know it."

Jamie's cool. I like her; she stands her ground and tells it like it is, which not a lot of the women around here tend to do. She gets away with it because she's good at her job. Hence why it's not even seven a.m. and she's here ready to clean up before anyone else gets here.

"Not that it's any of your business, but I'm fine, thanks for asking."

"You don't look fine," she repeats, folding her arms over her chest. "Moping around here won't get her back, you know."

I take a sip and burn my tongue. "Make this hot enough?"

"A simple thank you would be nice."

I give her an eyeroll instead.

She takes a seat on the small amount of space near my feet.

"I think we're friendly enough by now for me to say that you need to take a good, long look at yourself."

I look at her like she's lost her mind. "Do you now?"

"Yes," she says firmly. "You're the only one of the boys that won't shoot me for speaking freely, so I'm going to come out and say it."

"Don't be so sure," I mutter.

"Rubble. You're fucking miserable. You're not going to any of your therapy appointments. You're falling apart at the seams. I saw you the night before last, and you're not even boning any of the sweet butts. You've got it bad, and for what it's worth, I think she's good for you."

I pinch the bridge of my nose.

She's right. I am the only one in this club who will listen to this shit.

The fact that she's right has absolutely nothing to do with it.

"You got a big fuckin' mouth, you know that?"

She gives me a beaming smile, which I do not appreciate. "Yup."

"She doesn't want me. I gave her an out, and she took it."

She shakes her head. "No, you drove her away. There's a difference."

"You know, for a bartender, you seem to know an awful lot about shit you've got no business poking your nose into."

She remains unperturbed. "Someone has to say it. If you let her go, you'll only regret it, and you're a good guy, Rubble." She gives me a playful punch on the arm. "I've never seen you like how you've been these past few weeks, you're different. If I were you, I'd go bang down her door and beg for forgiveness for whatever it was you did to drive her away."

I want to tell her to shut her goddamn mouth, even if she is right. I know no other patched member would sit here and listen to this, but maybe I need to hear it from a female.

Maybe she's actually right.

"She's too good for me," I say after a few moments of silence. "If you really must know. She was gonna break up with me before the accident. She had reservations about the M.C., and I can't have that; she's either in or she's out. And she would only have stayed because of the accident. I'm nobody's pity party."

She stares at me like I've got two heads. "You know why I'm still single?" she asks suddenly.

I'm not sure I wanna hear this, but it doesn't seem like I've got much option. "Enlighten me."

"Because of shit like this." She waves a hand at me. "Stubborn asswipes who want to sit around feeling sorry for themselves when they could be going to therapy and getting themselves better for their woman. Instead, you're sitting around here with a face like a bucket of worms."

"Are you finished?"

"Are you going to call her?"

"If you weren't like a sister to me, I'd wash that mouth out of yours."

She snorts. "Lucky for me huh?"

"Somethin' like that."

"You've got a brain in your head, I'm sure you'll work it out eventually, that's if she hasn't moved on by the time you do." She turns serious and I know she's right. I know she means well, she has a good heart, and maybe I need to hear that I'm a schmuck. There's also a sadness in her eyes that I don't miss.

Her and Smokey hooked up a few times, but they never had anything serious. I still see the way he looks at her, though. He's never looked at anyone else like that.

And while I should tell her to get gone, I probably needed a kick up the ass. I just never expected it to come from her.

"I'll think about it."

She rolls her eyes. "Don't wait too long. One thing I know for sure; time doesn't go on forever. You've never been a guy who did anything halfway, Rubble, and I think you're short-changing yourself if you don't go beat down her door and find out what could be, for what it's worth."

I glance at her again. "When did you fuckin' grow up?"

She shrugs. "Don't be stupid. I'm the all-knowing bartender, honey. I've heard it all, trust me. I've got an answer for everything. Any problem I can fix."

I snort, then give her a nod. "Haven't you got work to do?" I take another sip of the coffee she made me; it tastes like liquid gold.

She goes to stand. "Call her. If you don't, I'll tell her your real name."

"She already knows my real name, wiseass," I say as she marches off.

She sashays away, looking over her shoulder as she goes. "She's a keeper, then. Mark my words, if you let her go, you've only got yourself to blame, and then you're the one who has to live with it."

The only trouble with that sentiment is not only is she

absolutely right, but it makes me want to punch something because I know I'm just copping out.

I was a dick. I didn't trust us enough, and I never wanted to be a burden. My Lucy deserves the world and I want to be the one to give it to her.

I never really thought about the fact that she may actually *really* want me, so giving her an out was the right thing to do.

And now, I might have just made her hate me for good.

13

LUCY

ONE WEEK LATER

I SOMEHOW MANAGE TO DRAG MYSELF TO WORK, EVEN THOUGH I really wanted to just stay in bed and eat cheerios while binge watching Netflix.

It's been days since Rubble and I had our fight, in truth I've lost count, and I haven't heard from him since.

I know I should let it go, but I'm hurt. I'm hurt because of what he said and how I feel about him, even when everything was screaming at me to run the other way. Yes, he's part of the Phoenix Fury, but he's not a bad person. Not underneath.

These past few months being with him have been amazing. I've never felt more alive than when I'm on the back of his motorcycle, cruising along the highway or up to one of the Canyons. Or when we're just chilling, enjoying each other's company. I never expected stability from a dirty, hot biker who I met in a strip club.

I miss him.

The way we left things has made a gaping hole in my heart.

I don't want to be one of *those* women who loves what she can't have, who is enticed by the bad boy and he gets to treat me however he wants. That's not it at all. Rubble's not like that.

He's always treated me like a queen, up until the other day. And I know that was out of embarrassment and fear. He can't fucking walk. And now, I've run away like a coward because he told me to leave. The truth is, I've never seen him like that. He's never been that angry with me, though I now know he was only angry with himself.

His words did sting me, I can't lie. I know I'm made of stronger stuff than this, but just for once, it would have been a nice change to have the guy run around after me. I'm always the one doing the giving, and after my ex, I promised I wouldn't do that again. The partnership has to be equal, or else it won't work.

I stare at my computer screen and realize fifteen minutes have gone by, and I haven't done a damned thing.

Jemma is off with the flu, but the workshop isn't busy at the moment, meaning I've got more time to sit around and mope.

I stop at the grocery store on the way home and pick up a couple of things for dinner. Emerson wants to go out this weekend with a bunch of our other friends, and while the last thing I feel like doing is going out and having a good time, it may just be what the doctor ordered.

I'm not going to sit around at home and wait for a man or feel sorry for myself, even if that sounds like the best damned thing in the world.

He didn't want me, and I don't want to grovel; I shouldn't have to. A part of me does wonder if I should have called his bluff, fought him on it, tried to break down his walls.

I know where all of this physical therapy stuff is concerned, it's a sore subject. I also know that none of his *brothers* will likely be encouraging him to go to rehabilitation, and he needs that right now.

The only one who's remotely supportive is Smokey and that Nitro guy who always looks like he wants to say something but never does. It's weird. Hoax can be forgiven because he's still in hospital.

I get to my car and decide to hell with it. I'm going to text him; he needs to keep going to therapy, no matter what happened with us. If he doesn't start trying to walk again, he may never get the use of his leg back properly and healing will take so much longer.

Me: Don't forget your appointment Friday...

I backspace over it. It sounds like I'm a nagging housewife. And why should I care anyway? It wasn't like he gave a shit when he basically told me to fuck off.

I breathe in and out and try to let my temper go, remembering it's his pride that did this.

I try again.

Me: I know you're not in a good place right now, but you still need to be going to therapy. Whatever we were, whatever you said, it's okay. I'll never forget you, Barney. Please just don't give up x

Okay, a little more dramatic than I was going for, but it's better than goodbye.

Tears well in my eyes, and I haven't cried in as long as I can remember.

Why has he had this effect on me so profoundly?

Maybe he did offer that masculine, alpha, protective side that I've been searching for. Maybe the woman in me needed that. Even though I'm strong and capable, it was still nice having him around. Doing things to me that no man has ever been able to do. He knows exactly what I like and how I like it, but most of all, I just miss him being around.

His smell. His crooked smile. His cheeky, dirty talk. The way he looks at me when I open the door and I know exactly what's on his mind.

I sob in the car for a good ten minutes before I dry my eyes and turn the ignition on.

I straighten my back and pull myself together.

I'm a strong, capable woman. I don't need a man.

I hold on to the steering wheel just as my phone vibrates on the seat next to me. I pick it up, and my heart skips a beat.

It's him.

Rubble: Baby, I need to see you.

I bite my lip and shake it off. I drop my phone back on the seat and don't reply.

I need to see him too, but I can't forget about the things he said. I want him so bad, but by taking him back, it means that nothing's going to change. He's still part of a one percent motorcycle club with no ethics; they're criminals and will likely all end up in jail or dead. Added to that, the shit they sell out on the streets; it turns my stomach.

I just wish things could be different, but I can't be with someone who has no moral compass.

If only I hadn't turned up at the clubhouse that weekend, seeking him out for sex, then I wouldn't be in this predicament now. But I also wouldn't know how this feels either, how it feels to be desired, to be really wanted… and that's the part I can't forget.

How I can know him for such little time but all the dots join. I've never joined with anyone before.

I get to my apartment and retrieve the shopping bags out of the trunk. It's then that I hear the loud engine of a truck raging up the street. Just as I unlock my front door, the tires squeal and pulls into the lot next to my car.

I see Nitro in the driver's seat and Rubble in the passenger. My heart skips a beat as he stares at me through the tinted window.

He looks like shit. Like he hasn't slept in days.

I drop the bags and stand there looking right back at him. The sincerity in his eyes tells me everything. *He missed me.*

Nitro hops out and gives me a chin lift. "Hey Lucy," he says, jogging around to the front of the car. "I drew the short straw."

He looks down at his feet as he talks to me and it's then I realize he may actually be a little bit shy. It's a conundrum. The bikers from the club all seem so confident and kinda full of themselves, but Nitro avoids looking at me.

I smile despite myself. "You drive like a maniac."

He meets my gaze and smiles back and it's then I realize he is sorta cute, in an eclectic kinda way with his shock of black hair and pale skin with piercing blue eyes. There's something endearing about him that I never really noticed before. All this time I thought he was just weird.

He goes to open the passenger door to help Rubble out, his gaze hasn't left mine.

Putting my hands on my hips, I shake my head. "Rubble, what are you doing?"

He runs a hand through his hair, the way he does when he's nervous. "I told you, I needed to see you, we need to talk."

He rests his arm around Nitro's strong shoulders as he helps lift him down. When his feet touch the ground, he holds onto the door keeping his bad leg bent as he hobbles, then Nitro reaches into the back and pulls out the crutches.

I walk closer to him. "How are you?"

He looks like he's in a fair bit of pain. "Seen better days."

"Looks like it," I muse.

He nods to Nitro as he helps secure the crutches under his arms. "Hate these fuckin' things."

"Quit bitchin'," Nitro says, closing the door as Rubble starts to move toward me.

Rubble gives him a chin lift. "Thanks for the ride, and for makin' sure you hit every bump."

He salutes with a smirk. "Anytime." Then he looks back at me. "See you around, Lucy."

I give him a small smile. "Bye, Nitro."

He hops back in the driver seat and reverses out into the street and drives away.

I stare at Rubble wordlessly. "I mean it, you look like you need a hot bath and a bowl of beef stew."

He grins as my heart kicks up a notch. His button-down shirt gapes wide, with his layers of jewelry and tattoos showing, his cut with the dirty patches, and that mop of shaggy hair.

My mouth goes dry. *I still want him.*

You're a strong, capable woman... oh, shut the fuck up.

"You gonna say somethin' or just stare at my body, babe?" He smirks when my eyes land back on his again. Stupid libido. It isn't my fault he's fucked me up for any other man. That's all on him.

"What are you doing here?" I demand. "You made it pretty clear you didn't want me around the last time I saw you."

He runs a hand over his face again; he looks so tired and like he's lost weight. Maybe he's not eating properly... *stop it!*

He takes a deep breath, like this is hard for him. "I came to say I'm sorry."

I'm taken aback for a moment before responding. "Well, that's a start I guess."

"Can I come in?"

"You're asking permission now?"

He chuckles. "I love it when you're mad."

I ignore him, moving aside so he can get by.

He swears under his breath as he moves awkwardly on the crutches. "Definitely didn't think it through," he mumbles.

I want to go to him, kiss him, tell him it's okay, that I'm here, but I don't. I may love him, but I can't look past what he does.

I love him? My heart crushes in my chest knowing that I do.

I follow behind as he moves slowly toward my door, which lucky for him is on the first floor.

I pick up the shopping bag and my purse where I dumped them and head for the kitchen. Then I put the cold things away while he makes himself at home at the kitchen island.

"Are you gonna look at me, babe?"

I continue putting the groceries away, then switch the kettle on before facing him.

The way he's looking at me makes me want to die.

There's sadness in his eyes, real genuine sadness, and it makes me want to weep.

"You been cryin'?" He gives me a chin lift as I pale a little, remembering that I sobbed in the car. I wear enough mascara to make a drag queen jealous, and I realize now that I must look like a mess.

"Am I a mess?" I ask, my hands on my face.

"No, but I can tell when you're upset."

I swallow hard. "I'm fine."

"Who made you cry?"

"You," I say, finally meeting his gaze.

He lets out a slow breath. "I missed you, baby."

"Did you want water, coffee, bourbon?"

"I don't drink anymore," he says as I flick my eyes to him.

"What?"

"It's been a shitty week, and I've done some soul-searching, Sparkles. I've realized some things since you've been gone, and if you'll hear me out, I'd like you to hear what I've got to say. Then you can kick me out if you want."

I bite on the inner cheek of my mouth, unsure what to say to that. It's not like I don't want to hear him out, but I don't know where any of it leaves us.

"Fine. You've got five minutes."

He gives me a chin lift. "Come here."

I keep my feet planted exactly where they are.

"No, you don't get any sugar right now. I'm still mad at you."

His eyes blaze. "I'm just scoring up those spankings, baby, so just keep that mouth runnin'."

I roll my eyes.

"Was that an eyeroll?"

I give him another one, very deliberately. He reaches out to me before I can dart away and pulls me to him, crushing me against his chest. Despite his injury, he's still strong.

His scent, musky, masculine, with faded cigarettes makes me want to melt into his arms. He feels like home and he shouldn't; he can't keep doing this to me. I just cave whenever I'm within a ten-foot radius.

"You can't just try and seduce me and expect me to just fall over with my legs in the air," I huff. "That isn't how this is going to work, Rubble. What you said hurt me."

He leans in and rubs his nose with mine. "I know, I'm sorry. Fuck I missed you."

He kisses me with a little tongue, and the heat goes straight to my belly. I want him so bad, but I can't let my libido cloud my judgment.

I don't resist his tight hold on me, and I don't need to cup his crotch to know he's rock-hard.

A whimper escapes me when he pulls back, my chest heaving as he spares a glance downwards.

"Missed those too."

"Well, better take your last look at them, because this is the end of the line…"

"Is that so?"

"Rubble, you can't push me away like I'm nothing then come crawling back. I've been a wreck. No amount of coercion with your penis is going to make that better."

He smirks. "Coercion with my penis?"

"You know what I mean."

He sobers. "I'm sorry, I didn't mean to push you away. Watching the pity in your eyes when I couldn't do it… it fucked with my head. I'd also been drinkin' pretty heavily. I was hungover, but that's no excuse. I shouldn't have taken it out on you, Sparkles. You know I'm a fuckin' mess without you. It's been the worst week of my life."

Butterflies buzz in my stomach at his confession. It's not like I want to hear he's had a shitty week, but the fact he's here at least says a lot.

"I just wanted you to try. It didn't matter to me if you were in a wheelchair or not…"

"I know that, Luce. I was a fuckin' asshole, and I regret it. Makin' you leave like that, it was a dick move. I've made some decisions this last week, but there's no point in me sayin' anythin', baby girl, unless I know you're with me. I need to know."

Tears well in my eyes at his sincerity. "It's been a shitty week for me too," I admit. "It hasn't been great…"

"You were right to walk away, you deserve better, but I'm still here. I want you, Luce. I want you to be mine. You are fuckin' *mine*, and I'm not leavin' until you know it, until you really fuckin' know it from head to toe what you mean to me. Then, if you decide you don't want me, I'll go, and you'll never hear from me again and that'll be that. I know I don't deserve it."

"Rubble," I whisper. I bury my head into his shoulder as he holds me. "I thought I'd lost you for good."

He rubs my back soothingly. "I thought I'd lost you too, the best thing that's ever happened to me. I don't wanna make that mistake again."

"We're so wrong for each other," I say. "We're so different."

"I know I'm bad for you. I could lead you down a dark path, and I know you'd follow, but that isn't what I want, baby. So, if you'll hear me out, I got an idea. For us, for our future. If you'll still have me."

I close my eyes. I want him so badly. This moment is either make or break; there's no going back now.

"Okay," I whisper, as I hold him tight in case he goes away again. "I'll listen, Rubble. I promise I'll hear you out."

"I love you," he whispers.

I gasp as he holds me closer than he ever has before.

I never thought I'd hear those three words coming from his lips, and I can't help but feel the fire burn deep inside me.

14

RUBBLE

I PULL BACK, AND SHE LOOKS DOWN AT ME. I MOVE MY LIPS TO hers and kiss her gently.

"You love me?" she whispers.

I nod. "Yeah, baby, tried to fight it, but you got me all fucked up inside."

She doesn't need to say it back. That's okay. But I need her to know.

I want to take her right here, right now, but that can wait. She needs to hear me out first, this can't be all about sex.

"I don't know if my leg will ever be better, my shoulder's fucked too, and heavy lifting is out for at least twelve months," I say. "Been talkin' to a buddy of mine, out in Bracken Ridge. He's lookin' for a partner in a tow truck business he's thinkin' about buying, as I've got some skills and he's a mechanic, so I'm thinkin' about going in with him. Starting a business."

She stares at me with those blue eyes I love so much.

"I want to leave," I go on. "Start a new life with you, away from all this shit. I don't wanna end up dead or in a concrete cell, anything that would take you away from me would be like hell. So maybe gettin' shot at and almost gettin' killed did me some good; it's made me realize a lot of shit I've been doin' wrong for a long time."

She frowns. "Can you just leave the club?"

"The club is in disarray," I tell her. "Tex started a turf war that didn't need to begin in the first place, and the club has been dismantling slowly for some time because of the decisions he's made. The fact that I'm of no use to them for twelve months gets me off the hook, so to speak. When you patch in, you're in it for life, you don't get to leave. But I can use this to my advantage. Sure, it's like tuckin' tail and runnin', but I don't give a shit how it looks. I was there when Hoax almost died. He didn't deserve that, and I don't wanna leave the house one day and never come home. I couldn't do that to you. If Tex doesn't like it, he can get fucked."

Her beautiful eyes stare at me wordlessly. "Are you sure he won't take you out to the desert instead?"

I know she's never taken to Tex, and he's always had an eye for her I didn't like. I don't respect him or where he's takin' the club, that's the truth of it. I don't like the danger he puts the club in by playin' everyone off against one another.

"I don't know if the club can withstand the war he has created. And though I feel like a coward takin' the easy way out, it may just be the opportunity I need to start fresh. To move on from here. To start a life with you somewhere else, where nobody knows us. If you'll still have me."

I've slowly learned over the last few months who my real brothers are. Smokey. Hoax. Griller, too. Nitro just recently. They've always had my back. I wouldn't trust the others as far as I could throw them.

She stares at me with her mouth open. "Are you for real right now?"

I shrug. "You're always sayin' how you hate your job, and how it's not goin' anywhere, and you've got no family here. I know you have your friends, and it's a lot to ask, but I want you to come with me, Luce. I want us to move to Bracken Ridge and start a new life."

She swallows hard. "You'd really leave the club?"

I rub my chin. "Well, before we go gettin' all joyful' over it, my friend Steel is in an M.C. too. They're not one percenters, though. They're all legit, but party hard, just with no drugs, guns or any shit like that. They're a small club; everybody has legit businesses and put into the club coffers. I'd probably have to wait a year until I join, just to be sure the Fury don't get wind of it and stir up trouble, but somethin' tells me they've got bigger fish to fry at the moment. And Steel's a good guy. This way, we both win. I can keep in with the M.C., and you won't have to worry about me gettin' shot."

"This is a lot," she whispers, clearly taken aback.

"But you didn't say no, so that's promising, right?"

Her eyes go wide. "Rubble…"

I brush a hand over her sweet, delicate skin. "Will you come with me, Lucy? I want you by my side, baby girl. I want it to be us, somewhere far away from all this shit, somewhere that's new, that's *ours*, that hasn't been tainted and shot at and fucked over."

Tears well in her eyes, and I don't know if that's a good sign or not.

"Isn't this all kind of sudden? I mean, what happens if we have another fight next week?"

I laugh. "We had one fight, and that's because I was bein' an ass. If you don't want me and can't see a future with me, then you have to say so now, baby, because I want you. It's that simple."

"I want you too," she says, and my life just got made. "Thinking we were done wrecked me. I know that we barely know each other, but we have a connection that I can't deny exists, even if I have tried to fight it. I know you're a good person, Rubble, I really do, and I don't want you to leave your club if that's not what you truly want, despite your injury and the club going to shit. You could do other stuff…"

I place a finger over her lips. "It wrecked me too, and that's when I knew. I don't wanna be without you, not for one fuckin' second." I kiss her, pulling her to me by clutching my hands in her hair. It turns urgent quickly.

"I love you," she whispers. "You drive me crazy, but I fucking love you."

"Love you too, baby," I say in between kisses, our tongues meeting each time. "I need you so fuckin' bad."

She reaches down and cups my dick. "Is this thing still working?"

I smile into her skin. "You tell me."

She unbuckles my belt and undoes the top button. I watch as she slides my zipper down and reaches her hand inside. I groan, moving my hands down to grasp her tits.

Those big juicy puppies that give me a hard on every single time I look at them.

I pluck her nipples through the fabric of her blouse as she rubs me up.

"Lucy," I whisper as she reaches under the elastic to grasp me in her hot little palm.

I try to undo her buttons but get annoyed, so I just rip the thing open. She gasps as I laugh against her mouth. "Let's take this to the bedroom. You're gonna have to ride me till I can move properly."

She shakes her head. "I don't know, you seem like you're in a lot of pain."

I spank her ass as she moves out of my hold. "I'm fine."

Once I'm on my crutches, I follow her to the bedroom and sit on the edge of the bed. She pulls my boots off, then my socks, then tugs at my jeans, pulling them free, along with my briefs. I sheath my dick; it's hard and ready for her. It's been fuckin' ages since I was inside her perfect pussy.

Her blouse hangs open and her bra barely contains her tits.

"Pull them out," I tell her, nodding to her chest. "Then come over here."

She does as I say, pulling her bra down and her tits bounce out as my mouth waters just staring at them. She stands in between my legs and reaches for my dick, then she takes over, jerking me off with her palm as I hiss at the grip.

I spank her ass.

"That's for talkin' back earlier," I grunt. Then I give her another. "And that's for not answering my text when I said I needed to see you."

She bites her lip, and I roll up her skirt and move to cup her sex. "This pussy is mine, and only mine from now on."

"Fuck," she swears when I clutch her hard. But I don't rub her there; she's gonna beg me for it, and I'm gonna keep her right on the edge.

I pull her to me, sucking one nipple into my mouth as I cup her and push her tits up and together. Fuckin' perfect specimens, I wanna shoot my load all over them like I did before, marking her as mine. Marking all of her.

I suck and nip at one and pull at the other as she groans, squeezing my dick tighter, precum dripping off the end, and she brushes it with her thumb as I watch her. She knows how to handle me, just how I like it.

I move my mouth to the other one, sucking and nipping, giving it the same attention as the first. I knead and cup her tits, playing with them like a fuckin' teenager because that's how she makes me feel. Then I dip a hand down to her panties and slide my hand inside.

I smirk. "Your pussy's beggin' for me," I mumble.

She rocks her hips, trying to get some friction as I swipe through her folds, brushing her clit.

"I need you," she whispers. "I need you so much, Rubble."

It's like music to my ears. I continue to pleasure her until she's almost ready to blow, then I bite down on her breast as she whimpers and cries out my name. She comes, grasping my cock as I dip a finger inside her, and her tits continue to bounce in my face. It's fucking glorious.

She moans, and when she opens her eyes again, there's a heat in them that I see clear as day.

She drops to her knees, and I caress her face as she licks my tip and teases me with her tongue. Watching her beneath me, taking charge of my cock has me swelling even more. I've so much cum in my fuckin' balls, I'm surprised they're not blue.

"Gonna come all over those tits," I tell her.

She smiles as she laps and swirls her tongue over my head, then works her tongue down as I reach down and pull both her nipples, loving how she groans at the pleasure of it.

She takes more of me into her mouth, and it's so damn good, I can't bear it. It's gonna be so fuckin' embarrassing, but her hot little mouth is teasing me so good. When she grabs my balls with one hand, I lose it, pumping my hips, ignoring all the pain in my leg and hip, choking her as she takes me, and I shoot my load down her throat.

"Fuck, sorry, baby," I say when I pull out, and she releases me with a big smile on her face. My load dribbling down her chin. She looks like a goddess.

"I love the taste of you. I could drink you up all night," she says mischievously.

"I wanna taste you so bad, but I need your pussy on my dick, baby. Sit on me 'cause I can't do any other position right now."

She stands and does as she's told.

"Are you clean?" she asks, kissing me. I can taste myself on her mouth, but I don't fuckin' care.

"Yeah, baby. Why?" I don't dare to believe that she wants me bareback.

"I'm on birth control. I want all of you. I hate condoms."

I pull her by the hair and kiss her hard and rough. "Sit on my cock. Now," I demand, lifting her by the hips as she slides down, taking all of me.

It feels so fuckin' good. I've never not used a rubber before, and the sensation is like nothing else. She's so beautifully tight, my cock filling every inch of her.

"Ride me, baby. Fuck me like you mean it."

She places her hands on my shoulders and moves up and down slowly at first, her body flush as I grab her ass and give her a spank on one cheek, then one on the other. I love the sound it makes.

"I want this fuckin' ass when I'm better," I warn her. "I'm gonna take it. Your body's mine, Luce, you hear me? Tell me."

"It's yours," she moans, sliding her soaking wet pussy up and down on my aching cock. "It's all yours."

I reach forward and suck one nipple, then the other. I love these babies in my face while she fucks me.

I grasp her hips and lift her, slamming her down. Pain shoots through my leg, but I don't give a fuck. All I care about is getting her off and watching her come undone.

I bounce her up and down as she grips my shoulders, her tits so fuckin' beautiful; it's like something out of a porno, only better.

"Fuck, Lucy, fuck..." I try to hold on. I need her to come first. I want to hear her scream again. "Come for me, baby, tell me how much you like ridin' my cock."

"Oh, God..." she trails off as I reach a hand between us to rub her clit.

"You're so fuckin' dirty," I grunt, pulling on a nipple with my teeth. "Ride me harder, baby, milk my cock…"

She grips my shoulders, and we're fucking so hard the bed sounds like it's in agony, then she lets go and makes the most glorious sound I've ever heard. I follow right behind her, shooting my load deep inside her as I shout her name until I slow and then we still, both breathing hard, flush up against each other.

I fall back against the bed as she follows on top of me, her tits crushing into my chest.

I'm fucking home with her, that's all I know.

"Was that angry make up sex?" she pants. "Because if it was, I'd like to order some of that every week."

And just like that, my baby's back.

THREE MONTHS LATER

I stare up at the shop front and feel pride swell in my chest.

I had to sell everything I own, except my bike, to be able to put down the deposit to go into partnership with Steel. It's amazing what you can do in a short space of time when you put your mind to it.

I've never had much to my name, but this is kinda cool, especially when Lucy looks at me so proudly.

Of course, I've taken a long time to heal, and I'm not there yet, but I'm back on my feet after months and months of agonizing physical therapy. My leg will never be one hundred percent what it was, but I can walk all right again and lift shit, and more importantly, work.

A large slap on my back wakes me from my reverie.

"You gonna stare at that sign all day, bro?" Steel asks, looking down at me.

The man's a machine, six-three and wide as a door. Nobody in their right mind would mess with him, which is why I guess they wanted him to be the Sergeant at Arms and the enforcer for the Rebels. He just got back from deployment; serious shit went down, which makes me glad I never got into the military.

"Fuck yeah, it's a pretty good sign."

He grunts. "Well, hold that thought. I found the fuckers who beat and left my baby girl for dead. I wanna go pay them a visit. My baseball bat is ready for a coupla hit and runs."

His baby girl is the one-year-old Pitbull, Lola, he recently adopted. He found her on the roadside, her face half chewed off after she'd been dumped by these assholes who run an illegal dog fighting ring. She was clearly used as a bait dog.

It's sad because she's such a nice dog, very submissive, how she trusts humans after that is beyond me.

He's been stewing for a couple of weeks, and the poor thing is still at the vets. It wasn't lookin' good there for a hot minute.

"Feel like fuckin' up some assholes?"

I give him a smirk. "Shit, yeah. When's Lola out of the hospital?"

The only time I ever see him show any emotion is over that damn dog.

"They kept her in after the last surgery, just so her ear heals and doesn't get infected. Or should I say, the muscle where her ear used to be, since they had to remove it."

"I'm sorry, man. People are fucked."

"Not as sorry as they're gonna be. Roundin' up Brock and a couple of dudes in town who hate this kinda shit too. She's such a sweet little thing, wouldn't hurt a fly. Gonna go postal on the ringleader. Whoever he is, we'll leave him for last; he's mine."

I do not envy him right at this moment.

"Sometimes I hate humans," I grunt. "They fuckin' ruin everything."

"Not wrong there." He turns to me. "You still thinkin' about joining the Rebels?"

"Gotta give it some time," I reply. "Still gotta bit of heat from Phoenix, though. I hear they're deeper in the shitter than ever before. Shit goin' down with the Vipers now. It's messy, pigs are gettin' involved. It won't be long before Tex either ends up arrested or in a wooden box. I never really gelled with him, definitely not as my Prez, he lacks common decency. He's done one too many deals on the side and now they're comin' back for payment."

I do miss some of the guys, though. Hoax was a good friend. Smokey, too. To get out when I did feels like a miracle. I knew there was a silver lining to me gettin' hurt, and this is it. I'm where I'm supposed to be, even if I do miss the guys I was close to.

They were the only family I ever really had, but the heat was getting too much. The things I wanted changed in a short space of time. I started to care about somebody more than myself, which I never had before.

Shit changed in the club so fast. It was like Tex was determined to play all sides, and at some point or another, something had to give.

I know for a fact Smokey doesn't like the way Tex was running things, and the members will eventually vote him out. I'm surprised they haven't nailed his ass already. Rachet is a fuckin' half-assed prick, and I never trusted him. He was always runnin' to Prez about every shitty little thing, disrespecting other brothers, and he beat a couple of girls, not that Tex did anything about that either; he was no better. Nitro helped me out when I was injured, but a part of me still thinks he's Tex's bitch and he has somethin' over him. Call it a hunch.

"I hear ya. That illegal shit's gotta catch up with you at some point; it never interested me. Don't wanna end up six feet under over some fuckin' bullshit or spend twenty years in a cell. Can think of about a million other ways to spend my time and it ain't in the joint."

That's the one thing that I always dreaded during the drop-offs, being caught by the pigs and locked away. Having my freedom taken away from me would have been the end of my existence. I couldn't be a caged man. The accident was a huge wake up call for a lot of things.

"Hear ya. Gettin' out didn't come before time, and now there's Lucy to think of and our future. Shit changes when you get an ol' lady."

He turns to look at me. "You plannin' on havin' kids?"

I shrug. For the first time in my life, it is a possibility.

I always just thought it'd be me, and the club, and maybe someone would come along that I'd wanna stick with. But kids? Nah, never on my radar, until now.

I slap him on the back. "Don't look so worried. If we do, we won't ask you to babysit."

He shakes his head. "I don't deal with baby shit. Got enough baggage with my own life without bringin' a kid into the mix."

"I used to think that too." I laugh. "You'll find a good woman one of these days, bud, then I'll be the one tellin' you I told you so."

He snorts. "Not gonna happen."

But like everything in life. It's always changing.

PART II

PRESENT DAY...

15

LUCY

PRESENT DAY

I FEEL THE BABY KICK AND RUN MY HAND OVER MY STOMACH.

I'm almost twenty-five weeks, and finally, I'm starting to look like I'm pregnant. I'm not one of these women who cares about getting fat. I want the world to know I'm having Rubble's baby. It's been a long time coming, after two miscarriages and IVF, we're finally having a baby of our own. I couldn't be more excited.

Cassidy knocks on the office door, and I pop my head up to see that she's brought snacks.

Cassidy is Colt's ol' lady. He got patched in about six months ago and runs the security business next door to us.

Cassidy learned early. Don't come near the pregnant lady first thing in the morning without coffee and snacks, though now I have to drink decaf while I'm carrying, but it's still better than giving it up altogether.

I smell the donuts in the greasy paper bag she's carrying.

Cassidy took over Colt's reception for a short time when she first moved here, but she works part-time at Lily's salon now, doing nails and spray tans and other beauty stuff. Even though she's only been in town for a few months, she's really fit in with the club and with the girls.

"Thank God, you must have heard my stomach rumbling," I say as she hands me the entire bag.

Cassidy glances around. "The boys around?"

I shake my head, peeling the bag open and devouring a donut like it's my last meal.

If Rubble sees me eating this crap, he'll go ape shit. He's gone really weird now I'm pregnant. He even refused to have sex with me for a few weeks when we first found out. I put a stop to that shit immediately. I get he wants to be cautious, but there's cautious and then there's ridiculous.

"Nope. Emergency meeting at the clubhouse. I don't know what's going on lately. They're having all kinds of secret meetings, and Rubble hasn't said anything about it. Has Colt mentioned anything?"

She sits in the chair opposite and takes the coffee cups out of the holder, handing me mine.

"Nope. I asked Sienna the same thing, and she's at a loss. Something's definitely up, but nobody's saying shit."

I know Rubble doesn't like to involve me in stuff when it's not necessary, and usually, I can get anything out of him anytime I want, but this is different.

It's well known among the women of the M.C. that pillow talk is the best form of getting information about what's happening in the club. As much as the boys like to say that it's "club business," they need an outlet to let some steam off when shit goes down. The club is nothing like the Fury, thank God. And Hutch, the club Prez, is one of the most decent men I know. He's helped us so much over the years and while he has a commanding presence and I wouldn't like to cross him, to compare him to someone like that creep Tex is just an insult.

I just hope nobody's in any kind of big trouble because the fact that not one of us girls know about it, has me even more on edge.

"Oww!" I say again, pressing a hand to my belly.

Cassidy's eyes go wide. "Is the baby kicking?"

I smile as I lick my sugary fingers. "You betcha. The little muffin has become very active these past few days. Do you want to feel?"

She nods enthusiastically, coming around the side of my desk and squatting down. I place her hand on one side of my stomach where the baby just kicked, and we wait. About a minute later, she giggles.

"Oh my God!"

"I know, it's so weird."

"Does it hurt?"

"At the moment, it feels like popcorn popping, but they say going into the third trimester, they can start to kick ribs or the bladder. Can't say I'm looking forward to that."

Her eyes go wide. "That's insane."

I laugh. "It is pretty neat. Rubble can't keep his hands to himself, though I wish it were to do something other than feel my stomach. Ever since I've been knocked up, I'm so horny all the time. I'm sure he goes off to hide from me because he disappears for hours at a time some days."

Cassidy stifles a laugh. "It's different when the shoes on the other foot."

She gets up, and I snaffle another donut and take a big bite. "Speaking of which, how are you and Colt getting along?"

"Great." She beams. "I love living with Amelia, but her questionable taste in men leaves a lot to be desired. I tend to stay at Colt's more than he stays at mine."

Amelia is Brock, the V. P's. younger sister, and she just moved back to Bracken Ridge a few months back.

"Ya'll gonna get a place together?"

She shrugs. "Someday. I'd like that. He's a good guy; I got really lucky."

I give her a warm smile. "So did he. Look at you. No wonder he took you off the market, girl, someone had to."

"You do wonders for my ego," she muses.

The front door swings open and Bones barrels through it.

He eyes the donuts, and I'm too slow at snatching them up before he's digging his dirty fingers into the bag.

"Hey! Those are mine and Cassidy's."

"Hello to you too," he grunts as he takes two big bites and the donut is gone.

He nods to Cass, and she gives him a small wave.

"Where is everyone?" he asks with his mouth full.

Hmm. Could be time to get some intel. He obviously missed the *get to church now* memo.

"Everyone went to the clubhouse." I shrug. "Thought you'd be there, seeing as you're one of the committee members and the road captain."

He gives me a look for my snide comment, then he pulls out his phone and curses.

"Fuck. I've got a million missed calls. I need to get a new phone, this fuckin' thing doesn't ring." He looks up at me. "How are you goin' with everything?"

I rub my stomach. "Fine, thanks, baby's been kicking, want to feel?"

He frowns. "Uh, no. And I meant with the Fury."

My eyes go wide. *Do not panic.*

"Umm, fine. I'm sure Rubble's sorting it out." He assumes I know. I don't fucking know.

What the fuck?

"That's what the meeting was about, I suspect." I swallow hard.

He curses again. "I better get goin', if they're comin' to Bracken Ridge, then we gotta be prepared."

I nod mechanically as he gives me and Cass a chin lift and then leaves just as fast as he arrived.

I turn to Cassidy. "This isn't good."

"Who are the Fury?" she asks.

I bite my lip. "The old club Rubble was in. I'm sure it's nothing to worry about." I don't want Cassidy saying anything to Colt until I can find out more. "Let's keep it between us till I talk to Rubble, okay? I'm sure it's nothing bad."

She nods. "Sure. Hey, I gotta go. I've got a shift in fifteen minutes. I just stopped in to feed you."

I smile but I can tell it doesn't quite reach my eyes. "Thanks for stopping by, sweetie, and for the treats."

"You're welcome. I'll see you later."

I sit in a daze as I try to scrap together what I just heard.

The Fury are coming to Bracken Ridge? What the hell for?

I know I should wait until Rubble comes home before I interrogate him, and it's not a good idea going to the clubhouse when there's a meeting in progress, but I can't help myself.

If something's going on with his old club, I need to know. It's been six years, and as far as we were aware, the Phoenix Fury fell apart years ago, and Tex was in jail.

After Rubble left it took a few months but everything came back to bite Tex on the ass. He wasn't happy about Rubble leaving, even though at the time he was in a wheelchair and crutches on his good days. Tex thought he deserted the club, lucky for us he had bigger things going on than us skipping town, but I know he's the type of man to hold a grudge. Surely that's not what this is about. And Smokey and Rubble were on good terms.

I lock the shop and turn the phones over to the machine, then hop in my SUV and drive the hell over there.

Way to go, Bones. He's usually the one to put his foot in his mouth, but I never expected that.

I make my way to the other side of town, and when I get to the clubhouse, I see all the bikes parked in the lot. I frown because I know I shouldn't be here right now, but that doesn't stop me parking in a free spot as I try not to let my heart rate run away with me.

It's going to be okay, I tell myself. *Nothing bad is going to happen.*

Ever since I got pregnant, I have become a little bit more paranoid and definitely more sensitive to things, which isn't like me, so I blame it on the hormones.

When I get out of the car and through the front doors, Ginger is behind the bar, washing up some glasses.

I give her a smile. "Hey, Ginger."

She looks up from the sink. "Hey, doll, how are you?"

"Good," I reply. "The boys just about done?"

She shakes her head. "Been in there a while."

I lean on the bar. "Who's in there?"

She shrugs. "Just the boys, but they're expecting company, I think."

My heart plunges. So, it is true. I know we didn't leave on bad blood with the club, but a visit from anyone to do with the Fury can't be good.

I try not to show my fear but I'm also mad at Rubble.

She looks up at me. "Can I get you anything to drink, doll?"

I nod. "Just an orange juice, thank you, Ging." I look toward the door.

Ginger's one of us, but she doesn't get too involved in club business. She's worked here forever and a day. When Knuckles, her husband, used to fight, he was the enforcer for the club until he had a stroke and had to give it up. He still comes to the club from time to time to hang out and give the boys shit.

"Are you all right, hon? You look a little pale," say says, placing a glass of orange juice in front of me.

My gut pangs. I need to see Rubble now but barging in there isn't something I really want to do. For one, it's their meeting room. Hutch may be easy-going most of the time, but he sure wouldn't appreciate me doing that, and I don't want to piss anyone off needlessly. It would only look bad on Rubble, but I don't know how long I can contain myself.

There's a baby in the mix now.

I take a sip and try to calm my nerves. "I'm good, sugar, just a little warm out there today, and the baby is being very active."

Her eyes light up. "I got six grandkids and another on the way. Love 'em when they're babies and can't talk back or get into trouble, then they grow up. Did you find out the baby's sex?"

I pat my stomach. "No, we thought it would be a hoot to be surprised. I know people always say they don't care, as long as it's healthy, but I'm in a conundrum. On one hand, if it's a boy, Rubble will be happy to keep the family name and he can - in his eyes - grow up to be part of the M.C. On the other hand, if it's a girl, Rubble will be sharpening his knives and carrying a piece with him wherever he goes, and she won't be able to date until she's forty."

She smiles wistfully. "It's always different when it's a girl; they become apes. It's like they don't want to think about all the shit they did to women over the years, they only just realize that they were someone's daughter, too. Reality hits them hard in the face."

She's right. There is definitely a fine line between the two. In my eyes, they are equal.

I wouldn't let our son do whatever he wanted and keep our daughter under lock and key, they'd both have the same rules. I don't know who will be the strictest out of the two of us. Rubble is very protective; he always has been.

"You said a mouthful there. Once the baby comes, I'll be giving up work, I want to dedicate all my time to being a mom. It's what I've always wanted." My heart feels heavy when I think about how much we both want this, what we've been through to get here. I also notice my mind is elsewhere. It's in that meeting room.

I shouldn't be here.

But the longer I sit here, the worse my temper grows.

I'm mad at Rubble. I shouldn't have had to hear about the Fury from Bones. I'm Rubble's fucking wife, and he should have told me. They're the main reason we left Phoenix.

The rational part of my brain reminds me that he would tell me, if it were something vitally important. We don't keep shit like that to ourselves, we never have.

I reason with myself that he would only do that if it were to protect me. But the longer the minutes tick on, the more agitated I get.

"You sure you're okay?"

I nod. "I really need to...I need to see Rubble."

I don't think, I just act.

"Lucy," Ginger starts, but I'm already heading that way, toward the meeting room door.

Rubble will kill me for interrupting but I don't give a shit. Everyone here knows me and they know what I'm like, I never think things through before I act. They can stick their stupid rules up their asses.

I barge through the door and all six of them glance up at me at once. Hutch, who sits at the head of the table, stops speaking. Next to him is Brock, then Gunner, Bones, Rubble and lastly Steel. They all seem surprised to see me standing there.

My heart races but I'm way past the point of self-control.

"Rubble," I begin, "we need to talk."

"Luce." He starts to stand, but Hutch cuts him off.

"You all right Lucy?" Hutch asks, looking concerned.

"I'm fine. Well, no, actually I'm not fine, in fact, I'm far from fine."

"Here we go," Steel mutters.

"We're having a meeting, babe," Rubble says, his tone a little strained, like I don't get it. "Can we talk about this in a bit?"

"Is it true?" I demand, staring him down.

"I am six inches, babe," Gunner pipes up. "Those rumors can be put to bed."

I shoot him a glare. "Shut up Guns."

He holds up his hands. "Can you hold five while I go get the popcorn?"

More chuckles.

Rubble stands, his face insistent. "Lucy, we can talk about this at home."

"Don't you try and shoosh me," I fire back. "I'm sorry I've barged in on your super secret meeting, but it might be an idea to let your *wife* know that Phoenix Fury are coming to town!"

"Who told you that?" Rubble asks, looking around the table.

His eyes land on Gunner. "Don't look at me, I didn't say shit."

Bones slinks down in his chair.

"That doesn't matter," I retort. I don't want to land Bones in it. "And that isn't the point, the fact is, I can see by your faces that it is true and I want to know why you didn't tell me."

Rubble isn't the kind of man who gets mad at me, in fact, he never does, even now when he should be livid, he just looks like he wants me to calm down. But I don't care, what are they gonna do, throw the fat, pregnant women out the room? I don't think so.

"He didn't tell you because we don't exactly know what this threat is," Hutch says as my eyes dart back to him. "We just know some shit's been goin' down with some of the old members of the club, they mentioned Rubble and that they were lookin' for him, for what exactly we're not entirely sure."

I blink a couple of times, I kind of thought it was just a vicious rumor. I also know Hutch is sugar coating it. "So it's true, they're coming here?"

"Smokey is and Griller and Hoax," Rubble says as I swing my gaze back to him. "And we'll talk about what they want when they get here. They're my friends, it's gonna be okay."

I narrow my eyes, he knows I'm gonna chew his ass later for lying to me, but I don't want to completely annihilate him in front of his brothers.

"Which is in a few minutes," Brock reminds us. "Might wanna get her outta here."

I look back at Rubble and he runs a hand under my jaw and holds my face, he lowers his voice. "Should've called me first."

"I don't know, kinda like the look of a woman in here." Gunner laughs. "Brightens the place up a bit, like fourth of July."

"Yeah, especially from havin' to look at your ugly mug," Bones fires across at Guns.

"Is there anything else you'd like to add, Luce?" Steel says, always the voice of reason, though he looks far from impressed at my outburst. "Since you barreled your way in here knowing fine well a meetings in progress."

I'm about to tell Steel to bite me when Rubble pulls me to him and squeezes my ass. "Gonna walk you out to your car before they arrive, and we'll talk later, when we've figured shit out."

"I'm not done with you," I warn him.

I hear snickers around the table and when I look over that way, I even see Hutch's shoulders shake. So I'm not in *that* much trouble, but Rubble probably will be. Serves him right.

"Sorry for interrupting your precious meeting," I go on, because what the Hell, I'm cactus anyway. "Must be the hormones."

"Can't blame the baby," Gunner says. "Unless it takes after it's momma, God help us if it does."

I shoot him a look too but he doesn't seem fazed by it. Nothing shocks Guns and he's always out to rib someone and get a rise out of them.

Steel clears his throat, because he's the only one not seeing the funny side, and Rubble grasps my hand and leads me out of the room.

My short-lived victory lap is quickly replaced with Rubble's disapproval.

"Lucy? What were you thinkin'?" he says, when we're outside and out of earshot of the others.

"I had to get your attention somehow."

He runs a hand through his short hair and shakes his head. "They're gonna chew my ass out in there, you know that?"

"You deserve it, last time I checked we were still married and yet the boys know more about what's goin' on with you than I do. That's not okay."

He frowns. "That isn't fair. I didn't want you involved until I knew the details, now you've left me no choice. I was gonna to tell you after the meeting with Smokey. Some shit's goin' down from the past, stuff I thought was long gone, until I know what it is exactly, I don't want you here."

I don't get time to respond as I hear the distinct sound of straight pipes in the distance.

"Fuck," Rubble mutters.

I swallow hard. "I'm sorry..."

He turns and looks down at me, his eyes dancing. "You always were my little firecracker, Sparkles." He leans down to peck me on the lips gently. "Still not done with you, though."

A few moments later, three motorcycles pull into the gates and park right next to my car in the lot. My stomach fills with dread.

Smokey pulls his helmet off and shakes out his shaggy hair.

Holy shit.

I straighten my back and steel myself for what's to come. I don't see how any of this can be good. Even if Rubble wasn't ever on bad terms with anyone except Tex, them coming all the way out here makes me nervous.

I notice, as Smokey's back is momentarily turned, that the patches now read: Sons of Phoenix Fury.

I frown.

He climbs off his bike, and then, noticing me for the first time, he pulls his sunglasses off and squints at me.

"Lucy?" he says, disbelief in his tone. "Well, I'll be damned."

My eyes must go wide because he chuckles.

"Hey, Smokey." I go for cheerful and hope for the best.

"What, no tearful greeting?"

I will him to disappear. "What are y'all doing here?" I try to sound casual.

"Came to visit your old man." He nods to Rubble, they clasp hands over my head.

"It's been too long," Rubble says, I can tell he's on edge.

When Smokey steps back he grins at me, raising his eyebrows. "That it has." His eyes flick down to my stomach, and I place my hand there protectively. "I see you've been busy."

Behind him, I see the one named Griller, the Sergeant at Arms, and then, Hoax of all people climb off their bikes. When Hoax sees me, he does a double take.

"Lucy?"

"Hey, Hoax."

I flick my eyes to Griller, he doesn't smile, then again, no Sergeant at Arms ever does. I think it's part of the whole deal. He gives me a subtle chin lift but doesn't speak.

Look mean and scary, check. Don't crack a smile, check, check. Tower over you like a force to be reckoned with, check, check, check.

Before I can protest, Hoax grabs me by the hips and lifts me up into a big bear hug.

"Hey, careful!" I say, as my arms are pinned at my sides.

"Been a fuckin' stranger." He laughs, then when he's finally done manhandling me, he sets me down. "Let me take a good long look at you."

Griller slaps him upside the head. "Bitch is pregnant, half-wit. You probably just squashed the baby."

Aww. Sweet.

I give him an appreciative smile and don't take offense to being called a bitch; to them, it's a term of endearment I'm sure.

All three of them glance over my shoulder at the same time, and before I even get to turn around, hands are wrapping around me, and I feel Rubble pull me behind him.

He stands in front of me, and his stance is rigid. Ready if needed, though I honestly don't think these three post a threat.

I notice Steel sidle up next to me, then Brock on the other side.

I don't know if this is suddenly turning into a pissing competition, but the testosterone level just went up about five hundred notches.

"Hoax," Rubble says, still holding onto my upper arms as I try to wriggle free.

They clasp hands do the chest bump thing as Hoax grins from ear to ear. "My old friend. See you still haven't got this one under control." He nods to me.

I immediately stop fighting him.

"When did I ever?" Rubble agrees.

When I glance to my right, Steel stares down at me, unimpressed.

I poke a tongue at him behind Rubble's back because nobody can see. His eyes go wide, and I know he doesn't appreciate my random acts of rebellion, especially when faced with what could be – in their eyes – a potential threat.

Still, they seem to be in friendly enough spirits.

"She was just leavin', weren't you, babe?" Rubble lets go of me and brings me into his arms. I narrow my eyes back at him.

"Meetin's inside," Brock grunts. "This way."

"See ya, Luce!" Hoax gives me a wink.

They're not here for beef, then. I can only hope my instincts aren't getting rusty.

The others take off inside, and Rubble lets go of me and places his hands on his hips.

Looks like I'm in trouble.

"Why do you always gotta fight me?"

I copy his stance; except I point a finger in his face. "I could say the same about you," I accuse. "You know how I feel about being kept in the dark, Rubble."

"I didn't want you to know," he replies. "Until I get this

shit sorted out, told you that. There's no point in worrying you without good cause."

"So you keep saying."

He runs a hand through his hair, exasperated. "I gotta go."

He sees the disappointment in my eyes because he gives me a kiss on the nose.

"I thought the past was behind us," I start, but he places a finger over my mouth.

"Go home. I'll be there when I can. I don't want you here while they're here. You shouldn't have come knowing full well we had club business in the first place."

I ignore that last comment. "I'm fine. Aside from Hoax trying to squash our baby."

I see his lips twitch. I know he's missed his friend over the years, and Hoax hasn't changed a bit.

I still have that uneasy feeling in my stomach, though. We are so far from being done with this.

"I don't want them havin' any leverage over me, with you and the baby…" he trails off.

I cup his face. "Rubble, you're scaring me, you said they're your friends."

He kisses me gently. "They are. As far as I'm aware, but it's been years. There's nothin' to be scared of, just takin' precautions. Just like I did when we got married in Vegas. I told Elvis I'll look after you till I die, and I meant it."

Tears well in my eyes. "I'm mad at you, but I love you so fucking much."

His lips twitch again as a slow grin spreads across his face. "Give me some sugar."

"No," I retort, pushing back off his chest. "You don't get any sugar after this stunt."

"I'm the one who should be mad, you just stormed into our meeting and grilled me."

Despite that, he pulls me to him and kisses me hard. I can feel his hard on pushing against me, and my eyes go wide.

"Babe..." I groan.

"Fuck," he mutters. "You know I can never stay mad at you, Sparkles."

A few moments later, Steel yells across the lot. "You already knocked her up once, Rubble, can't get her pregnant twice so fuckin' get your ass in here now before I come and drag you inside."

He gives me a look. "Now look at what you did."

He pinches my chin and goes to open my car door, and I settle inside.

"I love you," I say.

"Ditto. Now go home, and don't be makin' any more house calls. I'll be there soon."

He kisses me again through the open window, then I start the car and he taps the roof as I drive away.

I wish I could be a fly on the wall and listen to what's going on in there.

I'm scared. I thought our past was just that, in the past.

Now I'm not so sure.

16

RUBBLE

Seeing Lucy out in the parking lot surrounded by my old club brothers shouldn't make me as mad as I am. Sure, I didn't leave on bad blood, but that still doesn't give fuckin' Hoax the okay to manhandle my woman.

Hutch is at the head of the table. With no fear of a mad little Texan woman barging in here again, I settle in my usual seat.

"It's good to see you," Smokey says, offering Hutch his hand as he stands to greet them. Griller gives us his usual curt nod. Hoax gives me another hard pat on the back as he sits next to me.

"You been okay?" Hoax asks. He doesn't look too much different, a little hairier, he's filled out a little too.

"Can't complain," I say, giving him a chin lift. "Shit's pretty good in the country."

Smokey and Griller take a seat around the table, and Ginger appears with a tray of drinks.

I never thought I'd see Smokey, or any of my old club sitting here at church.

"Thanks darlin'," Hutch says as she walks around the table delivering beer and bourbon.

I get my usual non-alcoholic moonshine that Ginger stores special for me. It's our little secret. I've been sober for six years and seventeen days. Quite an achievement for someone like me. When I make a promise, I stick to it, and I'm in the best shape of my life. I don't touch the stuff anymore. Someone like me can't ever go there, because as much as I say I'm a social user, I know that isn't the truth. I've got too much to lose.

We wait until Ginger has left and closed the doors behind her before the meeting begins.

I purposely didn't tell Lucy because I've no idea what this is about or if the rumors about some missing coke are actually true. Or why they're wearing cuts that say: *Sons of Phoenix Fury*.

I had heard through the M.C. grapevine that after the destruction of the original Fury, and Tex going to prison, the club disbanded and had only recently tried to come back together.

"Boys, it's good of you to come down," Hutch goes on, taking a sip from his glass. "With all the talk goin' on, it's better to clear these things up in person. Appreciate you takin' the time."

Both Griller and Hoax look at Smokey.

"Nothin' like catchin' up on old times over a bourbon at ten in the mornin'," Smokey says, raising his glass to take a sip. He's gone a little gray, his face tan from the elements, his hair still wild and free.

"Well, the floor is yours." Hutch interlocks his fingers and waits.

Smokey keeps his eyes on Hutch. "First, I should start by givin' you the background story to why we started up Sons of the Phoenix Fury, and I guess you figured most of that has to do with Tex and the dismantlement of the original club. Took him a few months after Rubble left, but he finally ran the club into the ground, not before voting him out. Started off makin' deals he couldn't keep, and little did we know, he was borrowing from Peter to pay Paul, added to that, some of the shit he was gettin' into wasn't cuttin' the grade. The Mexicans weren't happy with the shit the Vipers were distributing, then he pissed off the Cubans over promising and not delivering. We knew he was mixin' a bit of this with a bit of that to make more profit by splittin' the bricks and takin more of a slice for himself. It wasn't pure grade anymore, but he was still sellin' it as such. He wanted a slice of all the pie but wanted to deliver shit and hope nobody would notice. He got too greedy."

Silence ensues.

Though it's been a while since Hutch was in a one percent club, he knows the ropes, fuck – he knows it better than anyone. He was born into M.C. life and made the decision in his late twenties when he took over the club to go a different route. That split decision to either complete a drop or walk away turned out to be the biggest decision of his life. That night there was a surprise attack and a shootout. Almost everyone from the two clubs involved ended up dead or locked up.

When I asked him one time why he decided to take the club in a new direction, he told me that he'd just found out Kirsty was pregnant with Deanna, and he had a premonition, a gut feeling that shit was gonna go wrong.

When I think about that moment, I knew that I made the right decision in leaving Phoenix. Especially when I hear about what Tex did to the club.

"Sounds like he created one too many enemies," Hutch remarks. "Did the fucker have a death wish? How did he not think he wasn't gonna get caught? Playin' everyone from all sides can't last forever."

"He thought he was smarter than everyone else." Smokey shrugs. "He thought he could bluff his way out of it and nothin' would happen. God complex or some shit, I don't fuckin' know. A part of me thinks he was snorting the shit he was sellin'; would explain a lot."

I give him a chin lift. "So, your Sons of Phoenix Fury now, for real?"

He flicks his eyes to mine, with a dangerous glint in them, which reminds me of why he was always gonna be a President of a club at some point or another. He just has that air about him. People stop and listen when he talks; they respect him. Something Tex never had.

"We laid low for a while. We're tryin' to piece a new club together with the help of some of the Sons from the Cali chapter. The Dragons – as you probably heard – went under after Tex started a turf war. Was the perfect time for the Vipers to move in and dismantle everything, take charge, but by doing that, they also got in the middle of everything, though I think they knew what they were doin' from day one."

"One that evidently cleaned out most of the Sons," Hutch finishes.

"We were lucky, but Tex had doubled-crossed the Vipers and that shit sticks. They're still out for vengeance, so startin' up again hasn't been easy. I've been recruiting some old members, but we're not there yet. There was a lot of scum in the old club, guys that couldn't be trusted. When shit went south, I wasn't goin' down with Tex – he started the war and, in the end, he paid the price. He made decisions that went against what we voted on; cardinal rule number one is you don't go against the committee. He had no respect for the members, and personally, I think he was crooked from way back."

Now more than ever I'm thankful I didn't go down that road.

"What happened to some of the other boys?" I ask. "Ratchet, Nitro…"

"We don't know for sure, but Ratchet went underground, and we think Nitro's gone rogue, but we believe he's been workin' for Tex while he's been locked up," Smokey continues. "When the bricks supposedly went missin' from the warehouse that night– which I still don't believe even happened – it was an excuse for Tex to take out the trash. You're glad you got out when you did. They blamed Needles, one of the prospects, then buried him out in the desert. I still don't know if it were true or if he was just a scapegoat to cover up Tex's lies. Tex then made up some shit about one of us bein' there that night, and he wants payback when he gets out. In his fucked-up brain, he wants all of us gone. We weren't loyal to him – we think that Nitro or Rachet, and anyone else they've got workin' for them, may come out of the shadows to try and finish off the club before we get off the ground. Payback."

I can see it with Rachet, but Nitro kinda surprises me. Then again, the guy was always hot and cold.

Steel nods to me. "But you left the club before any of this shit went down and detonated, on good enough terms," he says, then looks to Smokey. "So, what does any of this shit have to do with threatening Rubble? He was free and clear."

"They've been threatening all of us. Scare tactic," Hoax answers. "They're workin' underground, never stayin' in one place long. Trouble is, we can't pinpoint where their HQ is – or if it is even Nitro and Rachet and the old members behind it. Like Smokey said, Tex is a sewer rat, and he's still got plenty of minions around him to settle the score, even from prison."

Smokey nods. "Makes us uneasy. Tex knows that we're forming a new club. He's still got plenty of loyalty from scumbags on the outside. We believe he's still got old members working for him, but they're on the DL. We got wind that there's a new lab bein' set up, and it's got Tex's name all over it. If we play our cards right, the Vipers will move on in and settle it before shit gets out of hand. They own Phoenix now, and since we don't wanna be gettin' into hauling coke, they're welcome to it. The question is, why now? Tex isn't up for parole for four more years, so it isn't like he's gettin' out anytime soon, but it's as though he's settin' shit up, ready for his return."

Low mumbles go around the table.

"With there bein' no sightings of Rachet, he could even be dead, we just don't know. Some of the slimeballs live in the shadows for years then reappear," Griller adds, his gravelly voice booming across the room. "Nitro was always a bit of a loose cannon. There was something about him where it was never clear if he was in or out. We figure if we can give the Vipers the tip that they're tryin' to start up some shit, they can move in and sort it and take the rest of them out. Might mean we make amends of sorts with the Vipers and stay off their radar. We'll be even."

I run a hand down my face. While the news isn't great, the threat all seems to be centered around Phoenix and the underground shit goin' on, not here. I feel a little relieved.

"So you just wanted to give us a friendly warnin'?" Hutch asks, curling his hand around his whiskey glass. "Seems awful noble of you to come all this way."

Hutch is a player from way back; nothin' gets unnoticed around him, and it does beg the question.

Smokey looks him in the eye. "We don't trust any of them.

They'd put a bullet between our eyes for walkin' away from the club, and now startin' afresh with a new club – that shit right there is enough to cause a thirst for vengeance. We'd be rivals, and anyone that betrayed them in their eyes would be a target. We already lost a prospect, and two old members showed up dead in the last few months. One of the crew's girls got attacked a week ago while leavin' the bar she works at, beat her up pretty bad. Left her with a message that they'll fuck with all of us if we don't back down from reforming the Fury."

"They bein' who?" Steel asks. "They hidin' behind their old patches?"

"They call themselves the Rogue Warriors," Hoax snorts. "And they pop up whenever they please, hence why we're not really sure who's in charge, or what the agenda is."

Hutch's grip on the glass gets tighter. "That's not fuckin' good. I got a better idea, how about we take them out first?"

Griller grunts a sound of approval, and it's clear that that's exactly what he wants to do.

"We could, but we'd rather give the Vipers the heads up about their operation. We figure it'll be better for all sides if we involve them to do most of the dirty work, they'll defend their territory," Smokey says. "For all we know, Rubble is free and clear, but Tex and Ratchet had a thirst for vengeance even back then. Ratchet wasn't right in the head. Rubble and I have been brothers for a long time, and he saved this fuckers life." He thumbs to Hoax, who gives me a big grin.

"I never did say sorry that I fucked up your favorite t-shirt when you used it to keep me from bleeding to death," Hoax says, giving me a side eye.

"What are friends for?" I smirk.

Griller points at me. "Now you got an ol' lady and a kid on the way, I'd be keepin' a close eye on 'em. We'll do what we can and give you the heads up if Nitro or Rachet pop up on the grid again, or any of these so-called warrior dicks. Don't underestimate any of them; they might be slippery fuckers, but they got just enough balls to do somethin' stupid."

Unfortunately, I think Griller is right. I never gelled with Rachet to begin with – he always had the ability to take things too far, he was unstable. Again, I have a hard time seein' Nitro working for Tex and carrying out anyone's murder. But I guess nobody can be trusted, especially when they've got nothing to lose.

"Nothing's gonna happen," Brock says. "But we'll make sure the prospects keep an eye on things and someone needs to be with Lucy at all times. Better bein' safe than sorry."

"On it," Steel grunts. "Give Jax and Gears somethin' to do other than get into fuckin' trouble."

"I'd be makin' Gash a permanent fixture over at the office," Hutch adds. "He doesn't miss a trick, and he's fearless."

Gash, formally known as Lee, was recently patched in from being a prospect. He was also fundamental in rescuing Angel, Brock's ol' lady, when her ex stalked her and turned up at Angel's Ink.

"I'll be at Lily's most of the week," Gunner puts in. "I can watch the girls from the salon while I'm there, bring a prospect with me if need be, or take Bones?"

We all turn to look at Bones.

"What?" he says, though everyone knows he's gotta stay on the DL from the law.

I smirk and Hutch gives him an eyeroll. "You gotta lay low, so don't go gettin' so much as a parkin' fine, you got me. A fuckin' road captain is no good to me when you're behind bars."

"You rob a bank or somethin'?" Hoax laughs.

Bones smirks. "Nah, man, got some old shit catchin' up

with me. Speeding tickets, bail bonds, and parking fines from out of state. I got myself a good lawyer, though. I'll be fine."

"If you're referring to a voluptuous redhead with a whiplash tongue, I'll remind you she practically has a bounty on your head for harassment." I slap him on the back. "Might not wanna go pokin' the bear, bigshot. It might land you in jail quicker than a bounty hunter will."

He rubs both hands down the sides of his mohawk. Though he's let it grow out some, I don't know why the fuck he thinks it's fashionable anymore.

"The only thing I'll be pokin' is my dick down her throat," he says quite confidently. "Some chicks just take a little longer to come around."

I turn to Smokey. "What about you, get yourself an ol' lady?"

He laughs out loud. "Where did you get a crazy notion like that? I like my dick wet, and on the regular, though I admit, not bein' in the club environment means we gotta go out and find pussy rather than it bein' flung in our faces, but that's all gonna change soon."

"How long till you think you will have enough members?" Steel gives him a chin lift.

"Hopin' for a few more weeks, month tops. Hoax over here just got handed an inheritance, and the building we're lookin' at is perfect to set up our new HQ. Sooner we get some control back over Phoenix, the better. Vipers can keep the drugs, we want the guns, and we've got the connections. Made a few allies with the Sinners and Saints, but it's gonna take some time to get things back on their feet."

I know Smokey will make a great Prez and an even better alliance.

"Appreciate the heads up," Hutch says after a few moments of deliberating. "Offer still stands to come to Phoenix and help. We don't wanna get involved in any kind of turf war with the Vipers, but if you need help gettin' shit together before the takedown, then consider it done."

Smokey nods. "That means a lot. Appreciate it."

"Sure you don't want to stick around? Plenty of room upstairs if you wanna crash and drink here tonight," I add.

Smokey grins. "You got many women in this place who we won't get buried for approaching?"

"Hang arounds come and go, but there's plenty of sweet butts who hang out on the weekends, some lookin' for more trouble than others," Hutch grumbles, then adds, "Just stay away from a woman called Deanna. No matter what she tells you, she's off limits, trust me, it ain't worth dyin' for."

Our guys all snicker.

"Who's that?" Hoax asks with a sudden sound of interest.

"My daughter," he gruffs. "The reason I'm fuckin' old and gray." He looks at me, then at Brock. "You two better hope and pray you don't have girls. It'll be the end of sleep as you know it."

Smokey gives him a chin lift. "Don't I know it. Got a daughter too, just turned sixteen, only get to see her once or twice a year. It's a long story. Unfortunately, she takes more after me than her mother, which gives me more than one reason to worry."

Fuck me. I had no idea Smokey had a kid. Maybe he didn't either until recently.

"Rawlings gives me enough lip as it is," Brock complains. "And she's just turning seven."

Rawlings is Angel's kid who Brock adopted when they got together, and she's as cute as a button but has everyone wrapped around her little finger.

"Here's to havin' sons," Hutch says, raising his glass as the meeting adjourns. "And if we have daughters, let them take after their mommas, for fuck's sake."

A whoop of agreement rings though the room.

Now all I have to do is go and appease my wife. Not that that's ever an easy feat, but she'll be extra pissed because I kept this from her.

As if sensing my dilemma, Hutch calls me back as the guys disperse out to the bar.

"Got a minute?"

I sit back down. "Sounds serious."

"You worried about shit goin' down?"

I meet his gaze. "Crazy fucks will try anything to get under your skin, doesn't make me feel good that they took down an ol' lady. That's some fucked up shit."

"Yeah, none of it makes me feel good either, though the Rebels seem to be off the radar. I get that murky feelin' whenever this motherfucker Tex is mentioned."

"You're not wrong there." I feel it in my core just how fucked up he is.

He shakes his head. "This is exactly why I got out of the game."

"Hear ya. It's exactly why I got out too."

"I don't want to take any chances. I'll put the word out to keep an ear to the ground. Steel can get Linc to try and get a lead on Nitro and Rachet. If we can get any information, that is."

"I'll feel better when this bust is done and dusted."

"Me too," he agrees. "For now, we'll lay low and go about business as usual. No need to get our tails in a spin."

"Gotcha, Prez." I stand to leave, still feeling uneasy about the fact they've taken out three members and beaten up a woman and nobody knows who the fuck they are or where their hang out is.

"Oh, and Rubble?"

I turn on my heel.

"I'd take the woman flowers, son. Might make things a

little easier on you. Women like pretty things. Might keep you outta the doghouse."

I smirk. "One can only hope. Thanks for the tip."

When I get home, Lucy is in the kitchen making dinner.

"Luce," I call, pulling my boots off in the doorway. "I'm home."

She doesn't answer, and the minute I see her back to me as she leans over the pot on the stove, I know she's still pissed.

I come up behind her and slip my arms around her waist and hold her belly. "You ignorin' me?"

She wriggles her butt against me, trying to break free, but I don't let her.

"You know I'm not going to forgive you that easily," she huffs. "I shouldn't have to learn important information about my own husband from someone like Bones."

"Bones?"

"He came into the shop. He's the one who said the Fury were coming down, so it would've been nice to have a heads up, that's all."

"But you still came out to the clubhouse anyway?"

She turns in my arms, facing me. "I had a right to know. You always tell me important stuff, just not this time?"

She looks hurt, and I hate being the one who put that hurt on her face.

"Babe, don't overthink this. I didn't want to alarm you, with the baby and everything —" I trail off. We've had multiple miscarriages. My heart lurches when I think about the last time. Lucy was so happy, so sure that things felt different that time around.

I'm tentative with everything at the moment. I didn't even

want to have sex while she was in the first trimester, though she put her foot down and maintained the doctor said it would be healthy and wouldn't harm the baby.

We've been through so much shit, and we both really want this. We're both ready for it. The thought of jeopardizing that makes me feel sick.

"You can't use the baby as an excuse to keep me in the dark," she says. "I felt like a fucking idiot."

I kiss her chastely. "First of all, I'm not using our unborn baby as an excuse. I don't want you stressin' out over shit that isn't a problem. Second, there's no bigger idiot than Bones himself, so that's a moot point. If you want a third, then how about trusting in your husband? Have I ever not done what's best for you, what's best for us?"

Her face softens slightly. I know the signs. "Rubble, you know ties with that club don't sit well with me. They went underground for heaven's sake. A rival gang tried to kill you and Hoax, need I remind you?"

I pull her to me. "Baby—"

She puts her hand on my chest. "Tell me. If Tex is gettin' out, then I need to know…"

I frown. "He's not gettin' out. Some of the old club members have been snooping around and stirring' shit up again. That's all. It's nothin' to worry about."

She frowns. I don't want to tell her any more than that; there is no need to cause panic.

"But what does it matter now? It was six years ago. You're no longer a member. All that shit is dead and buried, right?"

I push her hair back off her face. Sometimes I think she's too innocent for this life, then she opens her mouth, and I know we're exactly where we need to be.

I run a hand through my hair, careful with my next words. As tough as she is, I don't need to scare the living daylights out of her. "It's just a precaution, but Hutch wants someone to be with you at the office when I'm not here."

Her eyes go wide, then she shakes her head. "I don't need a goddamn babysitter."

"It wouldn't be like that. But I don't want to take any chances. I'm not on the radar like we thought, but that doesn't mean shit. Better to be safe than sorry, for you and the baby."

"So I have no choice in it?"

"It'll just be a prospect, or Gash or Bones or Steel, you won't even know they're around."

She rolls her eyes. "A cloud of smoke appears before Steel walks into a room, like a warning signal. Bones makes an entrance as loud as a circus performer, and Gash — well, I suppose I can deal with him. Least he doesn't stare at my tits."

I frown. "Who else stares at them?"

She brushes my hair back with one hand. "Nobody, it's just a metaphor."

I shake my head. "If anyone looks at your tits, you tell me about it, especially a prospect."

Her lips curl into a smile. "You think I can't handle the prospects?"

"I know you can but I break bones with more force. What I meant was; tell me, so I know where they're buried. It's only polite to inform the families concerned."

She laughs, then kisses me. "I'm still mad at you."

I kiss her back. "No, you're not. I bet that hot little pussy is, though. Gonna give me some sugar, baby?"

She rubs her pussy against my thigh and sighs. "I'm gonna burn the stew."

"Fuck the stew." I reach over and turn it off, then I grab her by the hips and sit her on the counter. "Don't like you bein' mad at me."

"Good, because mad is putting it lightly."

I smirk as I cup her face. "I wish I could spank you right now."

"You can," she muses.

I shake my head; not while she's pregnant. I gotta be good.

"You know I'm saving' em up though for when I can tie you up again."

She pulls me to her. "Don't say things you know get me fired up when you can't deliver."

I know she thinks that comments funny. I nip her neck gently as she squeals.

"Oh, I can deliver, sweet cheeks, and for that comment, I'm gonna make you beg me to let you come."

She groans as I cup her pussy. "Baby…"

My hands find her breasts, and I give them a squeeze. "These are gettin' bigger," I muse into her neck. Hormones and shit are making her body change, and I fuckin' love it. She's all curves, all woman, so hot I want to take a bite out of her.

"Blame the man who knocked me up."

"Yeah. Wait till your husband finds out it was me, then you'll have some explainin' to do."

"I love you, Rubble," she whispers.

"When you're not mad at me, I love you too." *So fuckin' much.*

"Yeah? Well, now that we've established that, shut up and nail me, will you? A girl's gotta eat soon."

And this is the woman I chose.

17

LUCY

I wake up with a shooting pain in my stomach. I cry out as I sit straight up in bed.

Oh no. Not again. I know this pain.

I hear Rubble curse as he fumbles with the lamp on the bedside table, and then he turns to me as I double over.

"Shit, Rubble. Oh God…"

His face pales as he leaps out of bed and springs across to my side. "What can I do?"

I glance down and see red seeping through my sleep shorts. "No." I cup my sex. "No fucking way. This isn't happening."

"Just calm down," he tells me, already on his phone. "Hello, yes, I need an ambulance… my wife's… my wife's bleeding…. she may be… shit… she may be miscarrying…"

I burst into tears as I hold my stomach with one hand and try to stop the bleeding with the other. Rubble dashes to the bathroom with the phone still glued to his ear and comes back with a towel and holds it between my legs.

"Two fifty-two Oak Park Way, Bracken Ridge… I… I

don't know, hang on." He flicks his eyes to mine. "How far along are we?"

"Almost twenty-six weeks," I say, trying not to let the pain cripple me.

He repeats it back to the operator. "Okay... Yeah, uh, I don't fuckin' know, she's in pain, she just woke up screaming, and now there's blood everywhere..."

The conversation goes on for a few more minutes, and he stays on the line with her until we hear sirens. The one thing about living in a small town is how fast an ambulance can arrive.

He eventually hangs up, and I try to move. "Don't get up, just stay put," he says, and I hear the agony in his voice.

"I'm not losing this baby," I whisper. "I'm not, I can't, Rubble..." I sob. "Please, God, someone help us..."

His eyes cloud over as he holds me, and I sob into his shoulder. "It's going to be okay, baby. We're farther along this time. I'm sure this kind of thing happens, so let's not jump to conclusions."

We were only just feeling the baby kick a few hours ago. I start to panic, bile rising in my throat.

"I can't feel it," I say. "What if our baby died, and I didn't even know?" I can barely make out the words as sobs rack through my body. I want this baby so fucking much. I want to be a mom. I want us to be a family.

"Don't be sayin' crazy shit," he tells me firmly. "We're in this together, this baby's loved and wanted and nothin's gonna get in the way of that."

I know I should try not to panic and be rational, but I've been down this road three times. I've never made it this far in my pregnancy before. "Doctor Samuels is away," I say when I manage to come up for air. "I don't know who stands in for him..."

"I'll find out, just keep breathing and hold on to me. I'm not gonna let you go, baby."

I nod as he wipes the tears away from my face, and two minutes later, the ambulance pulls up. I say a prayer to God while I hear them at the front door. I'll do anything, *anything* to keep this baby. Please God, please, don't take my baby away…

I'm lying on the cot while Helen, Steel and Lily's mom, and Doctor Stevens try to find the baby's heartbeat. I got lucky; she's filling in for my regular obstetrician while he's on vacation. She repeatedly tells me to call her Frankie and that sets me at ease. She's about my age, tall with auburn hair and a kind smile.

She rushes an emergency ultrasound and Rubble squeezes my hand as I lie there and try not to scream with fear. She's thorough and professional as they work proficiently and silently.

Why can't they find it?

Then, a few moments later, she and Helen make eye contact, and then I hear the noise.

The baby's heartbeat sounds loud and clear, and everyone takes a visible breath.

"Lucy, your baby's doing just fine," she says, turning to smile at me. "It's common that babies can be very wriggly, even when you can't feel them, which is why we couldn't pick up the heartbeat right away."

Rubble and I both sigh at the same time as he holds me.

"Thank God," Rubble says, brushing his knuckles over my hand as he looks down at me.

"But the blood?" I blurt out, tears leaking down my face.

"I want to run some tests, with your permission. Being

that you've miscarried before, it's just a precaution. We don't want to put you or the baby under any stress. Though I know it's alarming, gushes of blood aren't this uncommon in a pregnancy this far along. Because you're past the first trimester and aren't clotting, we can rule out an SCH. I want to run a full exam, just to be sure."

I blink up at her. "What are you looking for? Are you sure the baby's okay?" I turn to look at the monitor for the first time. "Why couldn't you see the baby moving?"

"Sometimes the baby moving isn't an indication of anything until we find a heartbeat. I can assure you, it's fast and strong. I would suspect you're bleeding from the vaginal cavity, but we can't rule out that it isn't from the uterus or cervix, and that's what I'm concerned about. It could be an infection or a ruptured cyst. I want to keep you overnight for observation, if that's all right, so I'm close by and can monitor you and the baby."

Rubble nods, looking at the doctor like she's God. And right now, she is.

We'll do whatever she says.

"I'm just so scared, Rubble," I say, as he folds me into his chest and cry tears of happiness.

He won't cry in front of them, but I know he's feeling it. He kisses the top of my head.

"I told you it's all gonna be okay, baby doll, and the Doc just said the baby's fine. It's just a precaution. If they can find out what happened, then they can prevent it from happening again. Right Doc?"

She smiles at us kindly. "Exactly. I don't want you to worry, it'll put more stress on the baby, and we need a calm momma and healthy bub. I'll go arrange a bed for you in the maternity wing."

"Thanks, Doc," Rubble says as Helen pats his arm. "Thank

you, Helen, can you keep Lucy company for a second? I need to step out."

She nods. "Of course."

He leaves the room with Doctor Stevens, and I know he's going to corner her and give her an interrogation fit for a king. She's been amazing.

Helen hands me some tissues as she wipes the goop of my belly. "See, sweetheart, this baby's a little fighter, just like it's momma."

I sniff as I wipe my eyes. "God, I've never been so scared."

She rubs my arm. "When I was pregnant with Jayson, I had complications, him being my first baby, I had no idea what to expect. Of course, the little shit ended up being over ten pounds, so I thank his brute of a father for that one." She laughs. "Then I had Lily, and she was completely different, only six pounds and no problems at all. Each baby is different. When it's your first, everything is new, and you're not quite sure what to expect. The most important thing is not to stress; the baby will feel it, and we don't want that."

I nod like she's got all the answers. Then I laugh. "Steel was over ten pounds? You poor thing."

"Not exaggerating, the kid just about broke me. It's a wonder I ever walked again."

I can't wait to rib Steel about this, nothing like embarrassing birthing stories to bribe him with when I need something done.

"Do you think the baby's really okay?" I ask when we sober from laughing. All those old fears come rushing back.

She tugs my top down and pulls a blanket over me. "If the baby is anything like you, honey, then it's going to be just fine. It's better to be here while the Doctor runs those tests, just to get a clear answer, so you can rest and not have to worry. You're in the best hands. Doctor Stevens is an amazing obstetrician."

I nod. I have to believe it's true. I am in the best hands possible. If I bled but didn't lose the baby, then that has to be a good thing, right?

"Thanks, Helen, I'm so grateful."

"You just rest now, honey. We'll get you moved into a room shortly, just hang tight and I'll make you a cup of tea."

I smile gratefully. "Can you send that man back in here, please. He's probably out there grilling her as we speak."

"Sure thing."

She leaves, and I close my eyes and thank the almighty for this miracle. I don't think my heart could have taken a stillborn birth. In fact, I know it couldn't. I rub my stomach.

"It's okay, little one," I say. "Your mama's here, and I love you so much. Daddy loves you too. He's a good man, he'll look after us. We can't wait to meet you, little blip. We're going to have so much fun together. I can't wait to be your mommy."

I've never wanted anything so much in my life.

He or she is a fighter, and I know they get that from Rubble. He's my rock.

He's my everything.

By the time I get to leave the hospital, it's mid-afternoon.

Poor Rubble slept in the chair next to me even when I told him to go home and get some proper rest. He wouldn't leave my side.

Doctor Stevens confirmed that I didn't have an infection and as I wasn't bleeding from my uterus, they suspect it was a ruptured cyst. To say I've never been so relieved is an understatement, but now Rubble is insisting that I stop working and says I need to rest.

I love the man, but he drives me crazy. I can't sit around all day because I'll drive myself mad.

Deanna, her mom Kirsty, and Steel's ol' lady, Sienna, are all in the waiting room when I get discharged.

They all leap up the second I come into view.

"Lucy!" Deanna squeals, embracing me with a tight hug.

"Let the woman breathe, Deanna," Kirsty chastises. "How are you, sweetheart?"

I nod. "I'm good, the baby's good. They think it was a ruptured cyst, so nothing to really worry about, even though I was terrified out of my mind."

"You had us freaking out," Sienna says, when Deanna is done manhandling me. "Is there anything we can do?"

"Yes," Rubble pipes up. "You can make sure she stays off her feet and rests. Doctor's orders."

I roll my eyes. "He's being dramatic."

"I think Rubble has a point," Kirsty agrees, assessing me like a mom would. I feel a lump in my throat. She's always been like this, since the moment I met her. "I don't think it's wise to tempt fate. Exhaustion can creep up on you and that will put more stress on the baby."

"Don't you start," I mutter.

"I can help out," Deanna chirps. "I've got classes, and I'm committed to helping Angel for a couple of shifts this week working reception, but I can man the office in between."

"I can help too," Sienna agrees. "Between all of us, we can manage."

Deanna is in her final year of her interior design course. She often helps out here and there or where she's needed, but Sienna is busy running Steel's office at the garage next door. She can't be expected to run both.

"Thanks, guys, I really appreciate it, but I don't think we're quite at that point."

Rubble scoffs. "Something tells me you're outnumbered here, Sparkles."

Kirsty swings her arm around me as we exit and make our way out to the car. "That's what we're here for, to make sure you're not going to overdo it. The last thing anyone wants is you being run off your feet, Lucy. Listen to your man, he knows what he's talking about."

They're all so sweet, and I know they're just trying to do what's best for me because they care, but what happened wasn't because I work too much nor am I stressed. I know none of them will quit, though. The women of the M.C. aren't happy unless they're nagging someone.

When we get out to the car, Steel's leaning against the bonnet, talking to Rubble.

They both quieten when we get closer.

Steel gives me a nod. "You all right, beautiful?"

I nod. "Yeah, Steel, it seems this baby can't be kept down, though."

He gives Rubble a shove in the shoulder, which is his way of showing brotherly affection.

"You over workin' your ol' lady?"

I roll my eyes and answer for Rubble. "He's not doing anything, and don't you start too. I've had enough with these three rearranging my schedule and trying to send me to bed."

"Being in bed is what got you into this mess in the first place," Steel mutters.

"I'll have you know, it was probably more likely that it was the kitchen bench," Rubble corrects.

"Eww," Sienna and Deanna say simultaneously.

"Leave her alone, both of you," Kirsty scolds. "I think she's endured enough these last twenty-four hours, so why don't you both shoo, and I'll take Lucy back to my place."

It's funny, hearing Kirsty say "shoo" to Steel of all people, and actually get away with it. Of course, he can glare at her, but he won't tell her off. Nobody says boo to Hutch's wife.

"I'm fine," I assure her.

"I'm making French toast," she replies, giving me a warm smile. "And I've got the best maple syrup ever; it's homemade."

I wave to Rubble. "See you later, babe."

"Hey!" Rubble replies, alarmed.

"How come we don't get invited?" Steel asks, rising from the hood, his larger-than-life build towering over the rest of us. "A man's gotta eat too."

"Because Lucy won't complain about everything," Kirsty throws back at him as Deanna and Sienna try to hold back their snickers.

"Very funny. Sienna knows I don't complain, right, babe? I'm just vocal about what I like."

As much as Steel tries to tell everyone he's not grumpy, we all know it isn't true.

"Very vocal." She smiles sweetly as he frowns, then smacks her on the ass as she yelps, trying to swat his hand away.

Rubble pulls me to him as the girls work out who's driving with who.

"I don't want you by yourself for the time being. That's not a request."

"But…"

"No buts. I'll be sending a prospect over to Kirsty's when you're finished, and I don't want to hear any more about it."

I purse my lips; arguing is futile. When the men of the M.C. want something done, there is no point starting a storm in a teacup. I need to pick my battles, and this isn't one of those times.

"Fine, but they're not getting any French toast."

He kisses me chastely. "We got lucky last night."

"I know that," I whisper.

"If anything ever happened to you, or the baby…"

"It won't."

"The less I'm worrying about you, the better."

"I worry about you too, with this whole crazy shit with the Fury."

He cups my face with one hand. "That's club business. I'm not gonna put you in harm's way. That's not gonna happen, so you rest your pretty head knowing that I got this covered, you hear me?"

I nod, though I of all people know that you have to expect the unexpected. Even in this club, a legitimate club with no underworld ties or rivals with other clubs, there is still some small amount of danger. I can't help but think that it is impossible to outrun your past. Doesn't it always catch up with you at some stage?

"I hear you."

"I'll drop you off," he says.

I go to open my mouth, but he puts a finger over it.

"That smart little mouth is what got you into trouble when we first met."

I smile. "I could say the same about you, and that little skank that couldn't give you a decent lap dance."

"Bet you're glad now she didn't."

"Maybe I am," I whisper.

"Pass me a fuckin' bucket," Steel says, slapping Rubble hard on the back. "Some of us have work to do around here. Lucy, listen to your ol' man and stay put, or at the very least, have one of the girls with you till the prospect arrives."

I give him a blatant eyeroll.

He looks at Rubble. "This is exactly why I warned you about Southern women."

"I know you love me," I reply with a sweet smile. "When your nostrils flair like that, I know you really do care."

He gives me an exasperated head shake and climbs on his bike, calling Sienna to him with the crook of his finger.

The only one he shows any kind of affection to is his woman, which is kind of sweet, in a cave-mannish kind of way, yet to the rest of us, all he does is give us shit.

"You'll give him gray hair if you don't listen," Rubble muses, rubbing my stomach.

As part of Steel's job in the club as the Sergeant at Arms, he also acts as the enforcer and that means securing all property of the club. Not just buildings, businesses, and the prospects, but us too.

None of us want to believe we're *property,* and I'd smack anyone out that tried to say that in front of my face, but that's how the Sergeant at Arms sees it in the eyes of security.

He would never want anything bad to happen to any one of us. He's a good man.

"Since when I have not listened?" I huff.

Rubble gives me a chaste kiss. "Let's get gone. I gotta get to the workshop, and you need to feed this baby."

I've never heard such sweeter words come out of a man's mouth.

18

RUBBLE

I feel drained and tired. I didn't sleep a wink, and my back's fucked from sitting in that ramrod chair all night.

It's nothing compared to the relief I feel about Lucy and the baby being okay. My heart was in my throat as we sat there with Doc and Helen to see if our baby had a heartbeat. So many fuckin' emotions ran through me that I didn't know what to fuckin' do. All I could do was hold Lucy and pray that it was all gonna be okay.

My fingers twitch to have a drink, but I know I never can. Once an addict, always an addict.

I'd never touch the drugs again, but sometimes I do pine for a bourbon. I just know I'd never be able to stop at one. It doesn't do good things to me, which is why I don't keep any alcohol in the house or the office, or anywhere close by.

I'm never going back to that again. Almost losing Lucy was the worst time of my life, and I don't like who I am when I go past the line of no return. There is no happy medium, and I never want to be out of control, not when I'm the happiest I've ever been in my life and we've got a baby on the way.

Seeing Lucy like that, in the hospital bed, broke me.

I felt so fuckin' helpless with her lying there bleeding. If she'd have lost the baby... I don't know how we would have gotten through that. We've wanted this for so long.

I still feel uneasy about the visit from Smokey and the boys. If the old club is doin' shit on the sly, we want to be ready. Something inside me wants to go and fuckin' rip their throats out one by one. At least we can rest assured Tex is locked away for a good few years yet.

I know I need to keep myself busy, because sitting around and getting mad about what I can't physically control could send me over the edge.

I get a call out at the same time Bones comes barreling through the door, and as usual, he's stuffing his face. The man has hollow legs, I'm sure of it. He's wider set than me, slightly taller, and has this smart-assed look about him you either love or hate.

The sweet butts love it, but women in real life? Not so much.

"Sup, thought you were haulin' shit with Brock this mornin'?"

Brock and Bones run the junk and scrapyard just out of town, not that Bones is ever there. He has this knack of disappearing whenever he's supposed to be on the job.

"Somethin' came up at the school. Brock had to get Rawlings, so we're gonna go later."

I give him a chin lift. "I'm out myself, just got a breakdown, unless you wanna tag along."

He scoffs. "Why would I wanna do that?"

"It's your lawyer lady." I smirk.

His eyes light up. "You're shittin' me?"

I shake my head. "Nope. Seems she's not very good at changing a flat. Could be a way to break the ice, you comin' to her rescue and all."

He punches me in the arm. "You know damn well I've been breakin' the fuckin' ice for about six months. Bitch won't give me a look in. Fuck knows I've been squeezing it hard when I'm alone just thinkin' about her ridin' me…"

I give him a pointed look. "Thanks, I'll never jerk off again. I didn't think there was a woman out there able to resist your charms."

Of course that's a joke. Bones is about as charming as a rattlesnake.

"Neither did I." He frowns. "I mean, I'm up for anything. Doesn't have to be deep and meaningful, but she's hard as nails."

I shake my head. "You really have no fuckin' clue, do you? I thought Lucy explained it to you like a million fuckin' times. Oh, and just as a heads up, probably not best to refer to her as a bitch if she's anywhere in earshot. I find women don't tend to like that too much."

"What would you know? You've been pussy-whipped for like ten years."

"Six goin' on seven, actually. Let me tell you, pleasin' one woman, a woman who's got your back and is loyal, one you don't have to worry about fuckin' any other dude behind your back, that's a woman worth holdin' on to. If that makes me pussy-whipped, then that's fuckin' fine with me."

He gives me an exaggerated eyeroll. "Please, brother, don't make me puke my lunch back up. This dick ain't made for just one woman." He grabs himself, just to make sure the thing's still attached.

"Well, better keep it in your pants, big boy. Lawyers are smart, and I think if she was gonna fall over herself to sample your dick, she would've done it by now."

He looks at me like he finds that hard to believe. I gotta hand it to the man, he's persistent.

I grab the keys and we leave.

Kennedy broke down about five miles out of town. I spot her car on the side of the road, and Bones and I let out a low whistle at the same time.

It's a new silver, sleek Mercedes with the top down. Not practical for Arizona weather, of course, but it's an orgasm on wheels.

"So not only is she smart, successful, beautiful, has a whiplash tongue and doesn't fall for your charms, she's also got a Mercedes convertible that's worth more than my house." I laugh.

Bones does a half-assed job of tidying himself up, like it's just occurred to him that he's a little disheveled.

He tries to smooth out his mohawk as best he can. He's got his cut on without a shirt underneath, the fuckin' pussy boy.

"She's so fuckin' perfect," he mutters as I slow the truck and circle around, pulling up in front of her car.

"You got no chance in hell," I say as she gets out of the car, and Bones checks her out in his side mirror.

"Wanna bet?"

"No, I don't need to bet. I don't like takin' money off a man who can't operate a washing machine."

"Pussy-whipped," he quips, opening the door and jumping out of the truck and onto the asphalt.

I follow suit and meet her at the front of her car.

She smiles when she sees me, then the minute she spies Bones, that smile falters.

I don't even bother to hold in my smirk. He deserves it.

"Kennedy, right?"

She nods as I hold a hand out, then she takes it and we shake. She's got a firm grip.

"Thanks so much for coming out," she says.

"It's no problem." I nod to the idiot next to me. "You've met Bones before?"

She takes her hand back and places it firmly on her hip, not offering it to him.

"Bones. How could I forget?"

He gives her a solid once over, lingering on her assets that strain against the fabric of her blouse. She's a stunning woman. Curvy. Tall. Peaches and cream skin with dark, reddish hair, styled in long waves.

It's no wonder he's got his head in his ass.

"What, no happy greeting?"

She rolls her eyes. "Really?"

He gives her an exaggerated sigh. Way to go hot-shot. She looks like she wants to shoot lasers out of her eyeballs. I don't know what he did to her, but this really is hilarious.

"C'mon, doll. You know I've been tryin' to score a date with you ever since we met that day at the courthouse with Angel. Saw you checkin' me out." He grips the lapels of his jacket and tugs on the collar. Her eyes noticeably skirt down his torso, and I almost feel like I'm intruding. It seems even this hot-shot lawyer isn't completely immune to his physique.

"Let me take a look at the damage," I say, stepping around the side of the car.

She nods and gives me a smile.

"You've got a very vivid imagination if you think I was checking you out," she shoots back at Bones as he continues to bait her.

I don't know why he's so persistent. It's clear she's not impressed, but then again, that's never stopped him before.

"You've no fuckin' idea, babe," he replies. "My vivid imagination is X-rated."

I chuckle as I assess the fucked-up tire.

"You got a spare in the trunk?" Being she's ended up in a ditch, I'd still have to pull her out and change it.

She looks puzzled by the question, and I shake my head. "Its fine, I'll check."

She rounds the car, and I pop the trunk. These cars aren't exactly meant for practicality, as it's so tiny.

"Two-seater?" I hear Bones say, peering inside the tinted window. "Nice ride, what kind of mileage do these things get?"

"Is that a rhetorical question?" I hear her fire back.

Yup, she's definitely a spitfire.

"A what?"

I slap him on the back. "Gonna need to haul this out of the ditch before I can do anything."

"How'd you end up in the ditch, babe?" Bones asks as I check for the tire. It comes up empty. She's gonna have to ride with us back to the workshop. Lucky Bones.

"It's Kennedy," she replies. "And I don't know. I felt a pop, and then the car swerved, and I had to pull off as quick as possible."

"Looks like a nail in the tire," I say, rising from my knees. "Since there's no spare, you'll have to ride back with us, and I'll fix it at Steel's."

She nods gratefully. "That would be great. I have a meeting, and I'm already late." She checks her watch again and groans. "Excuse me, I just have to make a phone call and let my clients know I'm going to be delayed arriving."

"No problem," I say, sparing Bones a glance. He watches her as she turns to dial and get as far away from us as possible.

"I don't know what her problem is." He sighs when we start rigging up the back of the truck. "She was into it until she found out I was a part of the Rebels."

I shoot him another look. "Yeah, I don't think that's it, brother."

"You don't?"

"Nah, it's definitely you."

He shoves me in the shoulder. "Very funny, fucker."

"Maybe you just have to accept it, that she's just not that into you."

"Body language," he says, giving her a look. "See the way she glances at me, briefly, and then looks away when I catch her? She licked her lips at least once, and why is she playing with her hair?"

I chuckle. "You a body language expert now?"

"I was in the military, remember? You're trained to notice these things."

"So why is she playin' hard to get?"

"I don't fuckin' know, but aside from getting forcibly arrested, she's got no other reason to speak to me."

"Which is why some say it may be best to leave the beast alone. She's probably too much of a woman for you to handle anyway, look at her; smart, successful, super-hot… maybe you're just aiming too high…"

He tries to punch me, and I duck, so he misses. "Thanks, fuckface."

I glance at her as she talks on the phone, and I note she definitely was just looking at Bones.

"She may just need to see the softer, more feminine side of you?" I shrug, trying not to laugh at him. "Some chicks like that."

He looks at me like I've got two heads. "I'll show her my feminine side when my face is buried in her pussy all night long…"

"Hey, how'd it go?" I ask, giving Bones the side-eye as Kennedy approaches.

She does a lot of frowning when he's around. "All fixed. I've rescheduled my morning. How long is this going to take?"

"Shouldn't be long. We'll drive back to the workshop,

then it'll be another half an hour to change the tire and balance it properly."

"Shoot." She looks back down at her phone. "I knew I should have stayed in bed."

"You and me both," Bones says, giving her a wiggle of his eyebrows.

Man, I'd quit while ahead if I were him.

"If you wanna wait in the cab till we're done," I suggest. "You're more than welcome."

I refrain from a chuckle at how she's going to manage it in the tight pencil skirt she has on. That'll be fun for Bones watching her get up there.

"It's not like I dressed to go hiking up Camelback Mountain," she complains.

Bones doesn't waste a single second. "I can give you a hand, doll." He grins. "Getting up there, I mean, or two hands if you'd like?"

She turns on him. "I think I can manage."

"You sure? Looks pretty steep."

"Keep your hands to yourself. I'm fine."

He holds up his hands in surrender. "Whatever you say, but I'm here to catch you if you fall."

She gives him another withering look and takes a mighty stretch up onto the first step, hence her skirt making a loud ripping sound as she gasps at the same time.

"Jesus fucking shitting Christ!" she cries. "This is my favorite skirt!"

"I did offer to help," Bones replies with a casual shrug, tilting his head to get the best angle of her ass. "That's what you get for bein' a gentleman."

She regards him coolly, and fuck me if she doesn't kick her heels off, snatch them up, hitch up her skirt, straighten her back, and then she tries it again.

Bones stands back and lets her climb up, all the while his eyes are glued to her ass as he palms the back of his neck.

I'm tempted to throw something at his head in order to get him to come and fuckin' help me, though I admit, the show from over here ain't all that bad.

She smiles down triumphantly when she makes it safely.

Bones mutters all kinds of profanities as he walks back toward me. "I think I'm in love," he says as I lower the back of the tip tray.

"I dunno, brother, thought she might sock you in the head there for a minute."

"She wants me." He grins. "She might not realize it exactly, but she's comin' round."

"Right, you gonna show her what she's been missin' out on?" I laugh.

"It's gonna be worth it if she's anything like this behind closed doors. I like a challenge. I'm happy to surrender."

I feel my phone vibrate in my top pocket just as I'm hooking up the car to the rig.

It's Hutch.

The minute I answer, he says, "Rubble. We got a situation."

A pause for a moment, my mind going straight to Lucy. "Is everything okay?"

"Got a call from Smokey. They've got some news on Nitro."

"Okay."

"I'm calling a meeting at three o'clock, be there."

I rub my chin. "All right, boss. Bones is with me. I'll let him know."

There's a noticeable pause. "Kirsty said Lucy was doin' well, all things considered."

A lump forms in my throat. "She has a wonderful bunch of people around her, a real family."

"I'm glad about that. She's a good woman, fuck knows why she'd wanna have your baby, but we can't choose who we love, can we?"

"Long as the kid has her looks and charm, I won't be complainin.'" I pause. It isn't like him to leave long sentences hanging. "Is everything okay, Hutch?"

"Fine. Be there at three."

He hangs up, and I give Bones a chin lift. "Meeting at church at three, some shit goin' down with the Fury."

"No shit, hopefully they got some bodies strung up so we can use 'em for target practice."

"That'd be even better," I agree.

"Fuck knows I need to let off some steam." He glances up at the cab.

I give him a wink. "Just try not to get sued while we drive Miss Lawyer Lady back to the workshop. She'll have you in jail quicker than you can blink."

"Don't worry," he says, slapping me on the back. "I got a plan."

One can only hope it includes keeping his smart trap shut and not landing his ass in jail. She seems like the sort that would enjoy that kind of torture.

"Great," I drawl. "We're well and truly fucked, then."

He ignores me, then goes to the cab and climbs in, knowing full well that Kennedy is now going to be squished up in the middle of us.

Now I have to sit through these two going at it all the way back to Bracken Ridge as I slowly load Kennedy's car onto the back of the truck and pray that any news Hutch has is good news.

19

RUBBLE

"They've found him?" I can't help but feel slightly elated when Hutch drops a bombshell at the meeting.

"Smokey said they've found a hideout, but they're unsure who or what's in there. They need to make up numbers before goin' in and hauling his ass out, and they're not sure how many are there. It's an abandoned warehouse, and they wanna keep tabs on it till the weekend."

I know what this means. That we're going to Phoenix.

"At a guess?" Steel adds. "How many do they think?"

"Maybe a half dozen at the moment, though they could be the minions," Hutch replies.

Steel snorts. "Piece of cake."

"Any news on the Vipers?" I shoot at Steel.

I know Steel's been keeping close tabs with Griller, so we're all in the loop.

"Smokey's gonna move things up to this weekend pending what happens at the stakeout, then give the Vipers the drop in exchange for neutral ground," Steel replies. "It's still a good plan to make amends and gets us all off the hook.

Bury all this shit, once and for all, and the Sons of Fury can start their club."

That feels far off, but I can't wait for the day this is finally over

"Sounds like Nitro will bury himself eventually. Once the Sons are involved, then shit's gonna stick and they're gonna be potentially caught in the crossfire," Brock interjects. "And that means, we're implicated, too."

"Not if we let the Vipers take charge," Hutch says. "I only agreed to help from the shadows. This isn't our fight, and I'm not gonna send my guys to Phoenix to clean up the Sons' mess. I like the guys, but that doesn't mean I'm goin' to put a new target on our backs."

Steel looks a little disappointed, and Bones too. Both don't mind when things get a little fucked up. They don't mind wreaking havoc.

"With the rate they're movin' the new shipment, we're gonna have to move faster than we thought," says Brock. "If Smokey can time it right, then the Vipers can do the majority of the heavy liftin'. Bein' it's their turf that's bein' exploited, it's only fair."

I laugh. "You don't know the boys. Trust me, they'll be in the thick of it because it's what they do."

When all's said and done, Smokey has the loyal members with him. He knows what it takes to be almost taken out and rise from the ashes again once more, like a true Phoenix in flight.

He'll make it his mission in life to get the club back off the ground, and I know he'll do it. He just needs a kickstart and a helping hand. With the Vipers off their backs, he may just pull this crazy stunt off. That's if Nitro and Rachet don't just use their minions to do all the dirty work, and then go underground again. They've managed to live this long without being caught, but they'd have to be desperate for cash.

To catch a snake, you gotta act like one.

Steel frowns. "If we take off, we can't leave the club or the women unprotected. Smokey said he can call in members of the Sons of Cali chapter, and dependin' on numbers, it may not be a bad thing to have backup so some of us can stay put. We can't underestimate this operation. If they've gotten this far securing a warehouse, goods and clients, then they're not playin' around."

Hutch nods. "I think they're tougher than what we might think. Like Steel said, to get this far relatively unnoticed, it's gotta take some balls. I don't like how they've got nothin' to lose; it makes it all the more dangerous."

Nobody looks happy about the prospect of leaving the club less protected.

"Are we gettin' a little bit ahead of ourselves?" Gunner pipes up. "They couldn't keep a club together, but now they're gonna go down in a blaze of glory. They don't have a leg to stand on. Isn't our involvement just goin' to put us in the crossfires regardless? No offense, Rubble, but can't they just sort out their own mess?"

"Doesn't hurt to have allies on our side," I say, knowing that I do get where he's coming from. "And they did give us a heads up that Nitro or Rachet could be out for vengeance and workin' with Tex. What if they did come here and start some shit? Phoenix is closer than Cali for backup, that's all I'm sayin'."

"I hear your point, Guns." Hutch nods. "Which is why we gotta be smart. I don't wanna get involved about as much as anyone else, but as I say, I'm not gonna send any of you in to start some fuckin' war with one percent clubs just for the hell of it. I said we'd help where we can, and the surprise attack will be between the Sons, the old club, and the Vipers. Period."

"We still don't know who else is directly involved because the fuckers are slippery," Steel goes on. "Seems they want to keep things on the DL until they've got enough cash to set up digs somewhere. This is the part where it's crucial that the bust goes as planned. If they go underground again, and they've got numbers, all they're gonna do is come back and come back with force. We need to make sure this time that they stay down."

I know he's thinking it'll be a bloodbath, and while I would have been all for it six years ago, I've got a wife and a child to think of now. Things have changed. I left for a reason.

"I still don't trust any of them," Brock grunts. "Rogue clubs can do weird shit if they're backed into a corner. He's already killed at least two old members that they know of, and a prospect, and they attacked an ol' lady."

He's got a valid point.

"What about settin' up camp here so everyone's under one roof?" Bones suggests. "Just until we're back. That way, we won't have to worry about everyone bein' scattered across town."

Hutch looks up gravely. "I don't think we're at that point; it'll cause panic. I'll get Stevie to clean the vacant rooms upstairs, just in case, and the prospects can keep an eye on things from the front and back. Since Rubble will be goin' with you, I want eyes on Lucy at all times."

My gut clenches. I don't want to be away from Lucy, but the club and the safety of its members and the women and children come first. While I'd like nothing more than to see these fuckfaces six feet under, I still don't want to be away from her, especially after our recent scare.

Hutch must see the worry on my face. "We still gotta

work out the logistics, but I'd be thinkin' we keep Bones here, Dalton and Patch, Knuckles can cover things from the clubhouse, and if it comes to a lockdown, he knows the drill."

Dalton and Patch help out here and there and come to all the big club functions, they're good guys to have around.

Still, my mind ticks over. I know Bones is good with a rifle, hell, he used to be a sniper, but he'd be better use at the warehouse. Then again, Brock and Steel are both ex-military.

I don't like going against Hutch's wishes, but this whole thing feels pretty fuckin' personal.

"I don't know how I feel leavin' Lucy, Prez, after what we went through last night. Shit got real."

Mumbles go around the table, and I know everyone feels bad about what happened, but we got lucky. What if we don't get that lucky if it happens again?

Bones pats me on the back. "Lucy means a lot to all of us. I'm happy to trade places," he says. "Fuck knows I'm hangin' to get my hands on a sniper rifle again."

I was hoping that it wouldn't come to this, but the Sons were my brothers once, and I don't like the thought of turning my back on them while my Bracken Ridge brothers here go and fight my fight either.

I run a hand through my hair. "Appreciate that, Bones. I don't fuckin' know what to do. All this shit's got me fucked up in the head." Again, my fingers itch to clutch the neck of a bourbon bottle. Instead, I light a cigarette and take a long drag. "I'll do what you need me to do, Prez, you know that."

"What if we take shifts?" Brock suggests. "Rubble can take the first shift while they stake out the warehouse, and then swap with Bones before the weekend. Smokey said they need to get intel first, and that's probably gonna be a few days."

I don't want to see Lucy's face when I tell her I have to go. She's never been a needy woman, but at the moment, she needs me more than ever.

"She can stay with us," Hutch says. "Kirsty loves playin' mom and soon-to-be Grandma. It'll keep Lucy outta trouble and my ol' lady outta my hair."

It's not a bad plan. Lucy loves Kirsty, but I still think she's gonna go into panic mode. I don't want to lie to her, but I could play it down just slightly.

"Appreciate that. I don't wanna let anyone down. I'm here for the club, you all know that…"

"You don't have to tell us, we know," Gunner replies, giving me a chin lift. "We all love Lucy too. You gotta do what you gotta do; nobody here's gonna deny you that right. As long as I get to whoop some ass, I don't care."

"What you gonna do?" Bones counters. "Stun them all to death with your fake tan?"

"What's the matter asshole, jealous?" Gunner smirks. "Got my Christmas calendar comin' out soon, gonna need me some new props, like a fire extinguisher. Somethin' big enough to contain the rod in my pants."

Everyone groans.

"That's really fuckin' nice," Steel grunts. "Just what I want to be imaginin'. It's bad enough you chose my sister to shack up with, but I definitely don't need a running commentary on your dick pics."

"Could always lend you a toothpick, would do the same job," Bones fires back.

"Not what my ol' lady says," Gunner goes on. "She can't get enough of it."

"One more word, asshole," Steel warns. "You might be my actual brother now by association, but that doesn't mean I wanna hear about what my sister does to your limp dick."

"Trust me when I say, it's never limp." He laughs. "Lily likes my photo shoots. She finds new and interesting ways to get all that oil off me when I get home…"

"You keep talkin', fuckface, and I'll make sure it'll be limp from now till Remembrance Day," Steel barks.

Gunner laughs. "Ooh, promises, promises."

"Don't tell me your ol' lady actually doesn't mind you posing like that. I mean, *Gunner after dark?* Most ol' ladies would have your cock in a sling for that," Bones says with disbelief.

"She doesn't care. I get to bring some of the costumes home." He grins. "We keep the magic alive."

Steel just about blows steam out of his nostrils. It won't be long before Gunner gets a punch in the face, and it wouldn't be the first time. Out of all of us, he's the most protective of all the girls, but especially his little sister.

"Mom must've dropped her on her head at birth," Steel gripes. "That would explain a lot about her taste in men."

Gunner is unperturbed. "That or she's just got good taste. Anyway, your mama told me you always wanted a little brother."

"Yeah, one I could tie up and torture when he got too mouthy."

Gunner makes an *ooh, I'm scared gesture* and keeps laughing.

Though he and Steel fight like cats and dogs, they're as close as real brothers. When Gunner kept his relationship with Lily a secret, and Steel found out, things were shit for a while, and they had a brawl, but deep down, Gunner has a good heart, and he's a great brother. Lily's good for him.

We all just wish he'd keep his clothes on and stop reminding us that he gets paid more than us to strip naked and be photographed.

"If you two have quite finished, I'm tryin' to hatch out a plan here. The last thing I need to be thinkin' about is Gunner in any state of undress," Hutch barks.

"I say, we stake it out with Smokey and the boys, see how

many of them there are at the warehouse, and reconvene. It'll buy us time before makin' a move," Brock says. "That'll give us a chance to scope things out, see who's involved, and get the drop on them."

"I don't like it, but it's gotta be done," Hutch agrees. "I want you out there first thing tomorrow. I'll come down with Bones and swap shifts with Rubble and Gunner before the heavy shit goes down. This isn't somethin' I want to do from here."

"Sounds like a plan," I agree.

I feel uneasy, but I'll only be gone hopefully for a day or two at the most and I can't let my brothers down. Any of them.

"You good with that?" Hutch gives me a nod.

"Yeah, I'm good with that."

I know he's only giving me leniency because of Lucy and the baby and what we've been through, and for that I'm grateful.

"Stop worryin' about Lucy. She'll be fine. Bones will be on her at all times. I don't give a fuck what shit comes up, she's not to be out of your sight." He gives Bones a stern point across the table.

"Not like he can get pussy anyway," Gunner says with a smirk. "Been chasin' that hot fox lawyer he's got no chance with, and now he can't even get it up, so the sweet butts say."

"Since when have you been talkin' with sweet butts?" Steel interjects.

"I heard it through the grapevine." Gunner shrugs.

"I can assure you that hot fox lawyer is gonna be slurpin' on the end of my dick by Thanksgiving," Bones assures us all. "She's playin' hard to get. Women like her ain't used to bein' out of their comfort zone. She's not like other women; she'll take some work, but once she's had a walk on the wild side, she won't be goin' back to Kansas anytime soon."

Snickers ensue around the table. Of course, he's just setting himself up for a fall because we all know he's not gonna be tapping that any time soon, if ever.

Kennedy Hart is incorruptible, so it seems. Seeing him try is so fuckin' funny. It's like he's on a mission to prove to himself that he's still got it, even when Kennedy has other ideas.

"Don't think she's gonna be goin' to slurpy heaven either," Brock says. "Judging by the lack of action you're gettin' around here lately, it's safe to say that it may be more beneficial to invest in some lube and a thrust pro, that way, you'll have the happy ending you've always dreamed of. *Dreamed* being the optimal word."

Bones frisbees a coaster at his head.

"There's always one comedian," he grumbles. "And I'll have you know that thrust pros can only do so much."

"Thanks for that visual," Steel grunts. "Now I've gotta go home and bleach my brain."

"The sad thing is, he's determined." Gunner snickers. "You keep at it, big boy, and one day, you'll pop her cherry."

Bones gives him the finger.

"When you bunch of whipped little bitches have finished, it's time to clear out and get this mess over with. The sooner we find out when the raid is going to be, the sooner we can resume normal life as we know it," Hutch goes on, then nods to me. "And you need to go talk to your woman before you head out."

I nod. "Gotta love me a southern woman."

"And tell her to pack a bag."

I can't wait for that conversation. She's already hormonal enough, and after the ordeal at the hospital, I know she's not going to be thrilled about me going away. I do feel better knowing that she'll be with Kirsty, and Bones will be around, along with the prospects. Dalton, Patch, and Knuckles can handle things at church.

My gut is telling me one thing, and my club's saying another.

It's one night, two max.

Not that I want to tempt fate, but I wouldn't leave if I didn't think my wife and unborn baby were in good hands. I just know what it's taken us to get this far, and that's what worries me the most.

20

LUCY

Kirsty fusses over me on the couch, and while I insist I'm not on complete bed rest, she's taken it upon herself to play mother hen. I have been feeling really tired, but that could be lack of sleep and the trauma of thinking I was losing the baby.

When they couldn't find the heartbeat and had to do an emergency ultrasound, I didn't know if I could live through what was to come. I rub my belly and Kirsty smiles as she hands me a herbal tea.

"I could do with something a little stronger," I moan. "This is the downside of being pregnant; herbal tea doesn't quite take the edge off."

Kirsty tuts. "Well, you shouldn't overdo it on the caffeine, it's not good for high blood pressure, or for the baby."

And this is what all the girls have been like this morning, bless them. I really am so grateful to have a bunch of women that are more like my sisters than friends. I don't know what I'd do without them.

Deanna spent most of the morning, while Kirsty was out running errands, telling me about her and Cash, the President of New Orleans M.C. almost making out, which was news to me. And this happened months ago, though I'd heard rumors from Lily. All the girls know she's got a big, fat crush on him, but he's almost Hutch's age, and his friend, and I can only imagine what would go down if he were to find out. I mean, Deanna is almost twenty-eight years old, she's not exactly a little kid anymore, but when I think about our baby – boy or girl – out there in the world, I can understand how protective parents can be. Her banter takes my mind off things for a while.

Rubble has to go to Phoenix for a day or so for club business, business that's to do with Smokey, but he insists that it isn't dangerous. I know he's not being entirely truthful, and I know I got into this knowing that *club business* comes above everything else, hence why I've been summoned to staying with Kirsty and Hutch until he returns, which is ridiculous. I am a grown woman who can take care of herself, but apparently not in Rubble's eyes.

I close my eyes for a second when I think about how relieved his face was when the baby was given the all clear. I know he wants this as much as I do, and we're so damn close.

"He's not going to be long, honey," Kirsty says, catching my moments of reverie. "Hutch wouldn't send him away if it weren't important, you know that."

I nod. I love Kirsty, but she's still Hutch's wife, and they're a powerhouse in this town. I'd never bag him out to his own wife, even if I feel a little miffed that Rubble had to take off so quickly. Surely, someone else could have covered for him.

"I know, it's just hard sometimes. We're used to things being quiet around here. Club business is usually shutting down an illegal dog fighting ring or busting up Jack when he decides to rip off the club. Not doing favors for the ex-members of the Phoenix Fury."

She frowns. She of all people knows that as much as the

boys try to keep the personal things out of the details, we pick up on it. We hear things, and fuck them, we're gonna share things.

"Don't you worry yourself about it. Rubble's a big boy; he's street tough and knows how to handle himself. They'll be fine. Hutch thinks an alliance may come in useful down the track, if we ever need help, God forbid."

I sip the hot liquid; it tastes like peppermint. "I hope you're right. I'm just used to having him around all the time. When I woke up the other night –" I trail off.

She pats my knees as she perches on the end of the couch. "Sweetie, you've been through a lot. What happened to you is scary, and you've every right to be concerned, but you're in safe hands here. I'm not going to let anything happen, and when I spoke to Helen, she said you've probably been overdoing it at work. Stress can play havoc with the hormones."

"I'm fine," I plead.

"Nevertheless, Deanna is going to pick up the slack for the next few weeks until you're feeling better."

"I am better! Just a little tired. I can't just be sitting here with my feet up and drinking herbal tea," I protest. "You know I find it hard to stay still."

She shakes her head. "This is exactly why you should be. You've had a really big scare, sweetie, and I'm not saying it's anything to do with work, stress or being on your feet, but it makes sense to take things as easy as possible. The more rested you are, the more rested the baby will be."

I look down at my hands, and I can't help the tears welling in my eyes. The dam bursts before I can help myself. "I'm just so scared..." I trail off as Kirsty wraps her arms around me.

"It's okay, honey, this is your first baby. It's all new, and it's bound to feel strange," she says. "When I was carrying Deanna, I freaked out over the smallest of things, nothing like what you've been experiencing. I didn't know anything about being a mom or what felt normal in my body and what didn't. It's all a big change, and that's all part of the process. Big things are happening, and this is a time to be happy, enjoy your pregnancy, and don't be scared of it."

"I know." I nod. "I know. I'm just terrified of something bad happening."

"And that's completely understandable, but you can't worry day and night, because you're missing out on this joyous time of carrying your first baby. You won't get this time back. I was only blessed with one baby – not through a lack of trying – and I wish I'd slowed down a little more and smelled the roses. There will be bad days and there will be good days. Take it from me, you'll wish that you enjoyed every second of it, because all of it is precious."

I wipe my eyes as she passes me a tissue. "Thanks, Kirsty, you're like a mom to me."

"All my girls are angels," she says. "But I've always had a soft spot for you, Lucy. You stuck by Rubble when he was down and out. You came here with nothing and started up a new business and made it a success. And you've fought past demons together, I respect that. I hope that Deanna learns something from the strong women of this club and that when she decides to settle down, that it's with someone who has those traits; loyalty, honesty, and integrity."

I don't have the heart to tell her that Deanna wants to screw her father's best friend; that wouldn't be the saintly thing to do right now while we're having this moment.

Instead, I pat my eyes dry with the tissue and blow my nose ungraciously. "Thank you, Kirsty. When I came here, I didn't know anybody, and you were the first person to welcome me to Bracken Ridge. To move here was the best decision we ever made."

She smooths my hair back with her hands in a motherly

kind of way, and it tugs at my heartstrings because I didn't know up until this moment how much I miss that nurturing touch. Advice on the baby stuff and asking questions. My heart pangs for my family that will never be.

I don't have a relationship with my mom or my stepdad. My sister Tina and I don't get along and never will, and then there's Adam. Every time I get sad or think about family, Adam pops up in my thoughts. It's like I can never be truly happy until I find him and that's futile.

I wince at the thought of what happened because I know he wasn't a good kid all the time, but he was just a kid, brought up in a rough neighborhood with a heavy dose of fucked up parental guidance. I hope wherever he is that he's safe and making a life for himself. I miss him the most because to me he was just a sweet little boy. Someone who looked up to me, I was more a mom to him than my own mother was. She flat out ignored him and made his life hell. He didn't deserve that. Thirteen years old and on the run. My heart will never be quiet.

She lifts my chin. "Anything you want, Lucy, you just gotta ask, all right? I love doing this, and it's an excuse to get out of the office and let my assistant deal with some stuff."

Kelsey is also Angel's babysitter and Kirsty has just put her on as a junior.

Kirsty sells real estate and is *the* person you talk to when you move here. Sure, there is a rival real estate company in town, but they don't have half the clientele Kirsty and her firm do. Kelsey is lucky to be learning the ropes from someone so experienced, especially as she doesn't want to go to college.

"Okay. It's hard for me, asking for help. I'm so used to just doing what I need to do," I admit. "Rubble is amazing, of course. Don't tell the boys, but he is quite domestic at home. Ever since I fell pregnant, he's been so much more hands on;

it's like he thinks I'll break if the wind blows the wrong way, which is very sweet of him, and sometimes I know I don't deserve him."

She smiles kindly. "You're perfect for each other. He adores you, that much is obvious. He's going to make such a great father, Luce, and you're going to be the best mom – there's nothing more certain than the simplicity of two people loving each other and wanting a baby that will be cherished. I know it in my heart, and you do deserve him, as much as he deserves you."

It's times like this I wish I had my mom. But she didn't care. Kirsty is my saving grace, and I'll always be thankful for her in my life.

I know she's right; any reservations I have about motherhood are completely squashed when I think about how much we want this.

"And a bonus, the baby will have no shortage of babysitters." I laugh.

"Except maybe Steel," Kirsty says. "He's better with dogs than children."

"I've noticed."

I just hope Rubble comes back soon because he's only been gone a few hours and I'm like a broody, needy housewife already. I hate myself for it.

This will be good for me, and I know he has club shit to do to keep the bad people away; it's part of what they do, and I signed up for it. I just want whatever's going down with Smokey and the boys to be over with sooner rather than later. I can't go on treading on eggshells.

I sit back on the couch and take another sip. Maybe there's something in this peppermint tea after all.

"I really don't know if you should be eyeing up a prospect," I say with a chuckle as Amelia and Cassidy hang out with me and Deanna while I catch up on a few things and Gears hangs outside. Amelia is Brock's sister, and she's just moved back to town.

I've been banned from doing long hours, and there is no point arguing, but Deanna had questions, and I couldn't just leave her here alone. The office doesn't get really busy, which is just how I like it, but there's always something to catch up on.

"Tell that to Kelsey. She's the one eye-fucking Gears whenever they're in the same room together. She's barely of legal age."

"He's not made the moves on her, has he?" I frown. Even though Kelsey isn't technically part of the club, Hutch wouldn't stand for any underage shit going down. While Gears is a new prospect, he's hardly proven his worth in just a few months, and I don't know him too well myself. Our paths haven't really crossed much.

"No," Cassidy replies. "Colt said he'd kick his ass if he even thinks about it, though she graduates in a couple of months."

"Like that'll stop her if she really wants to get laid," Deanna chirps.

"Eww," me and Amelia say at the same time.

Deanna smirks. "What? Remember what any of us were like at that age, and Gears is pretty cute, when he's not shooting his mouth off."

Gears is definitely a wildcard.

"Hutch will have that beat out of him." Amelia laughs. "Then Axton will be out of jail in a little bit to become a prospect, too. I can't wait to see him."

I turn to her. "How are you feeling about that, honey? You must be really excited about having him home after so long."

Axton is the middle brother between Amelia and Brock. He went to jail ten years ago for armed robbery, and Hutch has given him a second chance at the club when he gets out. I just hope that he doesn't disappoint Brock; he's stuck his neck out to get him back on his feet.

It won't look good on him if he fucks up.

I know this is a soft spot for her because she was only a child when he got locked up. Axton was only about seventeen himself.

She nods, but her face looks somber. "Yeah, but dad is still really weird about it. Ever since he and Brock made up, things have been so much better between them, but I don't know if that will extend to Axton. I know he looked up to dad so much when we were younger, and it'll kill him to have dad reject him all over again."

I pat her arm. "It must be tough, but he's done his time. I'm sure your dad will come around. It can't be easy, but he's served his time. Everyone deserves a second chance."

"Rumor has it, he'll be stayin' at the Stone Crow to keep an eye on things now that Stef has stepped down," Deanna adds. "Heard dad telling mom about it, so least he's got a place to crash when he gets out. That's gotta be better than starting from scratch in a new place where you don't know anybody."

It's going to be hard on him, but he has an opportunity to turn his life around, and if he fucks it up, he's a damn fool.

"Plus, he's got the club," Cassidy says. "You all stick together like no family I've ever known. I can't say I ever thought a biker club would be quite like this one, where everyone has each other's backs and the guys are loyal, actually hot and not beer-bellied fat dudes who like to grope."

We all chuckle.

"I think we just got lucky," I reply, giving her a wink. "I see Colt can't keep his paws to himself, which is how it should be when you're in the honeymoon faze. Lord knows me and Rubble were at it like rabbits when we first got together."

"Oh Lord," Amelia says, slapping her forehead. "I should've brought earplugs."

I give her an eyeroll. I've never been one to shy away from sex talk, and when Rubble was being weird about having sex with me when I first got pregnant, the girls were a shoulder to cry on. I just seem to be one of those women who have a high sex drive, so sue me.

"Roll your eyes now, but don't come running to me when you find a guy who turns your world upside down, sugar. I'll just laugh and tell you to deal with it," I say, poking my tongue at her.

She snorts. "Like that's ever gonna happen. I moved from the city to snooze capital. At least I love my job. Kennedy is awesome."

"How is all of that going? It's great having a decent lawyer in town," I say, knowing how lucky we are.

"Amazing. I never imagined I'd ever find a legal secretary job in Bracken Ridge, but Kennedy made me an offer I couldn't refuse. And this place isn't so bad. I just gotta stay away from the club as much as possible, to say Brock is overprotective is an understatement." She sighs.

I smile. "He cares about you, as annoying as the big oaf can be, it could be worse… he could be Steel."

We all groan in unison.

Steel is not only famous for his grumpy exterior, but his reputation for being an overbearing protective asshole is well known around not just in the club, but the whole town.

He got over it when Gunner and Lily went behind his back, and I really do get where he's coming from. He has a lot of responsibility for everyone's welfare in his hands.

"No, worse is gettin' caught with a prospect." Deanna

waggles her finger. "So stay away from Jax and Gears at all costs."

Playing the field is so overrated. I'd never want to be back on the dating scene again, but I get it. Amelia is still young and is finding her feet. Just as long as she doesn't find it with a prospect, then everything will be fine. Gears is too pretty to have his face busted up by Brock, and then by Steel.

They may be a tad bit misogynistic at times, but their hearts are in the right place. I don't know what it is about gruff men in the club that can't express how they feel. It isn't healthy. But I do know that any one of them would put themselves in the way of danger to protect us. We really are a family, albeit a slightly dysfunctional one, but a family all the same.

They mean well even if they don't always know how to convey it. Especially Steel.

And as soppy as it sounds, I wouldn't want it any other way. I don't know any other way.

It's how it's supposed to be. And that makes me feel like a really lucky girl.

21

RUBBLE

"What the fuck are they doin' in there?" I nod to Smokey as I pass him back the binoculars.

There has been very little movement at the warehouse. Nothing has really happened aside from a couple of motorcycles pulling up with a van, then they all went inside.

Smokey doesn't recognize them or the bikes, nor did they have patches on. Now it's gone quiet again.

"Nobody's gone in or out for almost twenty-four hours," Smokey says. "Which means they're probably cuttin' the gear. Gotta do it somewhere."

"This whole thing is just super fuckin' ballsy," Steel interjects. "Do they really think the Vipers won't get wind of it? That's what I don't fuckin' get. They may as well sky write it."

"You're right, it does kinda feel a little brazen," I agree. "Like they've got balls of steel if they think they can pull it off. Maybe they plan on doin' it on the sly. Turnin' tricks in broad daylight where no one suspects it."

"Maybe they're just stupid," Brock says. "Dudes with nothin' to lose get desperate."

"Which is what leads me to believe that these assholes

must have financial backing from somewhere, to even get the gear in the first place," Smokey says. "To pull off a stunt with the Cubans, if that's who their main client is, is about as fuckin' suicidal as you can get. The Vipers will wipe them off the face of the earth."

"Good," Steel grunts. "Then we can get gone and go home."

He was all up for a fight initially, but he knows a rat when he smells one.

"What I want to know is, how will you get a sit down with the Vipers?" Brock asks,

as he takes a turn with the binoculars. "Not like they've got any reason to trust your ass."

"Thought about callin' it in, but that's the pussy's way out," Smokey replies. "Gotta take a chance and hope the Prez doesn't put a bullet in my brain. Thing is, I never had bad blood with the Vipers, but that don't mean shit, Tex did and so do we by association. If I give them intel, they'll have no choice but to listen. They can't ignore what we've got on these Rogue Warriors, and they also can't ignore the fact they're comin' in hard under cuttin' them. That's gonna hit them where it hurts."

The Vipers reputation for not being the most forgiving club in this city is well known, and I'm not so sure Smokey has thought things through. Gotta give him points for enthusiasm, though. He's a survivor.

"Need to get a read on where their hang out is," Smokey goes on. "Griller and Dice will keep tabs if they decide to take off. Hoax and Grip will take the night shift. Cali chapter is on stand-by. Until we can get a scope on exactly who the rest of these fuckers are, we're in the dark."

We've been lying on this uncomfortable ridge for hours.

"Sounds like a plan." I just wanna have a shower and call my ol' lady.

Hoax's place that they're using for the new clubhouse is out of the city and in a quieter suburb of Canon Valley. It's a quaint two-story with out-buildings, literally set on its own private valley so there's no neighbors. The house needs a lot of work, but it's in the perfect spot for a clubhouse.

We take off just before dusk and grab some burgers on the way. Since there're no extra beds at the house, we'll stay at a motel tonight and reconvene in the morning.

I'm beat by the time we chow down and then get to bed. I take a long hot shower, and though I've been texting Lucy all day, I need to call her.

I pull a towel around my waist and facetime her, sitting on the edge of the bed as I run a hand through my hair.

She picks up on the second ring. When her beautiful face comes on the screen, I wish even more than ever that I wasn't stuck in this shitty fuckin' motel room.

"Hey, babe," she says as I grin at her. She's dressed for bed in her silk Victoria's Secret pajamas.

"Hi, Sparkles." I give her a chin lift. "How was your day?"

"It was fine, honey. How are you?"

"I'm fine, babe. I'm just tired. What did you get up to?"

"I went and did a twelve-hour shift, then we sat around drinking margaritas and shook our tail feathers."

I shake my head. "You know I'm countin' your lippy remarks for the spank bank, and one day, you're gonna have to pay up."

She blows me a kiss. "How was your day?" she asks, sobering because she of all people knows that club business ain't ever good.

"It was fine, babe. We just sat around lookin' through binoculars at a warehouse."

"Sounds riveting. I had to make dinner for Bones, by the way. He's taking this looking out for me thing a little too seriously."

I frown. "Why didn't you tell him to fuck off?"

She shrugs. "I'm in the nesting phase and Kirsty has an amazing kitchen, so I whipped up a batch of lasagna."

"I thought I said you were meant to rest."

She rolls her eyes. "Cooking is like therapy, and it was fun, actually. I sent Gears out to the store to get all the stuff I needed."

"That's my girl. Hope he didn't make a fuss."

Most of the prospects are respectful enough, but I wouldn't put it past them to tell the women to fuck off when they don't wanna take orders from them. Lucky for Gears, he knows his place in the pecking order.

"He tried to, then I reminded him that I'm in Hutch's house, and he probably wouldn't take too kindly to me going out to the store when I've been told to stay here."

"I love how your mind works, baby."

"Speaking of which, I've got some kinda weird and exciting news."

I prop the phone up on the pillow and sit back against the headboard.

"Oh yeah, what's that?"

She giggles. "My breast milk came in."

I look at her blankly. "What the fuck does that mean?"

"It means that all the soreness I've been feeling lately is just my breasts making colostrum. Dr. Stevens said it's just my body's way of preparing for milk to come in for the baby."

I stare at her all excited and happy. "You're so fuckin' beautiful."

She bites her lip. "You're just saying that because you're picturing my tits."

I smile and bite my bottom lip. "Show me."

She frowns. "Rubble, I can't show you. I'm in Kirsty and Hutch's house."

I'm well aware of that, and I don't fuckin' care. "Where are you?"

"In the guest suite."

"Perfect." I give her a chin lift. "Lift your top up, I wanna see you."

"Rubble!"

"I don't know why you're acting all coy with me, Sparkles. I've seen every inch of you and my dick's hard. I've had a long day. I wanna see you."

She shakes her head, then gets up and disappears for a moment.

"Did you just close the door?" I smirk.

"You know I've never been able to resist your pretty face," she tells me as I settle back and take all of her in.

"Pretty? You know I've lost count how many spanks you're owed."

"I wish you could spank me right now."

I pull at the towel and free it from my waist, then adjust the phone so she can see all of me.

I fist my cock as she sets the phone somewhere and comes back into view.

"Jesus, Rubble," she whispers when she sees me holding my dick.

"Take your clothes off."

"You didn't say please," she muses.

"I'll count to one…"

She huffs and then pulls the silk pajama top off over her head.

Her large, very swollen tits come into view, and I just about lose it. I slow down the stroking because I want this to last longer than three minutes.

"Jesus, you're not kidding about them bein' huge," I mutter, staring at them and her pink, erect nipples. "Touch yourself."

She cups her breasts and lifts them, biting on her lip as she stares back at me.

I grip my cock harder, taking all of her in while I pull myself off.

"I missed you today," she whispers. "I hate it when you go away."

"I'll be back tomorrow, I promise," I say as her eyes flick to my cock.

"Like what you see, baby?"

"I wanna suck you off so bad. I want you to come all over my tits," she says, and I jerk at her dirty talk and stop for a second.

"Fuck, babe, almost shot my load then."

It feels so fuckin' good, especially imagining her mouth around my cock.

"Pull your panties off, I wanna see all of you."

"Rubble, I don't know about this…"

"Do it," I tell her. "Need to see you touch yourself."

She snakes a hand down the front of her little shorts and starts rubbing herself.

"Pull them down," I order her.

I start pulling my dick again as she rips off her shorts and panties.

She's so beautiful. I could stare at her naked body all day and never come up for air. I feel like driving home right now so I can fuck her properly.

"Part yourself."

She does, and I tighten my grip and pull my cock harder. I know I'm gonna come so fuckin' hard 'cause this is turning me on so bad.

She starts rubbing her fingers through her folds and up to her clit as my eyes dart from her tits to her pussy, and then she inserts a finger and lets out a small moan.

"Lean back a little, open your legs," I say.

She does, and I'm rewarded with a view fit for a king.

"Oh God, Rubble…" she whispers. I know she's trying to be quiet because she's in someone else's house, but this is so fuckin' hot.

"Tell me, baby."

"God, I want you." She tips her head back and plunges her fingers inside herself as I watch her beautiful, sexy body move to the rhythm. Her tits bounce at every small movement.

"Look at my cock, baby," I say through gritted teeth. "I want you to see me when I come all over myself."

"Oh, Rubble…"

I pull harder as she fingers herself with one hand and plays with her clit with the other.

"Tell me, baby, tell me what you want…"

She tips her head back. "I love you, oh God, Rubble… I love you so much…" She comes, and I watch as she does it silently, her face reddening, and her tits jiggling as she milks herself. I feel myself leaking at the sight of her losing it.

"Look at me," I demand. "Baby, watch me…"

Her eyes flick open, and I jerk myself harder, my eyes on hers as I come so hard, calling out her name as I shoot my load all over my stomach.

"Fuck," I moan. "Oh fuck, baby…"

When I finally slow and focus on her, she's biting down on her lip as she smirks at me. "God, that was so hot."

I groan because I'm so fuckin' frustrated right now. I need her body so bad.

"Not my fault you started talkin' about milk and tits and how swollen they were," I mutter, wiping myself with my damp towel. "You know what those things do to me. Imagining you all alone in that big bed got me goin'."

"Are you really back tomorrow?"

"Yeah." I nod. "Bones is gonna switch. Things are fine

down here, babe, so you go back to bakin' and shit, and I'll see you tomorrow night, okay?"

She nods, pulling the covers around over her. "Thank you for the orgasm. It was just what I needed." She stifles a yawn as I give her a grin.

"I should be thankin' you, but now I've gotta go have another shower."

"Goodnight, sweetie, be careful tomorrow."

She looks tired and sated, and I've done my job. "Love you. Night, baby."

"Love you too."

We hang up, and I run a hand through my hair.

It doesn't matter what tomorrow brings, or any other day. I'll do what I have to do to keep her safe.

Now and forever.

When we get to Canyon Valley the next morning, Hoax and the boys are already up and about.

I can tell straight away something has happened by the way they're moving around, getting shit ready for what looks like a takedown. There's a pile of guns and ammo on one table, and knives and weapons on another.

"What's up?" I nod, as Smokey and Hoax come into view.

"Meeting's been moved up to tonight," Smokey says. "I had no choice but to call it in. Last night, the boys said there were at least fifteen of them, and guess who was spotted? Our friend, Rachet. He's finally come out of the woodwork."

"Fuck," I mutter. "So, he really is behind it, just like you suspected."

"Unlucky for him, yeah, the fucker has enough crazy in him to pull a stunt like this," Smokey goes on. "Need to keep tailin' him so we can get as much information as possible. Griller's still out keepin' tabs on shit with the other boys."

"And the Vipers?"

"Sent them the texts. That got their interest, tonight we'll meet them on their turf. Can only hope we live to tell the tale, brother, it's all out of my hands now."

Fuckin' Rachet.

"Still no sign of Nitro, then, so makes sense if he's involved too. The pair of them cooked this shit up, and Tex is likely the driving force behind it. Even from prison, he's controlling everything," I say. "Not unheard of, but extremely fuckin' cavalier."

"There's no fallout for Tex if this goes bad," Smokey replies. "It's the perfect scenario. Not that he wants all his investment to be lost to the Vipers, but shit happens, and we're gonna rain on his parade after what he's done to us."

"Fucker needs to be taken out," Hoax agrees.

Smokey gives me a chin lift and then looks to Steel and Brock. "If you're okay watchin' the warehouse again, my crew will go to the meeting. We want to keep you out of it as much as possible."

"Appreciate that," Brock says, giving him a chin lift. "I just hope you know what the fuck you're doin', brother, for everyone's sake."

He gives us a dry smile, and I know that he's got this covered. It's how he is; he always has some kind of strategy, and just when you think all hope is lost, he pulls a zinger.

"What about you?" Gunner gives me a nod. "We headin' back or gonna wait it out?"

I promised Lucy I'd be home today. Fuck. But it seems a little crazy to leave now, just when things are goin' down.

Bones and Hutch could be here in a few hours, but still. Lucy is safe. I can't imagine that any of this is going to extend into Bracken Ridge. All the action seems to be happening right here, right now. This is where the drop is, and by tonight, they'll be all over it.

With the Vipers' involvement, they have the numbers and the strength to take them out.

"Nah," I say. "We'll wait it out. I'll call Hutch, tell him we may as well stay put. All goin' to plan, this shit should be cleared up one way or the other by tomorrow."

Famous last words.

"Last thing we want is Rachet gettin' wind that we're onto him," Hoax puts in. "I personally wanna nail his ass to the wall, but if he doesn't show up at the warehouse, it'll blow our cover, and the others will know somethin's wrong."

He's right, it isn't the smart thing to do.

I know Lucy will be pissed, but I gotta do what I gotta do right now. She's been an ol' lady for a while; she knows the drill. She'll understand.

"Rubble's right," Steel says, giving me a nod. "Best if we stay put for the time bein'. See what happens after the sit down. If you're still breathin' by then, brother, we might just see some fireworks after all."

"Here's hoping," Smokey replies as the tension in the room lifts slightly. He takes it all in his stride, and I don't know in this moment if that's incredibly brave or incredibly stupid, but I guess we're about to find out.

22

LUCY

I NEED TO GET OUT OF THE HOUSE.

Rubble called earlier and said he had to stay down there today as something had come up.

I can't hide that I'm disappointed, but it isn't his fault. He's got to do what he's expected, and I get that, but I was looking forward to being in my own house tonight, and in my own bed, with him.

Last night on facetime was so hot.

I shouldn't have been doing crazy stuff like that in someone else's house, but my hormones are in overdrive all the time at the moment, and we always find a way to keep the spark lit. I'm happy to say it's alive and well.

Since Deanna is busy at my office taking care of things, I offer to help Bones catch up on any paperwork over at the junkyard. It seems ridiculous that I'm not allowed in my own office, but I can escape to someone else's. He's dumb enough to accept, and I almost jump for joy when we get away unscathed because Kirsty had to go to work today, and she's already left the house. She's been watching me like a hawk.

I'm used to helping the boys out when I can, not that

there's much paperwork here; it's basically cash in hand and money on the side.

"This place is filthy," I say when Bones unlocks the office door.

Of course, it's his side of the office and his desk that's the pigsty. In typical Bones fashion, there's crap strewn everywhere.

"Honestly, Bones, I don't know how you think you're going to snatch that fancy lawyer when you've got fur covered donuts and cottage cheese in the bottom of your coffee cup," I go on, screwing my nose up.

He pats his chest like he's offended. "That's why I'm good in bed, darlin'." He gives me a wink.

I hold up a hand. "Please do not tell me that you've used that line recently to any woman with a pulse."

He rolls his eyes. "It's not that bad." He begins clearing shit off the desk, making just enough room for me to sit down. How chivalrous.

"I'm not starting anything until you clean this shit up," I tell him. "And you may as well bin that coffee cup. There is no coming back from that, sugar."

He puts his hands on his hips. "This how you got your man? Boss him into submission until he can't feel his balls anymore?"

I give him a sharp look. "Keeping a tidy workspace isn't just about having tight balls, sunshine. What if customers come in here and see this mess? It looks unprofessional."

He gives me a more exaggerated eyeroll. "There you go again. Did I ask for your *professional* opinion? And don't think I don't know you only asked if I needed help because you're tryin' to get away from Kirsty. These ears here ain't painted on." He brushes his ears with his fingertips and waggles them. "Not as dumb as I look."

I give him a look that begs to differ and shake my head. "Fine. I refuse to go anywhere near that desk until it's clean."

I watch as he goes to the wastepaper basket and then brings it to the edge of the desk, sweeping his arm across all the shit from plates, moldy food, and general bits of paper and broken tools, it all landing in the bin.

"There," he declares. "That better, your highness?"

I point at him. "It's that mouth of yours that'll get you in trouble."

"My mommas been sayin' that since I was five years old, sweet cheeks. Better come up with a better line than that."

"Fine. Let's talk in *biker boss mode,*" I say, well aware I'm trying his patience, but I don't care, 'cause he's trying mine. I cup my hand around my mouth and shout. "You're never going to get into Kennedy's pants when you're a fucking slob!"

His eyebrows shoot up. "I think I'm doin' just fine, thanks all the same."

I shake my head. "Really? You haven't even gotten to first base." I laugh. "And she won't look twice at you when your jeans look like they grew legs and crawled out of your hamper from two thousand and two."

"If you're such an expert on what high class women want, tell me then, what the fuck is it they actually want? And don't say to be wooed and taken out for romantic dinners because I don't do that shit."

"There!" I say as he swats my finger away from his face. "That attitude right there. She wants a man, not a little boy who stamps his feet when he can't get what he wants. Most women, now I'm not sayin' *all* women, but *most* want a guy who's nice, and says they look pretty and might want to do something that – and here is the clincher, Bones, pay attention – *they like doing!* It might be going to the movies, or grabbing a burger, or just chillin' out. *Don't* take her to the strip club. *Don't* take her to a seedy bar. *Don't* try and mount her on the first date. Voila. Not rocket science, but I'm sure in caveman land none of those things are even on your radar. No offense, honey, but for a good-looking guy, you do strike out a lot."

He frowns again, and I bite my lip and pat his cheek good-naturedly. We've been ribbing each other for years. Bones is like the little brother I miss so dearly. He lets me take a few shots in jest, and we get to have a laugh. And he does the same back.

"One." He starts counting on his fingers. "I *am* fuckin' nice. Two, there's no strip club in Bracken Ridge, so that's a moot point, and three, I only mount the women that give me the green light. I'm not some fuckin' horn dog; I've got some self-respect."

"Oh, and you say *fuck*, a lot," I add. "Most women don't really appreciate that in general conversation, it's considered rude."

He shakes his head, but his lips curl up like he's fighting a smile. "Says you, who swears like a sailor."

"I'm married." I shrug. "And not looking. It's different when you're playin' the field."

I give him a smile as I take the seat at his desk.

"You done, babe? It's like gettin' a verbal ass-whooping from my mama."

"I'm done, thank you."

"You know I'm gonna teach that kid all these bad habits when I babysit."

I snort. "Like I'd ever get you to babysit my child. You wouldn't know the first thing to do with a kid." I look up at him. "Would you?"

He waggles a finger at me. "I'm great with kids. I play with Rawlings all the time. She beats me at every fuckin' game we play, though. Kids love me. I think it's the mohawk, it kinda spells cool."

"I thought you were growing that out. That's another thing that could be off-putting," I go on, like he hasn't heard enough. "Tattoos on the side of your head kinda scream prison cell."

He looks at me seriously for a moment, then leans his butt against the desk and folds one foot over the other. "I'm not changin' for any chick, let's get that straight."

"You don't have to change your personality," I correct. "Just don't say *fuck* so much and make sure you wash your clothes. It's not really that hard. You're cute enough, and you're better when you smile more."

He grins at me like an idiot, and I throw a pencil at him just as his phone rings.

He throws it back as he answers it. "Hey, boss."

I fire up the computer and start looking through the papers to see what's trash and what isn't.

"Yeah," he says. "She's with me… Nah, just Gears. He's outside, got sortin' to do."

His eyes shift to mine, and he frowns. "Okay… Uh, when? Like, now?"

I glance back at the screen, trying to not make it seem like I'm listening in, which I am.

Bones steps away toward the staff room as he listens to whatever it is Hutch is saying, and I strain to hear as he walks away.

Something's obviously going on.

I set about going through any bills that need to be paid. When he returns a few minutes later, he's back to serious mode.

"We need to go," he says with urgency in his tone.

"Bones?" I frown. "What's the matter?"

"Just listen for once in your life, woman. Let's get going, we gotta meet Hutch."

"Is Rubble okay?" Dread fills me as I wait for his answer.

"He's fine," he says, motioning for me to get up. "I'll explain in the car."

I push myself out of the chair with a flair of annoyance as he plants the palm of his hand into my back. This is odd.

"Bones, you're scaring me," I say when he locks the door and calls out to Gears.

"Nothin' to be scared of, just a precaution."

My eyes go wide as we walk hurriedly to my car. "A precaution?" I squeak. "Bones, you're not making any sense."

To make matters worse, his eyes dart around everywhere, shielding me when Gears appears from out of nowhere as he pushes me back against the car door, and I'm trapped behind him.

"Holy shit," I whisper.

"Gears!" Bones barks.

I've never, in the time I've known him, heard him shout at anybody. It makes me jump.

"Sorry, dude." Gears frowns when he sees me peeking out from behind Bones' body.

"Some shit's going down, need you to follow behind us. You got me?"

He nods. "Sure thing."

I tap Bones on the shoulder. "You're squashing the baby," I say as he pushes off and frees me.

"Sorry, Luce," he says, running a hand over his hair, which does nothing to settle my nerves. "Didn't mean to scare you."

"Tell me what the hell is going on!" I demand.

Gears eyes go wide at my tone as I shoot him a glare. He raises his hands in protest as he gives Bones a look. "I'm on it."

Bones turns to me as I push him in the chest. "Give a

woman some room already."

"Please just get in the car," he says with finality. "I mean it. Get in the fuckin' car now!"

I don't argue this time. I grip the handle of the SUV and pull myself up to the passenger seat. He stands there in the open doorway until I'm buckled in, and only then, I try to calm myself.

He doesn't look nervous, but I know Bones used to be a sniper for a Special Ops unit when he was posted in the Middle East. You wouldn't believe it to look at him, but I know he's got the stoic look down pat.

He gets in the driver seat, and we take off, the tires skidding on the gravel as we pull out onto the road.

"There's no need to snap at me," I say after a few moments.

He glances at me with a now etched crease on his forehead that wasn't there before.

"Sorry, I got orders, babe. That's all."

I turn to him with my arms folded over my chest. "Care to explain?"

"Not till we get to church." He's as infuriating as they possibly come.

"You said you'd tell me in the car," I whine.

"Well, I changed my mind," he says. "Is that seatbelt fastened?"

I swat his hand away as he tries to reach over to check. "I don't need you pawing at me, I'm fine," I snap. "Aside from getting whiplash from being stuffed in a car without even so much as a please or a thank you!"

He snorts. "No offense, sugar lips, but I don't exactly gotta say please or fuckin' thank you to an ol' lady. You should just come when I say because you know I'd never put you in harm's way, and know that I'm here to protect you."

I glare at him. "Protect me from what, Bones? Tell me

what's going on!"

"Luce, you're killin' me here."

"I have a right to know!"

He stares at the road ahead with as much composure as I've ever seen. Usually, he's aloof and slightly crazy; nothing fazes him at all. But this is different. This is Bones in work mode, and I'm not sure I like it.

"One of the guys sent Hutch pictures of you," he blurts out suddenly.

My eyes go wide as I snap my mouth shut.

"What?"

"Recent pictures, okay. Of you at the store. At the coffee shop. Around town. At the office. Someone's been watchin', Lucy. They're sending a message, and I don't know what that message is till we get to church."

A cold shiver runs up my spine, and I've never been so grateful to have Bones in the same car with me before in my life.

"What do they want?" I whisper.

"I don't know that yet, babe."

"Where are we going?"

"To church."

I pull my knees up on the chair and hug them close to me, rubbing my stomach with one hand across my bump.

"Has this got something to do with what the boys are doin' in Phoenix, with the Fury?"

"You know I can't answer that," he says.

"You gotta give me something!" I squeak. "I know you're all on some secret squirrel mission to see who these dudes are that are giving Smokey and his guys a hard time."

"You call it a hard time; we call it a hostile takeover. It's not Kansas anymore, Lucy. It ain't like that anywhere anymore."

My gut twists.

"What is that supposed to mean?"

"It means, there's always bad guys out there, tryin' to hurt people, sometimes for no good reason. Smokey and the boys are tryin' to stop it, tryin' to make amends with the Vipers and take back some control, get rid of these rogue pissants or whatever they call themselves. Then hopefully, there won't be any more bloodshed."

"Oh shit." The way he says *any more bloodshed...* "Have they been killing people?"

I don't even want to form the words.

"That isn't your concern. I'm just sayin' that sometimes you gotta pull out the weeds and that involves risk. Sometimes when the threats are close to home, you gotta step in. That's why the boys are in Phoenix. If it involves our club, which it does with Rubble, then we gotta protect the club. We gotta protect what's ours by any means necessary." He runs a hand through his hair. "I've said too much, but it isn't like you're not gonna find out anyway."

"What message are they sending, Bones?"

He side-eyes me. "You ask a lotta questions, doll."

"I'm worried about Rubble," I say. "About all of them."

"I'm more worried about you at this minute, which is why we need to get to church to figure some stuff out. And now I'm gonna get my ass kicked for sayin' shit to you, which you had no business knowin'."

I stay quiet, biting on my thumbnail as I try to think.

They've no reason to come after me; it makes no sense.

To think someone has been watching me and taking photos? What kind of sick person does a thing like that?

"I'm scared, Bones," I say, unsure if he even hears me.

He reaches his hand out to me, and I take it with both hands and squeeze it.

At least he's not telling me to sit down and shut up like he was when he first hauled me out of the junkyard.

"It's gonna be okay, Luce. I won't let anything happen to you. You're forgettin' I'm better with a gun than I am with my fists."

My eyes go wide. "That started off kinda sweet until the gun part."

He shrugs. "You know I used to be a sniper, babe. I'm a good shot."

"That's all fine and dandy, Bones, but it doesn't do anything for my nerves."

He gives me a smile. "It's gonna be okay."

I hold up a hand. "Don't say that it's 'just a precaution.' This is serious. Whoever it is, they're sending a message loud and clear, aren't they?"

"We don't know anything yet," he maintains. "Just don't get your panties in a twist, got me? Not till we get to church and talk to Hutch."

I should message Rubble, but he probably already knows. He's probably already on his way back here... I need to talk to him.

I know what's coming.

We're going into lockdown.

Even if just the slightest threat is made or even implied, Hutch won't let it slide.

"Can we stop at mine; I need to pick a few things up."

"Can't do that, babe. This isn't a Sunday picnic."

"Please," I cry. "It's on the way."

"I got my orders, and it was to drive to church, no stop offs."

"I need pads!" I yell out.

He looks at me strangely.

"What the fuck?"

I've only been spotting, but Dr. Stevens said that was normal. I don't, however, want to be locked down at the clubhouse without my necessities.

"It's girl stuff, okay?"

"You're fuckin' kiddin' me?"

"Gears is behind us. I'll be like two seconds."

"I'm gonna get my ass kicked for this, you know that, don't you?"

"Is that a yes?" I say with pleading eyes.

He makes a turn toward Oak Park, and I let out a silent sigh of relief.

I try not to be scared out of my mind at who would be taking photos of me or why.

Pulling out my phone, I dial Rubble. It rings out.

I don't leave a message, but it makes me feel uneasy.

I stare out of the window and hope to Jesus that all of this is just some huge mistake, a mix up. But I know it isn't.

I knew deep down that when Rubble took off to Phoenix that bad shit was going to go down. What did I honestly expect?

I know Bracken Ridge isn't the type of place where a lot of stuff usually happens, but still.

Where there's a motorcycle club, one percenters or not, crazy shit can happen.

I think about all of this year with what's happened to all of us; Lily getting drugged and almost date raped. Sienna and her ex when Cassidy was kidnapped. Angel and her ex-husband who tried to kill her. Maybe I've been a bit too naïve in thinking that living in a small town is safe. It clearly isn't. Maybe nowhere is.

My heart feels heavy as I try to fit the pieces together.

I turn my head to the side so Bones won't see me cry.

I thought I was made of tougher stuff than this, but I'm not. All that is make believe.

All I know is, I want this to be over. Whatever the hell *this* is.

23

RUBBLE

"What the fuck?" Smokey says when Griller drags the prospect through the doors just as we're about to take over the night shift.

Smokey's sit down panned out. He didn't get shot, nobody did, thank fuck, even if it took everything they had to go in Viper territory and not get their heads blown off.

I thought fuckin' Hutch, Steel and Brock were the hardest men I know, but Smokey is something else. He'll do anything to get this club back on its feet, even put himself in the firing line.

The Vipers are clued up on the Rogue Warriors and what they've been up to, and needless to say, they were less than impressed about the warehouse operation and they want every last detail. The only logistics are when each of the clubs are going to strike and take them down.

The guy in the prospect jacket is battered and bruised and has blood running out of his nose. He seems like he's seen better days.

Griller seems quite pleased with himself as he drags him across the floor to face Smokey.

"Found this little pissant. Had tire problems on the side of the highway; seems like it was my lucky day," Griller says, shoving him toward the dining table that's being used as a storage area.

"Who the fuck are you?" he screams out, thrashing around like a little bitch.

Griller holds him up by the lapels of his jacket. "That's no way to speak to our Prez," he growls, then socks him in the stomach. The prospect barrels forward, clearly winded as I wince at the impact. Getting hit by Griller would be something to write home about.

You would think that struggling would be futile being that Griller is the size of a house, and you'd give up after a while, but this kid's got a bit of fight in him. I'll give him that.

Steel moves closer to them, blocking the only exit, just in case he tries to run for it, not that he'd get far. Only coyotes and cactus around these parts, and it's doubtful he'd be able to move fast or very far in the state he's in.

"So, let's try that again," Griller goes on. "Dear Mister President..."

"Fuck you!"

Griller cocks an eyebrow. "Wrong answer." He slugs him again; this time I hear a crack, and I know it's a rib. That's gotta hurt.

He wails and screams and doubles over, holding his torso as Griller rights him again so he's facing Smokey. The kid's gone bright red and is gasping for air.

"Dear Mister President," he growls like a lion. "We can do this all day, but the next shot I'm gonna take is your dick, and I've got a knuckle duster that's got your name written all over it. Or my switchblade, I just sharpened it this morning, and it slides through skin like butter."

I wince as I imagine that very unpleasant idea.

The prospect holds his ribs, trying his hardest to crouch

over. "D.. d… ear, Mis.. ter…Pre… s.. i… de.. nt," he begins but ends up in a coughing fit that lasts for about five minutes.

Griller pats him hard on the back. "See, that wasn't so hard, was it?"

Smokey rounds the table, his eyes lighting up at the dribbling fool before him.

"You're prospecting for who exactly?"

The kid is reluctant to answer still, but one shake from Griller, and he sings like a canary.

"The Rogue Warriors," he splutters. "They recruited me about six months ago. I do shit for them, I get them things, whatever they want me to do pretty much."

Smokey and Griller exchange glances.

I can see the cogs turning in their heads. This is a very good score.

A prospect is unlikely to be missed, as they're not high up in the pecking order for anyone to care about. Nobody really gives a shit about them until they patch in, and I doubt he's ever gonna patch anywhere, especially for a club who hides out and is displaced with no real leader.

"Listen to me very carefully," Smokey says, his voice dripping with danger. "This is either gonna go very good for you, and by that, I mean you may get to walk out of here and back to the rock you crawled out from under. Or it's gonna go the other way, and the other way is very fuckin' bad." He points to Griller, then to Steel. "These guys are experts in torture; they know how many bones to break in a person's body and which ones to make you scream more than the other. Ain't that right, Steel?"

"All two hundred and six of them," Steel replies, his arms folded over his chest. "I'm also very good with a hunting knife. I was gonna be a surgeon, but I don't really like saving lives as much as I like takin' em."

Snickers ring around the room.

If I were this kid, I'd be pissing my pants by now.

"I'll tell you what you need to know," the kid snivels.

"Very good, we don't want any more cracked ribs or missing dicks for that matter, now do we?" He whacks him on the back hard, then proceeds to roll up the sleeves of his Henley.

The kid pales, and I think it's sufficient to say he's on board with telling Smokey what he wants to know.

"Now start from the beginning," Smokey goes on, leaning his ass against the table. "Nice and slow."

The kid takes a couple of breaths. "I got recruited in a bar after I won a fight," he says. "Rachet was there, said that he was starting up a new club, that he was one of the leaders in the original Phoenix Fury. I'd heard the club had been abandoned, some of the members were kicked out, some shot, some locked up after the turf war between them and the Dragons and Vipers. Everyone knew about it, it was no secret. Some of the old members wanted back in, and Rachet had contacts, least that's what he told me. Said he could get shit at a better price, undercut the Vipers since they were kings around town, and nothing got past them. He wanted to take back what was once theirs. Which is why it all had to be underground to begin with; nobody could know what was really goin' on. Rachet figured he'd form a club strong enough to stand up to them when they realized what was goin' down, by then they'd have the numbers to fight back."

"Where's he gettin' the shit from?" Smokey asks.

The kid shrugs. "I don't know for sure, but I suspect the Mexicans bypassed the Vipers because Rachet gave them a better buy-in price. Then he split the bricks and mixed it with some other shit and planned to sell it as premium grade. The stuff he'd been mixing for years down in Nevada, and nobody suspected anything. This shit is lethal, blows your fuckin' head off."

"Why here, why now?" Smokey prods. "Why didn't he stay in fuckin' Nevada?"

He shakes his head. "I don't know, but he reports to someone else, some guy who's in prison. He never says his name, but he's the one who calls the shots."

"Tex," Hoax snorts. "Like we didn't know that already."

"How many of you are there?"

The prospect tries to think as he holds his hand on his ribs and attempts to suck air into his lungs. "Around twenty-five, maybe thirty or so, scattered around."

Smokey glances up. "That's more than I thought, but it's doable."

The kid frowns but doesn't say anything.

"Give us some names," Hoax demands. "You know a guy called Nitro?"

The kid shakes his head. "Never heard of a Nitro. Skank. Spyder. Deathtrap. Badger. Kermit."

"Jesus fuckin' Christ," Steel mutters at the same time Brock snickers.

"Kermit?" Gunner laughs. "Who the fuck thought of that?"

The kid laughs too, then quickly sobers when all eyes glare at him. He looks down at the floor while Smokey paces in front of him.

"Who are you supplyin' to?" Smokey asks, taking a cigarette from behind his ear and lighting it up.

"I don't know –" he begins but Griller grabs him by the throat and cuts off his circulation. He flaps his arms around and tries, but fails, to stop Griller's hand from choking him.

"Let's try that again," Griller spits close to his ear. He lets the grip loosen slightly as the kid grabs his throat and coughs and splutters while the Sergeant at Arms rolls his eyes.

"Jesus…" he chokes out.

"He won't help you," Brock states, leaning against the wall. "We're gettin' old here."

"I literally don't know the details of who," he starts, then quickly adds, "but I do know when the first drop's happening."

Smokey grins. "Now you're speakin' my language."

"Sunday night, ten p.m.; the majority of the Rogues will be there, bein' it's the first big haul."

"That means they also expect trouble," Steel says.

"They're gonna fuckin get it," I reply.

"Where numbnuts?" Griller shakes him again hard.

"There's a dirt trail, before you get to Superstition Mountains," he goes on. "About half a mile off the beaten track from U.S. Route 60, before you hit Canyon North."

"Nice and secluded," I say. "Hope Rachet isn't superstitious though, cause he's in for a hell of a surprise when he gets there."

The boys chuckle.

"Nothin' out there but fuckin' cactus," Hoax groans. "Me and cactus don't exactly see eye-to-eye."

"That's because you're not supposed to stick your dick in one," Griller says with a rare smile.

The kid laughs, and Griller gives him another shake until he wipes the smile off his face.

Smokey turns back to the prospect. "That all you know?"

"Yeah, that's about it."

"About it?" he shoots back. "What else you hidin'?"

"Nothing, I swear!"

"What about the old Fury members that wound up dead, the prospect, and one of the ol' ladies that got beat up last week?" Smokey points in his face. "What do you know about that?"

The kid is clearly shitting his pants right now because he

tries to think, and the more he tries, the more Griller tightens the grip on his throat.

"All right, all right!" he squeals; his voice is actually getting really fuckin' annoying. "Rachet had one of the guys make a list of all the ex-members who double crossed them, didn't want to join them, or ran away like a little bitch when the club exploded. The dude in prison, Tex, right? Yeah, he wanted to resurrect the club. Start something new and gain back control, and Rachet bein' his brother…"

"What?" Smokey says bewildered. "They're brothers?"

The prospect shrugs. "Stepbrothers, I think. They're tight, anyway. Rachet does everything he says. I heard, back when the club went under, that a few kilos were taken, and they blamed it on a prospect. Nobody really knew who it was, but Rachet was convinced it wasn't the prospect, that it was someone else from the old club tryin' to steal the profits. He's been hellbent on payback for the club goin' under. He's always goin' on about it, he said the old members owe him and Tex."

Smokey rubs his chin. Clearly, nobody knew that Rachet and Tex were that close, nor that were they brothers. Funny how they kept that a secret. "So now he's goin' around, takin' the old members out, one by one? Is that what you're sayin'?"

"Yeah, until recently," the prospect says. "He's been too fixated on this deal to keep up with it. Everyone's had their role to play, but it didn't matter since that Tex guy is out now, and he can finish the job for himself. I guess bein' locked up for that long makes you pretty bitter."

We all stare at him.

"But Tex is still in jail," I say, walking around so he can see me. "He's not gettin' out for at least four more years."

The prospect shakes his head. "Nah, he got an early release. Good behavior or some shit."

We all look at Smokey, who does a double take. "What the fuck?"

"Got out a week ago. If you ask me, he's got something on one of the parole board members because there was no way in hell he's been on any kind of good behavior," he snorts.

"Fuck," Smokey, Griller, and Hoax all say at the same time.

"So, you've seen him?" Hoax prompts. "Where is the fuckin' hideout?"

"I haven't seen him myself, but I overheard Rachet say he's layin' low until the night of the drop. He already fucked up one sweet butt and Rachet had to deal with it; the man's lost it if you ask me." The prospect looks up hopeful, like he's somehow redeemed himself and we'll let him go unscathed. He's had one too many punches to the head.

"Are you fuckin' kidding me?" Hoax kicks a chair and paces the room. "How the fuck did Tex get out with four years still left to serve, and we didn't know about it?"

"Dropped the fuckin' ball," Smokey mutters. "This is fucked up."

The prospect eyeballs Smokey. "Can't win 'em all."

"Did I ask for your fuckin' input?" he barks back at him, making him jump.

He holds up his hands. "Sorry, just tryin' to help."

"Where is your hang out?" Griller shouts. He's losing patience, and he also hasn't let go of the little prick since he hauled him in here.

"We've got several different locations," he spits. "The main one is downtown, under a shop selling fake Cuban cigars."

Smokey rubs a hand over his face. "He's been hidin' in plain sight this whole time."

"Slippery fucker," Brock agrees. "I say we take a trip down there, stake the place out."

"There's a basement entry at the back," the prospect tells us helpfully.

Brock nods. "Me, Steel, and Rubble can take a trip downtown, check things out. Just in case we get spotted, none of them will know us. Gonna need a cage, though."

"Rubble?" says the prospect.

We all turn to him.

"Yeah, fuckface?" I say, getting closer to him. "You hear that name before?"

"You're on the list," he says. "I remember the name. You're one of the few with an ol' lady."

All the blood drains from my face. "What the fuck do you know about my ol' lady?" I grab him by the lapels of his jacket as I hear Steel and Brock come up beside me, and Smokey mutters under his breath.

"Nothin', just that this Tex guy wanted to fuck up all the traitors to the club and the deserters. Ol' ladies were marked at the top of the list; nothin' like fuckin' up a brother by gettin' to his woman."

I stare at him like he's got two heads.

"I'm no fuckin' traitor or deserter," I spit at him. "We left on good terms, or so I thought. The prick has got a fuckin' screw loose."

"He's got a score to settle." Hoax sounds uneasy. "He's got it in his head that anyone that left the club or were involved when it went under is a traitor. Neither of them are convinced it wasn't one of us who stole some bricks. Fucked up shit goes on in prison. He's had a lot of time to stew over it, make a game plan, and he's got the element of surprise to carry out his vengeance."

"The man's crazy," Smokey mumbles. "There's no reasoning with crazy."

"And he's out," Steel barks, picking up his phone. "We gotta warn Hutch."

"Fuck," I say. I pull out my phone and see I've got three missed calls from Lucy. I dial her straight back, walking away from the fray, but she doesn't pick up.

Jesus fuckin' Christ. He could be anywhere now, he could be...

"Where is Tex now?" I scream at him, launching myself across the room. Steel grabs my shoulders and holds me back from pounding him into next week.

"I don't fuckin' know!" the prospect yells back at me. "He went out of town for a few days. He's gonna be back in time for the drop; as I say, he wanted to lay low for a while, blow the stink off, get cleaned up."

I turn to Brock. "Somethin' don't feel right about this. He fuckin' had it in for me from day one, I know it."

"I'll keep tryin' Hutch," says Steel. "Then Linc."

"Call everyone," Brock says to Gunner, who gives him a nod. "Give 'em the heads up what's goin' on until we find out where this fucker actually is."

"I need to get out of here," I say, just as I do the prospect snickers.

"He's probably not goin' to Disneyland, then." He laughs and doesn't even see the blow coming. I'm pounding his face like I'm a man with no soul as he howls at each blow until I feel hands on me, pulling me off as I try to kick him in the face.

"You think this is funny asshole?" I yell at him. My mind races, and my heart beats so fast I don't know which way to run. Like a caged animal.

"He's not gonna think it's so funny when we hand him over to the Vipers," Smokey warns, giving him a cruel smile. That shuts him up quick.

He's not gonna be in Bracken Ridge. He just got out of prison. He's got bigger fish to catch than paying back old club members, at least that's what I fuckin' hope.

Jesus, please let Lucy and the baby be all right.

I try Lucy again, but it rings out. "Fuck!" I yell to the wall.

I'm gonna lose it any second now if I don't get ahold of her. How could I be so fuckin' stupid?

I left her there... I left her and the baby.

Brock pats me on the shoulder. "She's with Bones twenty-four seven. Gunner's callin' him now. It's gonna be okay, brother, nothin's gonna happen to her."

I wish his words were comforting, but they're not. I know how sick fucks work, and I know Tex is depraved.

Lucy's my world, and if anything happens to her, I don't wanna be in a world without her by my side. I'll kill anyone that tries to take what I've got.

That's all I can think of as I dash out the door and out to my sled.

I've got to get to her...

24

LUCY

We turn into the driveway of my house and Bones jumps out of the car before me. Gears pulls up behind us.

"We takin' a detour, man?" he asks, frowning at Bones.

"Just pickin' somethin' up, keep the car runnin'," Bones barks back at him. "Then come and stand at the door."

He nods and jogs back to the car to turn the ignition back on.

Bones follows me up the drive, his hand on the small of my back as I unlock the front door.

"I hope you know that Hutch is gonna have my balls for this," Bones mutters as he steps in before me.

"You know you're kind of cute when you're goin' all commando on me," I say, giving him a little wink. "But I have to switch the alarm off first."

I step in too and disarm the thing.

"Very funny. Stay behind me until I've checked the perimeter."

"I just need to run to the bedroom," I tell him. "I'll be super quick."

"As I say, I'll be ball-less by tonight, I hope you'll be happy with yourself that I won't be able to reproduce. It'll be on your head, babe."

"That'd be a gift to everyone involved," I muse as he peers over my shoulder into the entryway. Everything looks completely normal. "What are you peering for?"

"It wouldn't matter. If there was a burglar or a break in, you'd be able to stun them to death with your chatter," he tells me, giving me a disapproving look.

"Is this you in stealth mode?" I try not to laugh, even though this is no laughing matter.

"I'm glad you think this situation is hilarious. Earth to Lucy, I ain't laughin'."

I give him a small pat on the cheek. "You're all right, you know?"

He grabs onto my wrist. "Shut the fuck up, woman," he whisper-shouts.

"Why are we whispering?" I say back as he tightens his grip on my wrist.

"Lucy, just do as you're fuckin' told for one single second, will you?"

"I don't see why I have to shut up, it's my house!" I retort indignantly. "And my bedroom's upstairs."

He ignores me and continues through the living room and checks out the kitchen. Everything looks fine there too, no signs of anything untoward.

"There's nobody here," I say, and just as I do, movement from the open doorway has me shrieking as Bones pulls his gun from nowhere and almost shoots the neighbor's cat.

"Holy shit!" he yells when the furry critter runs past us and down the hallway with a shriek.

My heart pounds as I clutch onto the back of the couch for support and try to get my breathing under control. "That scared the shit out of me."

"Since when do you have a fuckin' cat?" Bones quizzes, lowering his gun, not looking at all impressed.

"Will you put that goddamn gun away? You're freaking me out!" I cry, patting my chest, trying to slow my heart rate.

"Everything all right in there?" Gears calls from the front door, peering around to see what all the fuss is about.

"Fine," I say, waving him off. "The neighbor's cat scared us." I turn to Bones. "He sometimes uses the cat flap at the back. It was already here when we bought the place."

"Great," Bones replies, finally shoving the gun into the back of his jeans. "Tell that to my heart."

I head upstairs with Bones on my tail as I turn to him. "Don't tell Rubble I had another man in my bedroom."

"You should be so lucky," he snorts back. "And if you grabbed your stuff as fast as you run that mouth of yours, we'd be out of here by now."

"If you didn't go all Sonny Crocket on me, we'd be halfway to church."

"Sonny who?"

I tut. "Don't even insult me, please."

He gives me a gentle shove in the back as I ascend the stairs, and of course, he barges in front of me to check out the landing and the bedroom for intruders before I set foot in there. I get there's shit going on, but he's being a little bit over the top.

"You know, if you were this thorough with your tidiness at home and the office as well as your personal hygiene, you'd be killin' it with Kennedy Hart."

He blows out a puff of air. "Will you shut up about Kennedy Hart? Tryin' to concentrate here, and all I can hear is your voice like an annoying mosquito buzzing in my ear."

I quickly head to the bathroom, which he insists on sticking his head into first, then I grab my overnight bag and the pads from under the sink.

"See," I say, waving the box at him. "I wasn't lying."

He rolls his eyes and tells me to hurry up as I stuff in a change of underwear and grab my cardigan.

"We're not packin' for a vacation," he grumbles.

"Keep your hair on, I'm done."

I follow Bones out and down the stairs, and he takes the bag off me, throwing it over his shoulder.

"How updated is this security system?" Bones asks, reaching for the front door. "Maybe Colt needs to come check it out, just to be on the safe side. With everything goin' on, you can't be too careful."

"No you can't," says the man who barges in the front door, pointing a gun at Bones as I shriek and jump backward, expecting it to be Gears.

When I see Tex glaring at me over the top of Bones's head, the scream halts in my throat.

It's like time stops as I stare at him in disbelief.

"What the fuck?" Bones reaches for his gun, but Tex shoves him in the chest.

"Don't even think about it, fuckface. I'll put a bullet in your brain."

Bones holds up his hands, and all the while, I hide behind him as he hovers in front of me, not letting Tex in the door.

"Pity about your prospect," he sneers. "Kids these days spend too much time on their mobile phones. That shit could kill ya." He laughs and pushes Bones back farther.

Oh no, Gears was manning the door.

"Just take it easy," Bones says, waving his hands in the air.

"Shut the fuck up and get back," he barks as Bones walks backwards. I keep as close as I can to him and clutch on to the back of his cut. "Bet you never expected to see me again, did you, princess?"

"Hoped is a better word," I spit back.

He lets out a horrible laugh that makes me cringe. It's

clear he's high, and I'm still trying to get my head around how he's even here and not in prison when he tells Bones to turn around slowly, keeping his hands up. Bones does as he's told, looking down at me gravely when our eyes meet.

My heart accelerates as I swallow hard.

Holy fucking shit. Can this actually be happening? I feel like I'm trapped in some kind of nightmare.

Tex reaches into the back of Bones's jeans and takes his gun, spinning it around in his fingers with a low whistle. "Nice," he says, assessing it, keeping the other one pointed at the back of Bones' head. "Now don't move, or I'll blow your fuckin' brains out."

I want to scream, but I'm in so much shock that I now know what people mean when they say your legs feel like lead.

"What do you want?" Bones barks through gritted teeth. "You got beef with the club, we can sort it out man-to-man."

He shakes his head, his eyes glassing over. "The time for talkin' was a long time ago. I've had plenty of time to map this out."

"Who are you? What's your beef exactly?" Bones asks as I avoid looking directly at Tex. He's out of his fucking mind. I caress one hand over my belly and pray to God we get out of this.

"My beef is with thieves, deserters, and whores!" he spits.

"Yeah, how'd you figure?" Bones winces as Tex shoves his own gun into his back, so now he's got two guns pointed at him, and I don't think I've ever been so afraid.

"You let Rubble go fair and square!" I shoot back, my eyes snapping up as Bones gives me a look that says *keep quiet.* "What have we done to you to deserve this after all these years?"

He sneers at me. "Maybe I just changed my mind," he says. "Maybe lettin' him go wasn't on my agenda at all. I planned on killin' him a long time ago. He was useless to me when he couldn't walk anymore or do anything except moon after some two-bit whore. Thinkin' it was okay to just walk away from the club, that it was that easy?"

"He was in a wheelchair!" I cry as Bones gives me wide eyes. "What was he supposed to do?"

"The only reason he lived this long was because I got locked up, and then the M.C. went underground after shit fell apart, no thanks to club members who didn't stick with us. Same goes for Smokey and that fuckface Hoax, and let's not even discuss your precious Rubble. They were both meant to be taken out that night at the drop. I set it up; it's a pity I didn't get what I paid for."

I gasp. "You set up the execution of your own men? Why?"

"Don't look so shocked, like I said; I was takin' out the trash. I had to prove to the Cubans that I was serious. Sacrificing your own brothers is a strength of character. It sorts the men from the boys, and I did what I had to do. They were replaceable, nothin' to me. Some people count, and some people don't."

He is absolutely crazy.

We walk toward the couch as I back away, my feet wanting to run, but I know that'll be suicide, I need to think…

"Now you're gonna do as I say, or I swear to God, I'll put a bullet in him and then…" His eyes flick down to my belly as my hands fly down there protectively. "Well, first, I'll show you what a real man is made of, then I'll shoot you and your fuckin' baby."

Bile rises in my throat.

The thing is, he really is crazy enough to do it. Panic sweeps over me, and for the first time in my life, I feel helpless… I need Rubble.

If I'd ever hoped for a miracle, then it would be right about now.

"Nice place you got here," he goes on, looking around the den like he's casing the joint. "Pity your husband isn't around to see this go down. I would have paid money to see the look on his face."

Bones gives me a subtle head shake, telling me quietly to keep my mouth shut.

I don't exactly want to aggravate a crazy person any more than he already is, so I stay quiet.

"Did well for yourself, considering the company you keep," he goes on, circling the room, waving his gun around. "I'm impressed, though we all knew Rubble was shooting above his average when he landed you. You never were club material, though it seems you've made yourself at home in this shithole of a town."

I want to yell and scream at him that he knows nothing about me, nothing about Rubble, and definitely nothing about my home.

Instead, I swallow hard as his eyes glance over me, and he laughs. "What, no smartass taunts? I thought we were just gettin' warmed up. You disappoint me, Lucy."

Now is the time to be strong. Now is the time to use everything I know to keep calm and think. Inside I'm screaming and want to run, but outwardly I keep my head held high.

I've never wanted the ground to open up and swallow someone whole so bad in all my life.

Instead, I close my eyes and run a hand over my belly.

There is nothing that I won't do for you, little one. Nothing. I won't let anything bad happen. I'll guard you with my life. Bones will too... I know it. I know it more than I've ever known anything. I know because I love you more than I've ever loved anything.

I'll never be sorry.

25

LUCY

Times passes slowly when there's a gun pointed at you.

"It was you all along," Bones interrupts. "Settin' up your minions to do all the heavy liftin' while you plotted to gain more traction with the underworld figures, thinkin' you could outsmart them all, but your thirst for vengeance has made you sloppy. You tried this once before; remember how that turned out."

Tex takes the butt of the gun and slams it against Bones's head as I shriek.

"Shut the fuck up!" he yells. "Next time, that'll be the pointy end of the gun goin' into that thick skull of yours!"

Bones, bless him, doesn't make a sound, but I silently cry as I hold my hands over my mouth to stop any more noise coming out.

I don't know if Bones has a plan, but fear grips me like nothing I've ever felt before. I can hear the blood pounding in my ears as I try to hold onto the last of my resolve.

"You won't get away with this," Bones tells him, his words laced with poison. "You can run but you can't hide. You know they'll catch you eventually, and I'd love to be there when they cut your eyeballs out and feed them to you."

That earns Bones a swift kick to the stomach. "I said, shut the fuck up!" he yells as I cover my ears.

Then he points the gun to me. "If you make one more fuckin' peep, bitch, I'll kick you in the stomach too."

I bite my lip to avoid bursting out crying.

There's no way out of this.

Then, hope blooms in my chest as I hear the front door. Tex turns expectantly, and I gasp out loud when Nitro, of all fucking people, barrels through the door, a gun in his hand.

He looks different. His hair is black, longer, he has scruff over his face and his eyes are smudged with dark liner. His eyes look so green, like emeralds, and he stares at me with that weird expectant expression. He points a gun at me as I stare at him, unblinking.

"Ah," Tex says with a smile. "Here he is, my trusty counterpart. The thing about sewer rats is they stick together, don't they, Nitro? I kept this one well hidden. I think we can put all those rumors to bed about you bein' six feet under."

"Nitro?" I say in shock, as I try to make sense of it. Granted, I didn't have much to do with him at all, but still. He seemed so quiet, endearing almost, but not the type to stage something like this. To point guns at people.

"Long time no see, Lucy." His voice is deep and barely audible.

Something about his demeanor is completely off. He looks completely at ease yet conflicted somehow, and his brows furrow even deeper as he watches me.

My heart races as I try and get him to talk.

"Why are you doing this?" I whisper, tears leaking from my eyes.

"You're on a need-to-know basis," Tex says, turning and handing Nitro Bones's gun, then he shoves his own gun down the back of his jeans. "Now be a good little bitch while we tie you up. I'm sure that Rubble will pay whatever it takes to have you back, and that's if I decide not to slit your throat first and film it so he can watch."

I'm not gonna go down without a fight, that much is certain, so I just stay still.

I see Nitro's jaw tick as he points the gun between me and Bones, like he's unsure which one of us might make a run for it first. At this point, I might even be stupid enough to try.

It's my fault. I wanted to stop off...

I brush my tears away and straighten my back, if this is it, then I'm going out with dignity.

"Sit on the couch," Tex demands as I slide down into the recliner and Bones sits on the edge of the two-seater. If the look on Bones's face could kill, Tex would be dead a hundred times over.

"Throw me the duct tape," Tex says to Nitro. "This is the part that gets really fun, especially for you sweet cheeks." He gives me a once over that makes me want to shudder all the way down to my toes.

I never thought it was possible to hate anybody, but him threatening us, making me plead for me and my baby's life, for Bones too, which I'm about to do, makes me want to pull a gun on him and shoot.

Nitro keeps the gun pointed but doesn't move. As usual he doesn't say much and that to me is just cowardly.

"Cat got your tongue?" I spit at him.

"Don't Lucy," he warns.

"Do you really think they won't find you after you do this? That he cares about you?" I jab a finger toward Tex. "He doesn't, he'll probably shoot you too before the days out."

Tex laughs.

"I never wanted it to be like this," Nitro says, his voice quiet. "And I've waited a long time."

I close my eyes, fear grips me. He's insane too. They all are.

"You don't have to hurt her." Bones looks at both of them. "Let her go and you can do what you want to me. She doesn't deserve this."

"Bones!" I snap. "Don't you dare!"

"How gallant of you." Tex shakes his head. "But I've got a feeling Rubble's won't be as sad about me slittin' your throat as he will be hers."

"Don't be so sure about that," Bones replies. "Our club prides itself on true brotherhood, we're a family. We don't pull guns on innocent people and we sure as hell don't hurt women out of an act of vengeance that only you care about."

"I'm gonna enjoy killing you," Tex snarls as he turns around again. "Throw me the fuckin' duct tape, numb nuts!" he bellows at Nitro.

I swallow hard as Nitro stares at me, the gun still in his hand. His eyes cloud over before moving the gun toward Tex, pointing it at him.

Confusion crosses Tex's face when he glances up and their eyes meet. "What the fuck are you doin'? Don't point that thing at me, fuckface, point it at them!"

"I don't think so," Nitro says as he motions with the gun. "Keep your hands where I can see them, like I told Lucy, I've waited a long time for this."

"What the fuck?" Tex stutters.

"You see, you messed with the wrong person this time, Tex. I set it all up nice for you, made sure everything ran smoothly and stayed in the shadows just how you wanted. We let Rachet have his shot at playing the tough guy; that was a hoot. Word to the wise…" He cups his free hand around his mouth and whisper-shouts. "Rachet ain't that smart."

"I'll end you!" Tex bellows, but Nitro stays calm and still

as he cocks the gun as if he's ready to pull the trigger and end him.

My heart races as I grip the sides of the chair, and Bones gives me a *what the fuck is happening?* Look. I wish I knew.

"Admittedly, I didn't think you'd make parole, but I still sent all the information I had to Smokey and the boys anonymously. You gettin' out of prison early was just a bonus. The sting of seeing you go down for the second time would've been sweet all over again, after all, you ruined everything for all of us. But when I found out you had a list to settle the score, I knew I had to step in and make you pay."

Tex goes to reach for his gun, and Nitro fires. I scream and cover my ears, jumping back in the chair. Bones doesn't even flinch. In fact, he still holds his hands where they can be seen, and even though I know he's tempted to reach for Tex's gun too, he stays completely still.

Tex howls as he doubles over, clutching his shoulder.

"Purposely nicked the top left shoulder," Nitro says. "Pretty good with a rifle, even better with a gun. I won't miss your heart next time if you try that again."

"Fuck you!" Tex spits.

Nitro wants to take control? Has that been his plan all along?

"Nitro?" I cry before I can stop myself. "What are you really doing here?"

He flicks his eyes to mine, and I see something in them that I didn't see before. I see pain.

"I never wanted things to turn out like this," he says as I hug myself. "I never meant for you to get involved. The minute I heard that Rubble was next on the list, I had to intervene. This dumb fuck trusted me, so clearly he's not a very good judge of character. I'm rotten to the core, especially when it comes to family."

Family?

"You got a thing for her?" Tex sneers, holding his arm while the blood oozes out all over my rug.

"Nah, man, it's not like that, but we do know each other, better than she thinks…"

I stare back at him, then it hits me. Those emerald green eyes. "Adam?" I splutter.

He gives me a small smile. "Hey, Lucy Loo."

I stare at him as tears pool in my eyes. "Oh. My. God. Is it really you?"

"Yeah, it's me, sis."

My eyes go wide as I take him in. He looks nothing like how I remember. The last time I saw him, he was only thirteen, a child. That was almost fifteen years ago.

I burst into tears as he keeps the gun held toward Tex, but his eyes stay on me.

"Why didn't you say anything when I was at the Fury clubhouse?" I tug onto my emotions, ranging from angry, to sad, to shock. I don't know what the hell to think.

"I didn't want you involved with the Fury," he says calmly. "I wanted to say something back then, but I didn't want them to have something over me. I didn't want you havin' any ties to the club after you left. It was a clean break, one that I was happy you'd made. I didn't want to ruin anything for you, so I kept quiet."

"I was there for months!" I cry. "And you couldn't even tell me? I looked for you Adam…I looked for you everywhere…" I trail off and hide my face in my hands.

"When you two have finished catching up on old times, I'm fuckin' bleeding here!" Tex yells across the room.

"Who the fuck cares? Stay down and shut up," Nitro warns.

"You can't do this! One phone call, *one*, and you're gone! You're history. Sleep with one eye open, my friend," he snorts. "You're a dead man."

"I don't think so," Nitro says calmly. "You're all out of options, Tex. This is the end of the line, you've got nowhere else to run to."

"Please," I beg. "No more bloodshed. I can't bear any more…"

"After what he wanted to do to you?" Nitro looks repulsed. "There is no remorse. You got any final words, scumbag?"

"Yeah!" Tex says, his huge form splayed out like some fallen inmate, not a king, not a *Prez*, not even a man. He's weak. "Go to fucking hell!" He lunges across the floor toward me and pulls out a knife, and it all happens so fast.

Bones is faster, though; he darts off the couch and in front of me as the knife stabs into his arm just as Nitro pulls the trigger and puts a bullet through Tex's brain. Blood spatters everywhere, and he hits the floor with a thump, along with the knife in his hand which goes scattering.

I scream and put a hand over my mouth as I jolt back into the chair, shocked.

I've never seen anyone shot before, much less between the eyes, in my own fucking den, no less. An awful sound rings through the air and the smell of burning metal follows.

"Jesus, fuck," Bones mutters under his breath, his back to me as he shields me from the gun Nitro's still pointing.

His wound gapes as he assesses his arm and winces a little. "That fuckin' hurt."

Nitro tucks the gun into the band of his jeans as he looks down at Tex's dead body on the floor. "Fucker had it comin'."

"I'd feel better if you gave me back my gun," Bones says through gritted teeth, as I clutch onto the back of his shirt, trembling.

"I'm not gonna hurt her," he replies. "She's my sister for Christ's sake."

"It's okay, Bones," I say, patting him on his good shoulder.

"Let me up. I need to stop the bleeding, and I want to hug my brother. It's been fifteen years."

"Gun first," Bones reiterates, not letting me go anywhere.

Nitro hands him back his gun. Bones puts the safety back on and tucks it down the back of his jeans, then turns to me. "You okay?"

I nod. "You saved me, Bones," I whisper. "You fucking saved me."

"I almost got us killed," he mumbles. "Listenin' to you 'cause you wanted to do a stop off."

"Shut the hell up and let me get a towel." I wince as I step past Tex and rush to the hallway cupboard. I come back and press the hand towel to Bone's arm. "Jesus, is it deep?"

"I'll live."

"I'm sorry, I didn't listen," I say, feeling bad that he got hurt. This whole situation is insane.

"I'll be fine, sweet cheeks."

I turn to Nitro. "What happened, where did you go? Why did you run away?" I burst out because these are all questions I've been asking myself for so many years. He pulls me into his arms as we hug. I cry, my shoulders shaking with all the years of pent up emotion. And here he was, right under my nose the whole time.

"We'll get to that, we've plenty of time," he tells me as I hold his face, looking in his eyes and trying to see the resemblance of my stepbrother from so long ago.

He's changed so much, no longer the little boy with an earnest face and a whiplash tongue. The only thing that looks the same are his eyes. The last time I saw him, he was just a kid. Now he's a man. He cocks a brow as I stare at him, trying to figure it out.

"What happened to you?"

"A lot," he says with a small smile. "Not much of it was good, Luce, but none of it could have been worse than livin' with that asshole I called a father, and your mom, no offense, but she wasn't exactly what you'd call nurturing. I had to get out."

"I'm so glad you're safe," I whisper. "I worried about you for so many years. I never gave up hope. I tried to find you, so many times. It broke me, it broke me for so long..."

He shrugs. "It was too hard, Lucy. It was easier on the street than being target practice for dad when he drank too much. I know it was the coward's way out, leaving like that, but I couldn't stay there. I knew you'd be okay; you're stronger than me, always have been. I was a ticking time bomb, and honestly, aside from not seeing you, I regret nothing. It was meant to be like this."

"I could have helped you," I say. "We could have worked it out, you were just a child."

So much time has been lost, and the fact he was right under my nose and I had no idea makes me mad that he didn't say anything. I feel like a bad sister for not even knowing.

He holds me tight, and I can't help but to feel a little bit of happiness wash over me that I know he's safe, which is contradictory to the chaos surrounding us. Tex lies in the middle of the floor as Bones goes to him, and then looks up at us.

"Need to move him and fast before the pigs get wind of it. You fired two shots, and that probably won't go unnoticed by the neighbors."

"Shit," I say as the front door bursts open making me jump. Hutch appears in the doorway, gun in hand as he takes in the scene unfolding around him.

"What the fuck's going on?" he barks at Bones. "And who the fuck are you?" He points the gun at Nitro as I shake my head and wave my hands.

Jesus Christ with the guns already. If I never see another one in my life, it'll be too soon.

"He's not the bad guy, Hutch, this is Nitro – it's a long story, but he's my brother. He was part of the Phoenix Fury when Rubble was there, he doubled crossed Tex. Then he shot him when he lunged for me."

Hutch glances from the floor to Nitro, then finally to me again. He still doesn't lower his gun.

"She's right, it's a long fuckin' story," Bones replies, giving a nod in my direction. "But we gotta clean this shit up fast."

"You all right, son?" He nods to Bones.

"Just a flesh wound, I'm good," he replies. "Need to get Lucy outta here."

"Jesus fuckin' Christ," Hutch says, running a hand through his hair. "I thought I said to come straight to church."

"Yeah, about that…" Bones begins.

"Let's talk about that later," I add quickly. "Like you said, we've got to clean this up."

We can't stay here for much longer, though our neighbors aren't right on top of us, the whole street probably heard the shots.

He pulls out his phone, and then holds it out to me. "Your old man's been worried sick, better make sure he knows you're safe."

I wipe my tears as I take the phone gratefully.

I've never known loyalty like I have with this club, my family. The men who swore they'd protect me at all costs and didn't let me down. And now I have my brother back.

I clutch onto Nitro's t-shirt, then look around at the men in my life that I never knew how much I appreciated until now. And Bones… he got freaking stabbed. I cringe, it could have been so much worse if Tex had gotten that gun back.

"Looks like I'm gonna need a new rug," I say, nodding to the blood stains.

They snort and Hutch points at me.

"This is exactly why you stay away from women from the south."

26

RUBBLE

I've never rode my sled so fast in my entire life.

The journey home flashes by like it takes me minutes, not hours. I guess red-hot adrenaline will do that to a person, and the flames course through me like I'm a man possessed.

I don't even remember how I got home, or weaving through the traffic and not killing myself in the process. All I know is I need to get to her.

When I hit town, I head straight to Hutch's place and bang the door down, but nobody answers. I pull my phone out and see I've got missed calls from Hutch. Fuck.

I immediately dial back, and he answers on the first ring.

"Where the fuck is everyone?" I run a hand through my hair, feeling panicked.

"Calm down," Hutch tells me immediately. "Get over to your place, pronto."

"Is Lucy okay?" *Please let her be okay.*

"She's fine. Tex fuckin' showed up, though you probably figured that already. He pulled a gun on Bones, and then Nitro shot him."

"What the fuck? Nitro?"

"You've no idea. Get your ass over here," Hutch says, and I hang up, then jump back on my sled and hightail it to my place.

When I get to mine, I see Hutch and Patch's sled in the drive, along with Lucy's car and another one I don't recognize.

My head pounds as I make the journey to the front door, which seems to happen in slow motion as I move as fast as I can and storm through the door.

"Lucy!" I call out frantically.

The first thing I see is Hutch, Patch, and Bones and – fuck me – Nitro, all standing around Tex's body. Gears sits on the recliner, holding a pack of ice to the back of his head.

"What the fuck is he doin' here?" I bark pointing to Nitro. I'm on him in two seconds, pulling him by the lapels of his jacket as he stands his ground and doesn't fight back.

"No!" Lucy screams as she comes down the stairs. "Rubble, stop it! He didn't do anything!"

I hold Nitro's collar and turn to her. I shove him back as I take her in my arms.

"Baby," I say, holding her head, pushing her hair back and assessing her head to toe. I run my hands over her stomach as she clutches me. "Are you okay?"

"I'm fine. I'm just a little shaken up." Her eyes are red, and her makeup is smudged as I wipe a smear with my thumb.

"I'm sorry," I mumble into her hair.

She whimpers as she squeezes me around my waist. "It's okay, it's not your fault."

I kiss her and turn to the others. "Someone tell me fast," I bark, pointing at Tex's dead body on my carpet. "And you!" I snap at Nitro. "Better not be playin' any fuckin' games 'cause I'm all outta nice, get me?"

"He's not," Lucy pleads, tugging onto my cut. "Please stop yelling."

I stare down at her, and I feel my throat thicken. "Need to get you out of here, you shouldn't be here."

Hutch gives me a nod. "Kirsty is on her way. We gotta move the body pronto."

Jesus Christ.

I move Lucy toward the kitchen, away from everyone so we can talk in private.

As I pass by Bones, I say, "We need to talk."

He looks sheepish as he runs a hand through his hair, and it's then I see he's bleeding. "I'm sorry, man, he got the jump on us."

"You all right? What the fuck happened?"

"Fucker stabbed me."

Lucy pats him on his forearm gently. "He took a knife to the shoulder for me," she says as her eyes glaze over. "He saved me from being stabbed by that lowlife bastard, that's the truth."

I slap him on the back and he winces. "Thanks, brother."

When we're alone, I pull her to me and she folds into my arms as I kiss her on top of her head.

"I've never been so scared when that little fucker Griller caught told us that Tex was out," I blurt out as she stares up at me; the relief in her eyes that I'm here is all the reassurance I need. "I should've been here…"

She cups my face. "You're here now, that's all that matters."

I pull back. "Are you sure you don't need to go to the hospital?"

She shakes her head. "No, I'm fine. Bones may need stitches, though."

"Don't worry about him, he's had worse slaps from his mother."

Her eyes assess me as I hold her hips and stare down at her stomach. "This is the last thing I wanted. You're supposed to be resting and keeping your feet up, not being held at gunpoint by a fuckin' lunatic, and then there's that Nitro prick…"

She smiles and runs her hands up my arms. "He's not a prick, Rubble. He's my brother."

I frown. "What the fuck are you talkin' about?"

"I know," she says. "I haven't seen Adam since he was thirteen when he ran away from home, I thought he was gone for good."

"He's your brother?"

She nods. "I know, it's crazy. He's been working with Tex in order to protect me, pretending to do his dirty work. Tex admitted you and Hoax were meant to die in the car crash that night six years ago, Rubble, on the last drop you did. He set it up, all of this was payback."

I stare at her. "I know, baby. Rachet is involved too; they're half-brothers or some shit. He's been runnin' the operation in Phoenix while Tex has been busy bribing people on the parole board."

"Jesus."

"And Nitro?" I frown. "Why didn't he say something when he saw you in Phoenix all those years ago, seems a little convenient that he comes out of the woodwork now." Frankly, I don't trust any of these fuckers. Tex held my woman at gunpoint and I didn't even get to hurt the bastard.

"He didn't want the club to have anything over him. Tex would use anyone he could when it was for his own advantage," she goes on. "He didn't want to come back into my life and ruin it all over again knowing that we were out, so that's why he kept quiet about who he was."

"Sounds a little likely," I grunt, then I whisper, "I don't trust him!"

"Shh! He shot Tex dead; isn't that enough to prove he isn't trying to kill me?"

I snort. "Yeah, I'm really just gonna believe that he swooped in here and saved the day all for the greater good."

She glances over my shoulder. "Please, Rubble, just give him a chance. For me."

I cup her cheek with one hand. "Need to get you home; this is no place for a lady."

"I'll remind you; it is my own home!" she says incredulously.

"That's not what I meant. There's a dead body in our den right now, and I need to deal with that."

"I know that; I was here when he was waving a gun at me."

I close my eyes. "Jesus, Lucy, I'll never forgive myself."

The thought of her being hurt, of her lying on the floor like that sends chills through me.

"I just ask you to give him a chance," she whispers. "I haven't seen him in so long –"

I kiss her softly, loving the feel of her lips against mine.

"I want to kill anyone that puts you in harm's way," I say against her mouth. "Every last one of them. I'll bury them all."

"I know that, baby. But you can't be everywhere all of the time, that's impossible. Don't be hard on Bones, he didn't do anything wrong, he protected me."

It doesn't matter what she says. My job as a man and her husband is to protect her at all costs. The fact I wasn't here when this went down is on me; it's unforgivable.

I run a hand over my face as I take in her angelic face.

"You'd tell me if you were feelin' funny, wouldn't you?"

"Yes," she breathes. "Of course, I would. If it makes you feel better, I'll get Helen to check me out, check on the baby."

I nod. "Just don't want to take any chances, not with everything."

She looks down at her feet. "It's my fault," she whispers. "I convinced Bones to stop because I needed some pads."

"What did you need those for?"

"Just a precaution, I was spotting a little bit." She shrugs. "We were meant to go straight to church and I made him stop."

I lift her chin, so she's looking at me again. "Bones should've known better. I'll be havin' fuckin' words with him about not bein' bossed around by a woman who should know not to push his buttons so easily. You knew Hutch had these photos, and you still took the chance, *he* took the chance too."

"It wasn't like that."

I put my hands on my hips. "It *was* like that, Sparkles, don't try and cover up for him."

"Please don't. He's feelin' bad enough as it is, and he got stabbed, remember, it could've been his heart, he could be dead too...."

"Don't use that as an excuse, Luce."

"I'm not!"

"There's not gonna be a next time, so it won't matter. What if Nitro hadn't turned sides? What then?" I run a hand through my hair. I know that I couldn't live without her, I wouldn't want to. "Things could've been so much worse, baby, I get that, that's what scares me."

She cups my face, running a hand through my stubble. "But they didn't. I'm fine. Bones will recover, it's over now."

"I know what you're like," I mutter, giving her another quick kiss. "Are you gonna do as you're told and go with Kirsty now? Let us finish up here?"

"Yes." She nods. "It's not like I want to hang around here with Tex stinkin' the place up."

I shake my head. "You're the only woman I know that

could make a joke out of a corpse lying in our den instead of screaming the place down."

"Well, I married you, didn't I? That made me tough as nails."

I kiss her on the nose as I smirk. "Nah, Sparkles, I think you were tough as nails long before I came along."

EPILOGUE

LUCY

SIX MONTHS LATER

I hear Rubble pull into the driveway, and I smile to myself as he kills the engine. A few minutes later, he comes through the door and finds me in the kitchen. He's learnt not to call out loudly like he used to do, like Ricki Ricardo; *Lucy I'm home.* It wakes the baby.

The baby, *our* baby.

Avery Violet Cooper was born three months ago, and she's perfect. She's the apple of our eye. Frankie Stevens delivered her by C-section, and we couldn't be happier with the birth, first delivery nerves aside. She's absolutely perfect.

I can't say it was the easiest of pregnancies in the last trimester, but our baby was born healthy and happy with ten fingers and ten toes and a mop of dark hair just like her daddy.

She's so much like him but has my eyes and my nose, and she's a good baby. The girls can't believe she is already sleeping through the night, not that it would matter if she didn't. Just to have her in our life is a miracle.

I never realized how big my heart could actually expand to until she was born. When they laid her on my stomach and Rubble stared at me like I was his queen, no emotion on earth could top that. I've never seen him cry but he had tears in his eyes. He couldn't believe what my body had done in nurturing and growing this tiny human. And of course, he immediately stated he wanted more.

Rubble is obsessed with her, we both are.

He grins when he sees me in the kitchen with an apron on.

"Isn't this very domestic?" he muses, kissing me as he dumps a paper bag of Chinese food on the counter.

"What's this?" I ask, peering into the bag.

"Thought I'd give you the night off from cooking," he says, pulling me to him. "We can have our own little date night."

I grin up at him. "Is it a full-service date?"

He bumps my hips with his. "Only if you don't wake the baby."

I pull him down for another kiss, then he peers over to the oven. "What are you baking?"

I give him a look that says *nope, not before dinner*. "Sugar cookies."

He grins. "I think I like you as a homemaker. It's hot."

"Hey!" I slap him on the arm playfully. "I've always been one. Remember the woman who's kept you fed and alive all these years?"

He kisses me chastely. "Is that why I've got a dad bod?"

I can't help but grin back at him. "You don't have a dad bod, not that there's anything wrong with that…"

His hands grip my hips, and he gives me those come-hither eyes, the same ones that got me into this mess almost seven years ago. He's always been too hot to handle, but as a dad, it's like my heart has grown to love him so much more, if that were even possible.

"The baby's asleep…"

"No," I say, trying to wriggle free. I know what he's asking me. "Behave!"

He kisses me again and reaches behind, undoing my apron. "I can be quick."

"Yeah? Well, what about quiet? We both know the answer to that."

He chuckles. "It's not my fault I've got a hot wife who I can't keep my hands off of, she shouldn't be so temptin'."

"Flattery will get you everywhere."

"I hope so, since you owe me spank time, don't think I've forgotten."

This man.

But, I can't argue there; we had to wait just over six weeks before I could do anything physical after the baby was born, and it just about killed Rubble. He finds me even more attractive now that I've got mama curves, and he loves my body, though I'm no way the same size or shape I was pre-baby. All of that goes out the window when I look at Avery sleeping and know how lucky we are.

It's the furthest thing from my mind. All I care about is having a healthy baby and enjoying this time watching her grow. While motherhood has its challenges, and it's tested me, I wouldn't want it any other way.

"You want to get lucky? You can help me sort the laundry and do the folding."

He smirks. "You already tricked me into vacuuming, and while I admit that the payoff was worth it, I have been workin' all day."

"So have I," I fire back. "Feeding and changing your baby."

"Now it's my baby?"

His fingers brush the buttons on my blouse. "You're so fuckin' beautiful, did I ever tell you that?"

I stare at him and try not to let the tears well in my eyes. I love how much closer this has made us, and though he kids around about the housework, he is really hands-on as a father. He's even changed a few diapers.

When he looks at me like this, like I'm his everything, I know that I don't have to be anything or anyone else. This is why I fell for this man; he always lets me be myself. He's never tried to change me.

We have our ups and downs, we argue, but when it comes down to it, we work better as a team.

When all the shit with the Fury erupted, and the boys took care of everything, I knew that it was a turning point for us. A sign that things had to get better, 'cause it couldn't get any worse.

I'd already been held at gunpoint, lived through that terrorizing ordeal, and seen a man shot in the head and lying dead on my living room floor. Things could only go up from there.

I don't know what they ended up doing with Tex, and I didn't want to know. Sometimes there is a silver lining with club business, when we get to stay out of it. The less I think about that day the better.

"You tell me that all the time," I whisper as he continues to undress me.

"That's because it's true." He rubs his nose with mine, and then groans when his phone rings, interrupting our make out session. "Great, it's your brother."

Nitro and I have made up for lost time in these last six months, and subsequently, he and Rubble have become quite close. Sure, it's taken a little time to get to know him and earn trust, but we're headed in the right direction. And he's deciding whether to join back with Smokey and the boys or stay in Bracken Ridge. He's got options, something he's never really had before in his life, and I know he is a good person.

I never really understood why he didn't talk to me and tell me he was my brother all those years ago. I feel sad when I think about the lost time we had, then he reassures me he was a different person back then. Hooked on drugs, like most of the guys were, and that he was ashamed, and he didn't like the idea that I'd think less of him. That I'd be angry and disappointed when he'd run away all those years ago and never came back. He couldn't be further from the truth. I have had to put that aside otherwise we'd never move on.

I've always been a pretty forgiving person, and there is nothing to be gained by holding a grudge because of that. To me, that's in the past now. We can only move forward.

"Yeah, she's with me now. We're busy," Rubble says, giving me an eyeroll. "Probably not for at least an hour. Yeah, this weekend, okay. I'll tell her to call you later."

He hangs up.

"What did he want?"

"Your phone is on silent, and he was checking up on you. Said he's comin' down this weekend; he's got some things for Avery."

Needless to say, Avery is as spoiled a baby as you could ever imagine. Everyone dotes on her, including my brother; he loves her to bits.

I think having her in our life has healed some of the slightly traumatic childhood memories we all still have. None of us had it easy, especially Rubble. And he kept his word, he's never taken drugs or touched alcohol since we left Phoenix. His biggest fear is being like his father, but even on his worst days back then on the gear, he could never be like that.

We want to give Avery the best life she can possibly have. Give her all the love possible.

She won't suffer like that; she won't have drunks for parents or see her father beat up on her mother like what happened in Rubble's family, or be neglectful like mine. She'll only know love and compassion and loyalty. That's what we'll teach her.

"He spoils her," I muse.

"Doesn't everyone?" He grins. "Not like they can help it, with genes like hers."

"Well, we are slightly biased."

He slips his hand into my blouse and cups my breast. "What have you got here for daddy, Sparkles?"

I bite my lip. "You're insatiable ever since you couldn't have me for six weeks."

"Six weeks, five days, fifteen hours and three minutes, but who's counting?"

"Clearly, you are." I laugh as he snakes his other hand into the top of my pants and cups my sex. "Rubble, it's three in the afternoon!"

He grunts as he caresses my neck with his mouth, groping me any which way he can as I grind my pussy into his hand. "All the more reason to finish work early because you can't stop thinkin' about your hot, sexy wife at home, bakin' cookies in her skimpy little apron."

He dips a hand into my panties and slides his fingers through my wet heat.

I hold onto his shoulders as I grind against him, and he circles my clit, pushing my blouse open with one hand as he yanks my bra down and cups my breast in his palm.

"God, Rubble… you should finish work early more often…" I pant as he presses me back against the sink, and I part my legs as he loosens my jeans and then yanks them down to my knees.

"Been thinkin' about this all fuckin' morning since I didn't get to finish the job."

"Or start it," I remind him. "But thank you for letting me sleep in."

Rubble got up to feed Avery early and let me have an hour longer in bed, and then he brought me coffee. I even managed to have a shower, a luxury around here, while he was giving Avery her bottle.

"What are husbands for?" He grins and inserts a finger, then two, and moves in and out as I squeeze my eyes closed and get lost in the moment.

"That feels so good," I tell him. "So, so good."

"Look at me when I make you come, baby."

He curves his fingers, and at the same time brushes my clit with his thumb, and I moan through a long, hard, much needed orgasm as he pinches my nipple, and I dig my nails into his skin. I know this is going to be super-fast because my sex drive is up there with a playboy bunny at the moment.

"Rubble… oh God… yeah, right there… oh, don't stop…" I cry out as I grind down on his hand, milking the freaking thing for all I'm worth as I come hard and fast, gripping his shoulders and not letting go.

He looks very satisfied with himself when my eyes reach his as I come down from my high.

"You're very sexy in the throes of passion," he teases. "But I need to be inside you, Luce, like now…"

He undoes his button, and I help zip him down, brushing his waiting cock with my hand, and it's then that I hear the baby monitor. It's perched on the counter next to where I was cooking.

Avery, of course, chooses the most inopportune time to wake up.

"Hold that thought!" I say as I begin to put myself back together. Avery cries even harder, and I've almost got my jeans up when Rubble pulls me in.

"I love you in mama mode," he whispers against my lips.

I kiss him lightly. "Yeah? Well, I love you in daddy mode, and I want to finish this properly."

He swats my butt as I dash off to check on Avery. When I get to her bedroom door, he's right behind me as I go to her and pick her up and give her a little rock.

"I swear this kid just doesn't want me to get laid." Rubble chuckles, watching us.

"Nah, but I think she does like to keep us on our toes."

"Like mother like daughter," he says, as I turn to him and grin.

I bring her closer and Rubble kisses her on the head. "She's so fuckin' perfect," he whispers.

"Language. We don't want our innocent child's first words to be profanity," I scold. "That goes for all the boys at the club."

"I like you bossy."

"You better be listening."

"I also like you naked, and daddy's got a missile in his pants that's not goin' down."

"Let me put her back to sleep," I say when Avery quietens as I cradle her in my arms. "Then we can finish where we left off."

"I'll go clean up. Join me in the shower, I may need a hand with the soap." He gives me a wink as his eyes dance over us, a slow grin spreading across his face.

I glance up at him. "What?"

"Just lookin' at my two perfect girls and wonderin' how I got so lucky."

"We think you're pretty great too, daddy."

He gives me a chin lift. "You know when you call me daddy, it does things to me."

I try to hold in my laughter. "I know, that's why I say it."

He shakes his head. "Five minutes. I'll start runnin' the hot water."

I watch him as he turns to leave.

My heart swells. We're finally a family, and I'll never be sorry, everything is as it should be. We're not perfect, but we're exactly where we need to be, and I couldn't wish for anything more.

He really did turn out to be my Prince Charming, and I know I'm the luckiest girl in the world.

RUBBLE

It's not often that things change for the better, but after Lucy and Bones got held at gunpoint, I vowed that this was a turning point. Nobody should have to ever go through something like that and be terrified for their life, and their unborn baby.

It worried me that Lucy would be a little bit scared afterward, or a lot, but one thing I've learned about my girl over the years is she's resilient, and she's also one tough cookie.

We took out the trash, literally, and buried Tex's body out in the desert. Though I also didn't trust Nitro a hundred percent at first, he's proved his worth by not only shooting Tex and saving Lucy and Bones, but he's also been making up for lost time. He's really trying.

Smokey and the Vipers took out the Rogue Warriors on the drop that night, and whatever feud they have with the Mexicans and the Cubans is on them; the Rebels are stayin' well away from it. It isn't our fight, and it's not goin' to be.

We all know Smokey's itching to expand and get more members so he can start a real club again, and now he has an alliance with the Vipers after the takedown. I've no doubt he's goin' to succeed. All good things come to those who wait, that I know to be true.

The best part of my year was seeing our baby be born.

I smile when I think back to the day that our little miracle Avery came into the world, and I don't think I've ever been so fuckin' happy. Aside from the day when Lucy said she'd move to Bracken Ridge with me, because that was like music to my ears, and it changed everything. We grew stronger, changed both our lives for the better, and dumped all the toxic crap we had goin' on that no longer served a purpose.

My purpose is and always will be her, and Avery.

I watch her now, from the doorway while she hums away to our little girl as she tries to settle her.

She's such a good mom, as I knew she always would be. She was born to do this, to nurture another little human and teach her all the good things in the world that make it a better place. It makes me want to be a better man so I can teach her too, so all she will ever know is how much she's wanted. How hard we tried for her and how happy she makes us.

I don't know the first fuckin' thing about being a father, but I do know that being supportive and giving my girls everything I have is the way I know how. They'll never want for anything, and that's how it should be. They have my heart and my soul, there's nothing I won't do to protect them and keep them safe.

Lucy looks up at me from the nursing chair and gives me a smile.

"Hi, baby," she says.

I give her a nod. "Hi, beautiful." I walk toward her and give her a kiss, then I bend down and kiss Avery on her mop of dark hair. "How are my two girls doin' today?"

"Good." Lucy beams. "I went out to the coffee shop for the first time with her."

I crouch down on my haunches so I can watch Avery sleep. She's so cute, it melts my heart.

"Yeah? Was she good?"

Lucy nods. "A bit grizzly at first, but once she settled down and fell asleep, I drank a whole cup of coffee without interruption."

I smile up at her. The first few times of goin' out alone ended in disaster because Avery screamed the place down and Lucy ended up leavin'. She's self conscious about it, though I don't know why, most people are understanding when you have a new baby in a public place.

"She sleeps like her papa," I muse. Now she's into a routine, I can't believe what a good sleeper she actually is. Lucy does get up to her in the night, but she's only three months old, and I'm in total awe of my wife and what she's capable of. She's my fuckin' hero.

"Thank goodness," she sighs. "I think we've hit the jackpot with this kid, though."

"Must take after me, then."

She looks down at me. "Very funny. I bet you were a devil child."

He laughs. "You've no idea, babe. Rusty says he tried to suffocate me when I was a toddler because I never shut up, and he had to share a room with me."

"Rubble, that's awful," she says. "Though it does kind of explain your strained relationship."

That it does. I contacted Rusty after Avery was born to let him know he was an uncle. And, if all goes to plan, he's gonna come down and catch up.

A part of me does want to mend the relationship between us, but I know that it takes small steps. We've got a lot to catch up on. Something about becoming a dad makes you want to be better, I sound like a schmuck, but it makes you question everything. And, it would be nice to see my brother.

Lucy and Nitro have become almost inseparable when he's here. At the moment, he's sortin' shit out in Phoenix. Smokey allowed him back in the club after the loyalty shown to Lucy, and of course for being the one who shot Tex, but he's workin' out his options.

Hutch said he was welcome to join the Rebels, and I think he'd actually fit in here. We're all a little crazy, and that helps, so he's got some thinkin' to do. I know Lucy would love to have him around more so they can get back to where they left off all those years ago. It changed things when he came back, for the better.

Smokey, Griller, Hoax, and Dice are working hard at gettin' their club back on its feet, but it'll take time, they'll make a better club and only have members who are like a brotherhood. It makes me feel proud that we have that here, at the Rebels. I feel lucky that I never have to question my club brothers' loyalties.

The past has to stay in the past, and Bones bein' the one who saved Lucy and our baby, I can never repay him, but I am learning to forgive myself. It's not easy, and I can't even contemplate what would have happened if Tex had succeeded. All I know is I couldn't survive in this life without them. I wouldn't want to. They're my whole world.

"Yeah, well, I'm sure if Rusty really wanted to, he would've done it already. They say time heals all wounds, or some shit like that. We can only see what happens and if he'll meet me halfway," I reply, rubbing my chin. "Ball's in his court, I can't do any more."

One things for sure, I'm not puttin' Lucy or Avery at risk, family or not. If you want in the circle, and it's a pretty tight circle, you gotta prove your worth.

"It would be nice to have him meet Avery," Lucy says.

"Though she's got so many uncles and aunts, I can't keep track of them all."

Even the boys in the club dote on her, and of course, all the girls are as clucky as hens and never stop cooing and tryin' to steal her away.

As long as my girl's happy, that's all that matters.

I spent a lot of years of my life doing the wrong thing, and now I'm makin' up for it. Day by day.

"Why don't I run you a hot bath, then I can take over and you can have a soak," I say, knowing that Lucy doesn't get a lot of time to herself. Babies are hard work, and I didn't want her going off to the office and having all that to worry about, so we hired an office girl to help and that seems to be working well.

"I knew there was a reason I married you," she says, giving me a bright smile. I can see how tired she is, despite her glowing face and her gleaming eyes, but she needs a break. The baby gets her up a couple of times during the night.

I wanted to take her away for her birthday, but it's too soon to be leaving the baby with someone else. Lucy would panic too much, and bein' honest, I probably would too.

"Yeah, because I know how to get you to scream," I say, giving her a wink as I disappear to go run the bath. I tip in some of the scented bubble bath she likes and adjust the tap water until it's at the right temperature.

When I return, she hands Avery to me, and I hold her in my arms as she squeezes her little eyes, then does the cutest little yawn.

"She's almost out," Lucy tells me, having a stretch as she yawns too.

"Go on." I nod to the door. "Take your time."

She leans in and kisses me. "You could come join me, when you've put her down to sleep."

I give her an eyebrow lift. "Now you're talkin' my language, babe."

I try to swat her ass as she passes, but she's too fast for me, and I swipe air instead.

I cradle Avery as she stays quiet. She's always good for me; I like to joke that I'm a natural, but I've really got no idea really. She seems to like me, that's the main thing.

"You're the sweetest little thing, Avery Violet, you're just like your mama," I whisper.

Luckily, the only thing of mine she seems to have is the dark hair. Hopefully, she'll grow out of that. "Daddy's gonna give you and your mama the world, you hear me?"

She doesn't make a sound as I put her into her crib and tuck her in just how she likes it.

"Goodnight, angel," I whisper, turning on her little music box as I dim the light. Though her crib is in our room for now, we have set up a nursery for her. Deanna ended up decorating it for us and it's the perfect little girl's room. We just can't bear to put her in there all alone just yet, so she sleeps at the end of our bed where it's nice and close and we can check on her.

I walk down the hallway to our bathroom and find Lucy inside, bubbles overflowing since I'm an excess kinda guy.

"Well, well, looks like my night's lookin' up." I grin, putting the toilet lid down and sitting on top of it as I watch my wife under the suds.

"This feels so nice," she says, opening her eyes and gazing over at me. "Did she go down okay?"

"Like clockwork, mama, but you did all the hard work for me."

"We got lucky. I heard some crazy ass stories from the mother's group this week. I feel bad for some of the women who don't get any sleep at all, that could be me."

"Bein' a mom can kick your ass," I agree. "I get the easy part of goin' to work."

"You going for blow job of the year or something?"

I roll my eyes. "A man can't say anything nice without getting his head chewed off or insinuating he just wants sex."

"Come here and say that." She crooks a finger at me, and just as I'm about to slide down to her, my phone rings in my back pocket. I check the number, and I don't recognize it, but it's a local number.

"Hold that thought," I say to Lucy as I answer. "Yeah?"

"Rubble, it's me, Bones."

I frown. "Why are you callin' me so late?"

"'Cause I'm in deep shit."

I pinch the bridge of my nose. "What did you do now?" I brace myself for something stupid.

"I got arrested."

I guffaw. "You're shittin' me?"

"I wish I were. I'm in the fuckin' county lockup."

"Is this why I don't recognize the number? Did you only get one phone call?"

"I'm glad you think this is so funny," he grumbles.

"I don't *think* it's funny, it *is* funny."

"What's wrong?" Lucy questions.

I cup my hand away from the phone. "Bones got arrested."

"What?" she shrieks.

"You need to come get me. Like, now."

"Why me? Haven't you got anyone else's number memorized?"

"Brock's not pickin' up," he tells me. "They say I'm gonna need a fuckin' lawyer to make bail."

"And the only decent lawyer in town practically has a restraining order on your ass." This just gets better. "Isn't Stanley on vacation?"

Stanley is the only other lawyer in town and has done a couple of things for us in the past when needed.

"I need you to ring Hutch, get someone down here pronto." His voice then turns to a hush. "There's freaky people here; they're lookin' at me weird."

I snort with laughter as Lucy tries to work out what we're saying.

"You know I'd love to stay and chat, but aren't visitin' hours over anyway?"

"You're not leavin' me in here tonight!" he roars.

"I'll do my best, but I'm no miracle worker. Anyway, they can't grant bail until the morning. Looks like you might have to toughen up a bit, princess."

"Don't be a smartass," he warns. "All the times I've helped you out over the years."

"Helped me by taggin' along on a job to try and score pussy isn't the same thing, and it's the reason lawyer lady was throwin' daggers at you the last time you met, I told you to be nice."

"I was nice!" he yells.

I try not to chuckle but fuck it. "She seemed pretty hell bent on scowlin' at you, brother."

"I saved your wife and your kid!" he shouts. "Got a short memory? Was willin' to take a bullet *and* got stabbed. Least you can do is call me a goddamn lawyer."

I can't argue there. As much as we rib Bones to death, he's a good guy, the best. I know he literally would have taken that bullet if it came down to it, so I cut him some slack.

"That's true, and that's the reason I'll come and rescue you, so hang onto your panties a little longer till I sort somethin' out."

"Shut up and get down here!"

"You used to be a sniper," I remind him. "I think you're gonna be okay."

"Rubble…"

His time must be up because the call drops out.

I toss my phone onto the vanity and laugh. "What a dumb fuck. Told him all those speeding fines and unpaid parking tickets were gonna catch up with him, plus he's got a warrant out for his arrest in another state. Seems like he's past his due date, baby doll."

"You're so mean. Go get him, county is no place for a pretty boy like him."

I chuckle again. "You're right. I should…"

I drop to my knees and place my hands on the side of the bath. "But first, I gotta take care of my woman's needs."

"Rubble…"

I slide my arm into the water and across her stomach, then I move my hand up to grasp her tits, one by one.

"You've got needs, baby, and I'm here to take care of them."

"I suppose it won't do him any harm…" she trails off as I kiss her, softly at first, then our tongues meet, and she groans.

I love her like this. Relaxed and happy. She doesn't get much down time so I like to make it good for her. I know it's not all about me, but fuck me if I don't enjoy watchin' her fall apart when I touch her. Her face is as angelic as the day I met her, and her dirty little mouth has only gotten worse. My woman. There's nobody like her.

"I love you, Sparkles," I whisper on her lips as she pulls me closer and my hand snakes between her legs.

"I love you more," she whispers back. "Especially when you're hands-on."

I grin into her neck. "That you do, baby, that you do."

That's my girl.

Now and forever.

ACKNOWLEDGMENTS

Thank you firstly to Savannah and Brianna my amazing P.A. ladies who do a wonderful job promoting my books, making fabulous teasers, organizing everything from blog tours, newsletters and ARC's, I'm forever in your debt and I hope that we continue to work with one another for a loooong time to come!

I had an amazing bunch of Beta readers for Rubble, and they did not disappoint! Thank you to: Michelle, Brenda, Gemma, Kerri, Tianna and Nisha for all of your help, insights, questions and taking the time to help me better my writing. It certainly takes an army to produce a book. I look forward to working with you all for many books to come.

Thanks to my sister D for reading, re-reading and picking up all the mistakes I make before my books fly off to editing, and for cheer-leading in my corner when I doubted myself over and over. Life's better with a twin! I can't wait to announce our secret *shoosh* project together!

Thank you to my ARC team and my blogger friends for sharing my posts, graphics, reviewing, messaging me and taking the time to read my work and help me get my books out there. I'm thrilled I have such amazing support. Virtual hugs to you all.

It makes my heart happy to see my fellow indie authors succeeding. I'm so elated to call you my friends. I've met so many great authors (and readers!) on social media this last year. I can't wait to catch up with some of you in the near future.

Special thanks to my awesome editor Mackenzie @nicegirlnaughtyedits for yet again your wonderful work and words of wisdom. Can't wait for the next book!

Thanks LJ from Mayhem Cover Creations for another Yee-haw kick ass cover x

If you can spare the time to leave a review on GR and/or Amazon if you loved Rubble or any of my books that would be greatly appreciated and helps me so much as an indie author. Links are on the following pages.

I can't wait to bring you all many more books, buckle up because 2022 is going to be one hell of a bumpy ride!!

Love from Australia, MF xx

ABOUT THE AUTHOR

Mackenzy Fox is an author of contemporary, enemies to lovers, motorcycle and dark themed romance novels. When she's not writing she loves vegan cooking, walking her beloved pooch's, reading books and is an expert on online shopping.

She's slightly obsessed with drinking tea, testing bubbly Moscato, watching home decorating shows and has a black belt in origami. She strives to live a quiet and introverted life in Western Australia's North-West with her hubby, twin sister and her dogs.

FIND ME HERE:

Tiktok: https://www.tiktok.com/@mackenzyfoxauthor
Face book: https://www.facebook.com/mackenzy.foxauthor.5
Instagram: https://www.instagram.com/mackenzyfoxbooks/
Goodreads: http://bit.ly/3ql07a7

Don't forget to join my private Facebook Group: The Den – A Mackenzy Fox Readers Group here: https://bit.ly/3dgQfKk

Find all my books, newsletter sign ups, book links here in one easy spot: https://linktr.ee/mackenzyfox

Checkout my website:
https://mackenzyfox.com

WANT MORE?

BONES SNEAK PEAK (unedited)

Click here to get Chapter 1 of Bones now!

ABOUT Bones – Bracken Ridge Rebels MC Book 6

Bracken Ridge Arizona, where the Rebels M.C. rule and the only thing they ride or die for more than their club is their women, this is Bone's story

Bones:

They say good things come to those who wait, and I can safely say I've waited a lifetime for her.

She's the new lawyer in town. She's feisty. She's got a temper. And I can't get enough of it.

The trouble is, she won't have anything to do with me, aside from getting me out of jail.

I know she feels something, I can tell by her body language and how she can't take her eyes off me when she thinks I'm not looking.

The question is, what is she running from?

WANT MORE?

If she thinks she can banish me and keep me away, then she can think again.

The chaos that surrounds me has got nothing on the hurdles I know we'll have to face.

I'm all in.

She may have just met her match… because I'm not going away.

Kennedy:

I came to Bracken Ridge to start a new life. To get away from the past and all I left behind.

But the more I try to forget, the worst it gets, like my ghosts are set to haunt me forever.

He's the bad boy biker who's got a lazy smile, eyes that sparkle and a dirty mouth that he can't keep shut. I shouldn't be attracted to him, he's exactly what I don't need.

But the attraction calls to me on another level, one that I can't explain.

The trouble is, if I let myself fall again, I may not survive the fall out this time. And that's something I can't let happen, for both our sakes.

NOTE: This is book 6 in a series but is written as a standalone with no cliff hanger and a HEA. Recommended for mature readers only, it has adult content. Bracken Ridge Rebels rule...enter at own risk!

ALSO BY MACKENZY FOX

<u>Bracken Ridge Rebels MC:</u>

Steel

Gunner

Brock

Colt

Rubble

Bones (coming April 2022)

<u>Bad Boys of New York:</u>

Jaxon

<u>Standalone:</u>

Broken Wings

Made in the USA
Middletown, DE
04 April 2024